W9-AUU-705

OUT OF

TIME

by

MICHAEL McCARTY
&
CONNIE CORCORAN WILSON

Lachesis
Publishing

www.lachesispublishing.com

Published Internationally by Lachesis Publishing
Kingston, Nova Scotia, B0P 1R0

Copyright © 2008 Michael McCarty & Connie Corcoran Wilson
Exclusive cover © 2008 Laura Givens
Inside artwork © 2008 Carole Spencer

All rights reserved. The use of any part of this
publication reproduced, transmitted in any form or by
any means, electronic, mechanical, photocopying,
recording, or otherwise, without the prior written consent
of the publisher, Lachesis Publishing, is an infringement
of the copyright law.

A catalogue record for the print format of this title is
available from the
National Library of Canada
ISBN 978-1-897562-00-0

A catalogue record for the ebook is available from the
National Library of Canada
multiple ebook formats are available from
www.lachesispublishing.com
ISBN 978-1-897562-01-7

Credit: Jodi Lee, editor

This is a work of fiction. Names, characters, places
and incidents are either the product of the author's
imagination or are used fictitiously, and any resemblance
to any person or persons, living or dead, events or
locales is entirely coincidental.

TEASER

5:45 a.m.
Monday, November 22, 2010
The White House

Shortly before dawn, Renee Bellwood had one of the worst nightmares of her life.

She was walking in the ruins of a city. She wasn't sure what city. The devastation was extensive. Buildings were burned to the ground, reminiscent of the firebombing of Dresden in World War II. The city was still a raging inferno. Fire everywhere.

Concrete structures were rubble. All was chaos. Victims screamed, gestured with their hands, and then, one by one, collapsed, asphyxiated by oxygen deprivation. There seemed to be no other living soul in this nightmare. Everyone, except Renee, had fainted and burned to cinders. Streets, sidewalks were soot-blackened.

She wore a silky blue peignoir. Normally, at this time of night, she would have been cold, but the burned city was still very hot. The wind of the firestorm caused people fleeing from the burning houses to retreat into the doomed structures. Where the fire had burned itself out, the embers continued to smolder, warming the atmosphere and casting a grim haze of smoggy death over the landscape.

Dead bodies lay everywhere. Whole families huddled in grisly tableaus, burned to death. Cremated adults had shrunk to the size of small children. Pieces of arms, fragments of legs. Body parts burned so grotesquely, so badly distorted by the flames that they were unrecognizable as human remains. The victims were charred scarecrows. The corpses made Renee think of the Pompeii dead held prisoner forever after the eruption of Vesuvius in A.D. 78, suspended forever in time. Renee had to be careful not to step on corpses underfoot. All bodies still identifiable as human bore the look of victims who had seen unfathomable horror, unspeakable carnage.

Renee quivered with fear. There was a palpable sense of danger, yet there was no living thing nearby; only rotting corpses and dead bodies and dilapidated buildings. She couldn't shake the premonition that harm awaited. She wanted to run, but, as Bruce Springsteen sang, "Nowhere to run to, baby." In every direction, more destroyed buildings, more corpses littering the blackened streets.

She glimpsed a movement from the corner of her eye. Someone, or something, was alive. Despite her terror, she had to help. Instinctively, she knew she should just get out, but she needed answers. How could this happen? What had happened? Where was she? Were there other survivors?

A man crawled from beneath a putrefying pile of corpses. He smiled a menacing smile, a grisly broken grin.

Renee began to run, tripping over corpses, tripping the heavy fantastic. The man grabbed at her thin nightgown. She slapped away his cold, blistered hand. Gazing deep into his eyes, she was horrified to see that they were glowing a ghastly yellow.

The ghoulish figure knocked her down, loomed above her. Stooping, he pulled at the spaghetti straps of her nightgown, exposing her breasts. She wanted to scream, but no sound would come. The stranger tugged roughly at her gown. Pulling. Ripping. The fabric tearing. Brutally, he forced her legs apart, pinned her beneath him, and tried to thrust into her.

First Lady Renee Bellwood awakened wet with sweat, a sour taste in her mouth from the sleeping pill she had taken. Her husband was atop her. She struggled beneath William Buchman 'Bucky' Bellwood, pushing his dead weight from atop her slender form. She ran from the bed, fleeing the testosterone overload from this leader of the free world, escaping to the safety of their shared bathroom, screaming, "How can you think of sex at a time like this? Today we bury our daughter."

As the door to the bathroom slammed shut, she quickly turned the lock and sank, feeling sickened, to the cold tile floor. With her forehead leaning against the bathroom tile, her world returned to the familiarity of toilet and tub, her safety in the White House bathroom. She felt violated and disturbed.

DEDICATION

Connie Corcoran Wilson would like to dedicate this book to all the hard-working English teachers who taught me over the years (Florence Helt, Marie Turgasen, Dr. Barbara Croft, Patrick Somerville); to my friend and co-author, Michael McCarty (who convinced me to try my hand at fiction after 50 years spent in non-fiction); to my friends and family — especially my husband of 40 years, Craig — who encouraged me, and Karen Burgus Schootman, who proofed the document and made many excellent editorial suggestions; and to William F. Nolan, a Giant of the Genre, whose praise and encouragement made up for years of discouragement from others. (This one's for you, Bill!)

Michael McCarty would like to dedicate this book to: the science fiction writers, who time stood still reading: Connie Willis, Robert Heinlein, Richard Mattheson, William F. Nolan, Frederik Pohl and Ray Bradbury. I am very grateful for my collaborator Connie Corcoran Wilson for sharing this long and strange journey. I would also like to dedicate this to my father, who recently passed away at age 68. I wish he could have spent more time on this planet.

OUT OF

TIME

Change the past before it's too late….

PART 1
Minutes 'til Midnight

"Death began to call her name
In dulcet tones that sounded sane.
Lift the glass, take but a sip,
It will speed you on your trip.
Taste this fatal glass of doom.
Let me show you to your room.
Please, don't worry. Please, don't fret.
This is your best adventure yet."

—*Fatal Glass of Doom*, The One

PROLOGUE

Fatal Glass of Doom

5:45 a.m.
Monday, November 22, 2010
The White House

Shortly before dawn, Renee Bellwood had one of the worst
nightmares of her life.

*She was walking in the ruins of a city. She wasn't sure
what city. The devastation was extensive. Buildings were
burned to the ground, reminiscent of the firebombing of
Dresden in World War II. The city was still a raging inferno.
Fire everywhere.*

*Concrete structures were rubble. All was chaos. Victims
screamed, gestured with their hands, and then, one by one,
collapsed, asphyxiated by oxygen deprivation. There seemed
to be no other living soul in this nightmare. Everyone, except
Renee, had fainted and burned to cinders. Streets, sidewalks
were soot-blackened.*

*She wore a silky blue peignoir. Normally, at this time of
night, she would have been cold, but the burned city was still
very hot. The wind of the firestorm caused people fleeing from
the burning houses to retreat into the doomed structures.
Where the fire had burned itself out, the embers continued to
smolder, warming the atmosphere and casting a grim haze of
smoggy death over the landscape.*

*Dead bodies lay everywhere. Whole families huddled in
grisly tableaus, burned to death. Cremated adults had shrunk
to the size of small children. Pieces of arms, fragments of legs.
Body parts burned so grotesquely, so badly distorted by the
flames that they were unrecognizable as human remains. The
victims were charred scarecrows. The corpses made Renee
think of the Pompeii dead held prisoner forever after the*

3

eruption of Vesuvius in A.D. 78, suspended forever in time. Renee had to be careful not to step on corpses underfoot. All bodies still identifiable as human bore the look of victims who had seen unfathomable horror, unspeakable carnage.

Renee quivered with fear. There was a palpable sense of danger, yet there was no living thing nearby; only rotting corpses and dead bodies and dilapidated buildings. She couldn't shake the premonition that harm awaited. She wanted to run, but, as Bruce Springsteen sang, "Nowhere to run to, baby." In every direction, more destroyed buildings, more corpses littering the blackened streets.

She glimpsed a movement from the corner of her eye. Someone, or something, was alive. Despite her terror, she had to help. Instinctively, she knew she should just get out, but she needed answers. How could this happen? What had happened? Where was she? Were there other survivors?

A man crawled from beneath a putrefying pile of corpses. He smiled a menacing smile, a grisly broken grin.

Renee began to run, tripping over corpses, tripping the heavy fantastic. The man grabbed at her thin nightgown. She slapped away his cold, blistered hand. Gazing deep into his eyes, she was horrified to see that they were glowing a ghastly yellow.

The ghoulish figure knocked her down, loomed above her. Stooping, he pulled at the spaghetti straps of her nightgown, exposing her breasts. She wanted to scream, but no sound would come. The stranger tugged roughly at her gown. Pulling. Ripping. The fabric tearing. Brutally, he forced her legs apart, pinned her beneath him, and tried to thrust into her.

First Lady Renee Bellwood awakened wet with sweat, a sour taste in her mouth from the sleeping pill she had taken. Her husband was atop her. She struggled beneath William Buchman 'Bucky' Bellwood, pushing his dead weight from atop her slender form. She ran from the bed, fleeing the testosterone overload from this leader of the free world, escaping to the safety of their shared bathroom, screaming, "How can you think of sex at a time like this? Today we bury our daughter."

As the door to the bathroom slammed shut, she quickly

turned the lock and sank, feeling sickened, to the cold tile floor. With her forehead leaning against the bathroom tile, her world returned to the familiarity of toilet and tub, her safety in the White House bathroom. She felt violated and disturbed.

"Her comely features grace our past,
Her life a gift not meant to last,
Her days are spent and gone, alas!
A life lived well, but gone too fast.
We know so little of our fate.
Will we be good? Will we be great?"

—*Swan Song*, The One

CHAPTER 1

Embers in the Rain

12:00 a.m.
Thursday, November 18, 2010
Georgetown University

Isabella Bellwood died at midnight, and her secrets died with her. Her secrets were many and finally, the demons won the battle for Isabella's soul. She couldn't go on. Not after what she had done. There was no turning back. She had crossed the final threshold, ventured past the point of no return. Her actions would have repercussions; too many repercussions to comprehend right now. She didn't want to be around when blame was assessed. Isabella was ready to end her life.

She arranged the pills in neat piles. Next to the *Seconal* was a bottle of vodka and a Dramamine tablet. Outside her bedroom window, it was raining. From her window, had she looked, she would have seen a cold, miserable November downpour. The fire in the fireplace crackled.

Life is so meaningless.

As she brushed her long auburn hair, she gazed at herself for a moment in the mirror. A pretty but sad young woman in a flimsy black negligee stared back. She almost didn't recognize herself. Her hair was now combed and in place, but the luster and shine of good health and youth were missing. Dark, wraith-like circles pooled beneath her eyes. In place of her normal bright smile, a distraught scowl pulled her face down.

She glanced at the remaining fireplace sparks, flickering in her fireplace. Most of the fire had already burned out, like her life. Isabella had less than one hour to live.

Isabella Bellwood was twenty-one years old. Twenty-one

years of life. For what? To end up like this? Life was so unfair. She swallowed the pills. Dramamine to prevent nausea. Vodka to help the many Seconal pills she had stockpiled from various doctors. *Who will care? Who will really care?* But even as she thought this, she knew that her parents, for all their human frailties, would be devastated. Not as a unit, of course. They hadn't been a unit for years. They pretended to be a family, but the ties had been severed long ago. Individually, they loved her as best they could. She had failed them all. A sad sigh.

She felt as though her heart were dead and as though it had been dead for several weeks. Surprisingly, her heart kept beating in her chest. Inside, she felt empty. Love had vanished. She reasoned that the loss of true love, alone, excused her desire to end it. Reasoned was too strong a word. Isabella wasn't reasoning right now. Instead, she was wallowing in self-pity and remorse; she felt both scared and exhilarated. Part of her thought about what everyone would say after she was gone; how sorry they would be, how they would talk well of her.

A larger part of her wondered if it was going to hurt or if drifting into permanent unconsciousness would be like lapsing into a drug-induced coma. All she wanted was for it to be over. Peace. Black. Infinity. The End. *"The undiscovered country"* William Shakespeare called it. *"Eternal night"* was Algernon Swinburne's term for it. The Bible's *"pale horse, pale rider"* and *"dust to dust; ashes to ashes."* Grim metaphors, all of them. Isabella wanted to be remembered forever. But not the way she was going to be remembered. Not that way, at all.

She couldn't live with the guilt of what she had done to those she loved most. Death was the only punishment severe enough. Her parents' marriage would crumble because of her actions. The political structure of the United States would be shaken to the core. Her twin sister, Kaley, would be bereft. Worse than that, Kaley would be left to answer all the questions about Isabella. The hardest part of all would be leaving Kaley behind. Kaley was like another part of Isabella, an extension of Bella's heart and soul. Right now, Isabella was thinking only of herself. Selfish behavior was out-of-character for Isabella Bellwood. It was not her standard method of operation.

Selfish is as selfish does. She almost smiled at the rephrasing of the "Forrest Gump" quote, but she was too nervous. This is what she had become. Her lips twitched feebly, returning to a slight frown, as she swallowed the last of the pills.

As she drifted into unconsciousness from the Seconal, the pills and alcohol taking effect, she wondered if she would pull a Marilyn Monroe, and try to call for help at the last moment, her speech slurred beyond recognition. Peter Lawford – it was Peter Lawford Marilyn had called. Lawford could not understand Marilyn. Did not want to understand her, perhaps, or didn't realize what was happening to the vulnerable blonde movie star. Who knew?

Isabella now had less than thirty minutes to live. She slipped silently into a deep coma, wondering if it would hurt, thinking of Marilyn, and submitting to fate.

It was midnight. Isabella Bellwood, the President's youngest daughter, was dead.

"When daisies last in our garden grew
You were I and I was you.
List' closely now; I'll tell the tale
Before night falls and our world fails."

—*Before Night Falls,* The One

CHAPTER 2

Before Night Falls

8:00 a.m.
Friday, November 19, 2010
The White House

The phone call was put through to Renee Bellwood in her White House office on Thursday morning, after Isabella failed to show up for breakfast with her sister. Kaley had gone to Isabella's Georgetown condo, parked in her reserved spot and had gone to the top floor, using her special key. She entered the lavishly decorated marble foyer, followed the hallway to Bella's bedroom, and found her sister's now-cold and bluish corpse in bed, pupils fixed and dilated. Renee, busy in her White House office, was oblivious to the fact her youngest child was in danger.

Once the twins left for the university, Renee had let the baby birds fly. She didn't check on them daily, although usually no more than two days would go by without Mom or Dad calling the girls.

Observers thought Isabella would grow up to have a career in politics or international diplomacy. Her professors said that she might be the first daughter of a President elected President herself. A precedent-setter. Bella was studying law, following in her father's footsteps. Sometimes, that disturbed Renee.

Isabella, unlike her father William, had too much heart, too much soul for politics. Perhaps that had been the reason for her suicide? Politics was a dirty business, and it called for a tough hide. Bella was neither dirty nor tough, and her hide was as delicate and thin as fine silk.

Lately, the calls to Isabella produced no reassuring information. Isabella was down. Isabella was depressed. Isabella had thrown herself at a British boy, Kaley said. The romance hadn't worked out.

In their last conversation, Kaley tried to wheedle more details.

"Come on, Sis. You can tell me! After all, I'm your twin sister. We share everything, remember? Who is he? Where is he? What does he look like? Is he gorgeous? Tell me!"

Isabella had laughed merrily that day. "He's gorgeous, of course. He's tall, dark and handsome, Kaley. You know I go for that type."

"Yes. I've always favored blonde boys more," Kaley said. "But, to each their own. What color eyes?"

"Brown."

"How tall?"

"Six feet, give or take."

"Favorite expression?"

At this, Isabella laughed outright. "He says 'bollocks' a lot."

"Bollocks? What does that mean?"

"I'm not really sure, Kaley. He was educated in Britain. I think it might mean shit or balls. Something naughty like that." Both girls laughed at Bella's answer.

"I've been afraid to ask him what it means and reveal my ignorance of British slang. But, whenever he's pissed off at a soccer play on television, he says it."

The girls laughed together.

Isabella would say no more, but at least she had shared that much of the drama that might have driven her to the edge of the abyss and over the precipice into infinity. Throughout their lives as sisters, the girls had shared so many thoughts and secrets. It didn't make any sense to Kaley that her sister had suddenly closed down all communication. But she had, these last few weeks. Didn't tell their parents anything of real substance. It was obvious she'd brooded over something. Bella had dwelled on dark thoughts, but she'd kept them private. Now, she had taken her dark thoughts with her to the grave.

Isabella had been in love with someone? She wouldn't

even tell Kaley his name. Kaley remembered only that he was a young man from the Middle East who had been educated in England.

In the weeks before her death, Renee had asked Kaley why Isabella was moping around, sad and unhappy. The girls' mother had noticed that Bella's normally sparkling blue eyes were dull and darkly circled. Kaley at first denied any knowledge of the cause. Then she said, "Isabella has it bad for somebody. She won't say who it is. All I know is that he's from the Middle East somewhere, and he was educated in Great Britain."

"Elegant and curled are the roses", wrote Edna St. Vincent Millay. "Gone to feed the roses." Renee sobbed, soundlessly, now. After hours of loud, hysterical crying, all she had left was this pitiful noise.

Kaley's broken spirit and somber tone as she told her parents what she knew spoke volumes.

"Mom, Dad, I swear. I didn't know. I don't know anything that would have caused this. When I found her in bed, cold, blue." Kaley stopped and composed herself before continuing. "I was so petrified, I burst out crying. I didn't hold it together well. I felt so helpless. She broke down, sobbing.

"Don't try to talk now, honey. It's okay." Renee smoothed Kaley's hair, touched her troubled brow. She hugged her, and they cried together.

Renee wondered, over and over, "What happened to push Isabella over the edge? What or who caused Isabella to become suicidal?"

Renee couldn't think any more. She could only feel, and her feelings were eating her up inside. A throbbing, deep ache formed in the pit of Renee Bellwood's stomach, destroying her appetite, robbing her of energy. It was like the feeling that you were going to be sick, but then nothing. Renee was utterly exhausted. It was as though someone had stuck a hypodermic needle into her bones and sucked out the very marrow of her existence, drawing out every ounce of energy, like a vampire attacking its victim's neck, draining her dry, leaving behind only an empty husk. It was the feeling when you sat deathbed for hours and days and months. Deathwatch. Nobody had been on Deathwatch for Isabella. Isabella was only twenty-one years old. She had her whole life ahead of her. "What could be so serious that she would do this to herself?" Renee said this last sentence aloud, although she wasn't aware that she had spoken. It was just a quiet murmur.

After the initial hysterics, the convulsive sobbing that went on almost all of Tuesday, while the world spun out of control, the White House physician gave her something he said would relax her.

Thank God for drugs. She realized, ironically, it was drugs that had killed her beauty. But drugs were propping her up right now and keeping her alive, if you could call what she was feeling being alive.

Identifying your youngest child's body at the morgue laid out cold and dead on a slab, was a death, in itself. Renee's eyes were cried out. They still misted thinking of the image of her beautiful girl, her baby. Perfect. Young. Intensely blue, beautiful eyes closed in eternal slumber. Renee prayed, futilely, that this, too, would turn out to be just a dream, like her other recent nightmares. She hoped with all her heart this was an illusion, from which she would awaken. She would find her lovely daughters were both all right. They were just out for a night on the town, dancing the night away at a local club. But Isabella would never again dance, or breathe, or call Renee's name. She would never give birth to Renee's grandchildren.

The grief, when it came, was like a wave washing over her body. She vowed she'd remain strong. She needed to make the necessary arrangements. How could she ever get through this? But she knew that she would have to get through it, just like everyone else. One foot in front of the other. One day after another.

How can I endure? How is it possible to bend but not break? Renee's faith was not strong enough to sustain her. She was no Rose Kennedy. She was not capable of the heroism of Jacqueline Kennedy in the face of adversity. *How will I make it?*

Her jaw stiffened and she realized something. She would do what other mothers, in other lands, did since time immemorial. She would wail, weep, gnash her teeth. She

14

would beat her breast, as mothers did in newsreel footage from foreign lands.

If only that would bring Isabella back.

But it would not. She knew one more thing besides the fact that she must endure and persevere. Her life would never ever be the same.

She said a silent prayer, asking God, *Why didn't you take me, instead?*

No reply from the heavens.

Resuming an old habit developed in college, she took out her journal. Through the years, she had used this journal to pour out her feelings. The loss felt so great that the only thing that would come was this entry:

Why, God? Why, God? Why?
Why did you do this to Isabella? Why did you do this to me?
My sweet Bella? What was her offense? I don't understand. This seems so cruel.
What could this poor, beautiful broken bird have done?
Why did she take her own life?
How could we not know she was in such pain?
Please, give me back my little girl!

In the note she had left behind, Bella wrote only, "*I am so sorry for everything. Please forgive me.*"

What could Bella possibly have to be sorry for? She was a beautiful young lady with a passion for the environment, international law, human rights, the Constitution. She loved The One's music.

The One was a unifying theme for all the Bellwood women. Renee, Bella, and Kaley all loved the British singer's music. Renee had stopped following pop music years ago. When she'd first heard the name The One, she found it pompous. Her daughters had brought her around, introduced her to his music, convinced her to share their feelings regarding his talent. It didn't hurt that Dante Benedick was easy on the eyes, with flowing light brown hair, and piercing blue eyes.

The One's song *Path of Light* was the first thing Kaley learned to play on the piano as a child of five. Kaley could already pick out simple tunes. She was humming and plunking out a tune on the piano that Renee didn't recognize.

"What's that song, sweetie?" Renee called from the room next door.

"I dunno, Mommy, but I like it."

The melody played now in Renee's head. She remembered the words:

> *"Path of light*
> *Cast darkness away*
> *Illuminate this night,*
> *Brighten my world today"*

An image flashed in her mind. Isabella, also age five, wearing a white flowered sundress that matched her mother's. Renee was in the garden, watering the flowers. Isabella picked up the watering can. She began watering one daisy. The water didn't immediately come out, because the child was so small that she could not tip the container far enough. Bella held the container up and peered into the can. The water rushed forward, drenching her face and sundress. After a gulp of shock, Bella laughed uproariously in that high, giggly way little girls have, unconsciously, happily shrieking. Renee smiled, thinking of that day. Inside, her emotions were shrieking, and not in the giddy childish manner that echoed in her memory.

Renee began to sob. It had been a full twenty-four hours since the discovery of Isabella's body. The First Lady cried herself into restless slumber.

"In the day, in the night, to all, to each,
Sooner or later delicate death."

—*When Lilacs Last in the Dooryard Bloomed*, Walt Whitman

CHAPTER 3

The Funeral

11:00 a.m.
Monday, November 22, 2010
Arlington Cemetery

It was only a few days before Thanksgiving, but there was nothing to be thankful for here. The mourners gathered at Arlington for Isabella Bellwood's funeral. Hundreds were there on this bright but chilly fall day. Those present seemed anxious to get this over with and hurry home to their families for the Thanksgiving holiday.

Mia Akaihane-Black, the Vice President, gave her husband Roger a poke and whispered, "Do you have a tissue?" Her nose was beginning to run in the November chill.

"No, precious," Roger said, ever the docile servant.

"Great," said Mia under her breath in a surly tone. Leave it to Roger to be unprepared.

The Bellwood family was not holding up well. Kaley was a mess, crying and shaken. Renee Bellwood was in stoic mode...eerily reminiscent of Jacqueline Kennedy, a veiled chapeau concealing her tear-ravaged face. The President looked ashen. He seemed totally out of it.

Jake Jacobs, the Secret Service man assigned to Bucky spoke into his earpiece. "Hawk One looks more like Sparrow Shit today. He's really not doing well. Watch him."

"Roger that, Jake," responded Steve Johnson on the far left side of the crowd.

The Secret Service detail referred to William Bellwood as 'Bucky' in honor of his middle name, Buchman. Today, they were concerned he might fall like a Buckeye nut. Too bad Bucky had been a "hook 'em, Horns" fan, rather than an Ohio

State grad. The Secret Service considered the President of the Free World a nut job. They even used the term privately, amongst themselves, when drinking together off duty. The code name replaced Hawk One, Bucky's official code name. The Vice-President, Mia Akaihane-Black was Hawk Two, but, to the guys over beers, she was just plain Bitch Black.

To the President's left, Mia Akaihane-Black stood sniffling and clutching the arm of her husband, Roger Black. Mia appeared strained and preoccupied. She was stylishly attired in a black Gucci suit, with satin spiked heels that were sinking into the not-yet-frozen ground of the cemetery. She was upset that her brand-new Jimmy Choo shoes were never going to be the same. *Thank God I didn't wear the Manolo Blahniks!*

Being upset was to be expected. This was the burial of a twenty-one year old girl. Even Mia, Bitch Black, was sad and pensive. Unusual for her. She usually radiated a Nancy Reagan or Hillary Clinton-like vibe. Something was bothering Mia. But, then, something was bothering most of the mourners.

Celebrities were present in abundance, most of them foreign dignitaries: Princess Stephanie of Monaco; the young Windsors, the children of Princess Diana and Prince Charles, themselves no strangers to untimely death; the Prime Ministers of France, Greece, Canada, Australia and China; ambassadors from various United Nations countries. Turbaned sheiks and caftaned dignitaries galore.

Dante Benedick was clad all in white. White, the color of mourning in India, was Benedick's constant palette. The One was just back from a fact-finding mission to India, helping to set up a potable water supply for remote villages. He didn't look out of place, in a flowing white tunic that reminded of a longer version of the Nehru jackets of the sixties. If you were the world's most famous rock star, you could wear anything you wanted, anywhere you wanted. Dante had never gone to the extremes of a Michael Jackson, but he was always clad in white. His signature statement color: white. Girls screamed when he wore skin-tight white jeans or dressed more formally in all-white suits. He had started a fad by wearing white jeans. Until Dante initiated the trend, white jeans didn't even exist.

The color certainly hadn't formerly been the color favored by the world's teen-agers.

Right now, Dante Benedick just looked sad. Immeasurably sad. The sun was behind him in such a way that a nimbus of light radiated from behind his head, illuminating his thick flowing light-brown hair. His dark glasses hid the pain in his eyes. Every so often, The One would glance towards the First Lady, a darting glance to see how she was bearing up. He looked to see if she was wavering or unsteady on her feet. It was not as though he were near enough to help her if she stumbled. A number of Secret Service men would be much closer, to assist her if she felt faint.

Dante didn't know why he felt this odd sense of protectiveness for a woman whom he had only met once, at a White House command performance. They had spoken briefly, for under a minute. Even then, though, there had been an electric connection between them. Today, it was as though all her charismatic power, all her electricity, was just gone. Gone to feed the roses. He thought of Isabella, of his own dear musician friend Tony, dead too young. He shook his head sadly, the halo-like light further highlighting his abundant mane of hair. Only Jon Bon-Jovi, of rock stars currently performing, had ever boasted a mane of hair like Dante's, onstage, that held up so well while he performed. Tawny locks, light in color, thick and naturally curly, light brown, with natural highlights. He had a habit of tossing his head when playing, especially if, as he sometimes did, he took over the drums. It always drove the crowd wild. Dante Benedick was one handsome white man. At thirty-one, his slim sinewy build radiated power and presence, even though he was just six feet tall. Not tall, by American standards, but very respectable in his native England.

Under her veil, Dante knew, Renee Bellwood would be as white as paper, as white as snow, as white as the clouds scudding by above them on this glorious fall day. But he also knew that her face would be tear-ravaged. *What hell she must be going through!* he thought. The twin sister, Kaley, was the most vocal of the three immediate family members, since William Bellwood had chosen the stoic route, barely showing emotion of any kind. Kaley was sobbing hysterically.

Rhythmically. Gutturally. Kaley broke down even more as the white hearse bearing Isabella's body approached the gravesite.

Kaley held her mom's hand. Renee felt if she didn't clutch her daughter's hand, hang on to it hard, she'd totally collapse. The First Lady knew she had to be strong, not just for her family, but for her country, for the world that was watching.

The coffin was of rich mahogany, with yellow roses, a yellow ribbon attached spelled out "Beloved daughter and sister." Dante wondered if the yellow roses had been chosen because they were Isabella's favorite flower, or if William 'Bucky' Bellwood had ordered them because of the yellow rose of Texas, his home state. If Renee had been functioning in her normal, tasteful, efficient manner, she would have over-ruled Bucky and ordered Isabella's favorites: orchids and lilies. But, today, Renee was running on empty. Functioning was too kind a word for the Xanax-induced stupor she was moving through, as though lost in a heavy fog.

The minister spoke: "To close our service, The One has graciously consented to perform Isabella's favorite song." The selection wouldn't have pleased the President, had he known the lyrics beforehand. "Words," Dante's song, suited Isabella's vision of Washington, D.C., perfectly, as she had become more and more disenchanted during her father's term in office. Her view of politics as a career had been extinguished by his greedy profiteering. Lawyer, maybe. Politician? Never! She had developed a very low opinion of her father's policies and of politicians, in general. This was why Dante's song had particularly amused her.

The man in white stood next to the casket holding his white acoustic guitar. He began strumming, singing softly. The title "Words" didn't give away the song's ironic content to the audience. It was a cut from The One's first release and, therefore, one of his more obscure albums. It was likely that this was the first time most of them had heard it.

"If fewer words were spoken.
If fewer words were said,
If deeds alone were the mark of a man.
Not the 'catch' of an eloquent pledge.

If fewer words were spoken,
If fewer words were said,
If, for all the fake forensics,
There were simple words, instead.
And a man stated just what he started to state
Without false fuss or further ado.
If you weren't a politician,
I'd probably listen to you.
Words, words
Only words.
Words, words.
Only words."

He stopped, looked down at the coffin somberly, and exited. There was stunned stony silence. 75 percent of the assembled group consisted of politicians from one side of the aisle or the other. They all had just been soundly denounced.

At least ten Secret Service men surrounded the President, Vice President, First Lady and other close family members. Bucky Bellwood's approval ratings had dropped to an all-time low of eighteen per cent recently. It would be just like some rogue terrorist to use the occasion of his daughter's funeral to try to take a cheap shot at him.

That is what the Secret Service was thinking when a swarthy man moved quickly towards the coffin. He wanted to touch the wood of the casket. The Secret Service was on him immediately, wrestling him to the ground, nearly knocking the coffin off the wire stand where it stood prior to being lowered into the ground. The fake green astro-grass draping was askew. The thugs with earpieces handcuffed the man and quickly hustled him off, stage left. His name was Mosuma Hamad, although he had been nicknamed Zuma. Mosuma looked very angry as they took him away. He shouted something in Arabic, his eyes wild. None of them knew it then, but failing to let Mosuma say his own good-bye to Bella was going to be a very costly diplomatic error. Just how costly would soon become apparent.

Down into the darkness of the grave. The coffin was lowered. The swarthy Middle Eastern mourner quickly disappeared in a police car, to the accompaniment of a wailing police siren. Mia Akaihane-Black pulled her spike heels from the mud of the cemetery and tried to tiptoe on the balls of her feet toward her waiting limo. She was just glad to be leaving.

But people with real feelings, those who were not monsters, were mourning. The entire world seemed to be wailing, in sympathy with the Bellwoods. And so it ended. And so it began.

"We are but a cosmic speck
Of ash and dust, of finite dreck.
Yet our crimes, our sins, abound
As we destroy this planet found."

—*Cosmic Crimes*, The One

CHAPTER 4

Cosmic Crimes

10:30 p.m.
Monday, November 22, 2010
The White House

Renee took a long time trying to fall asleep. She had just buried her daughter. Her world was in turmoil. That evening she took a Halcyon and another ghastly nightmare plagued her restless slumber.

She was in a graveyard. Dusk fell against an autumn sky. As she walked through the cemetery, a brisk wind blew leaves across barren ground.

She approached a colossal crypt. Its huge stained glass windows and steeple made it appear to be a mini-mansion. She opened the door. It creaked loudly, the creaking of an iron door that hadn't been opened in centuries. She entered the crypt. Cold. It was so cold. She could see her breath before her face, frigid plumes, a ghastly fog.

The crypt's heavy lead door slammed shut.

In the midst of this mega-mausoleum sat a glass coffin. She slowly approached the coffin. Inside lay her husband, badly decomposed, dead for weeks.

I buried my daughter, not my husband!

Renee felt confined, claustrophobic. She tried to run for the door; the huge, heavy door wouldn't open. The door to the mausoleum was soldered shut.

A terrible noise. Her husband rose slowly from his coffin. He pushed the glass lid open and began rising from his final resting place.

"This is my mausoleum. I bought and paid for it!" His voice was strangulated, weird, eerie.

27

She tried again, frantically, to open the door, to escape, to run. It was futile. The door, resisted despite mustering all her strength to pull it free.

Slowly, William Buchwald Bellwood approached her. "You're wearing black. You always looked good in black." His rotting corpse voice cackled. Bucky's crumbling body fell atop her. Half of his face was rotted flesh; half of his face was skeletal. He kissed her, a grotesque parody of a kiss composed of bones and decaying flesh.

She tried to protest, to scream. He forced his swollen black tongue into her mouth. Renee gagged. Bony fingers ripped open her blouse; her pearls broke and fell to the floor, scattering, rolling everywhere.

Renee tried, again, to push Bucky away. He slapped her hard with his skeletal hand.

"It's just like old-times dear," he said, unzipping the moldy pants of his funeral suit. His organ was flaccid, purple, decomposed.

When he tried to take her, she screamed.

Renee awoke covered in sweat. In the darkness, she knew that she was lying in the safe confines of her bed, not inside some crypt. Lying next to her was Bucky Bellwood, her husband, naked, alive, and snoring like a snow blower.

She felt dirty, unclean. Renee rose, went to the bathroom, slipped from her negligee and took a long hot shower.

Even after the shower, Renee felt violated. She kept reminding herself, *It was only a dream.* Some dreams have the power to inspire, like Martin Luther King's dream. Some have the power to kill.

This dream was a killer.

Renee almost wished that, like her darling Isabella, she were dead.

"I've so much anger deep inside,
That there's no room for love to hide.
Kind has died and gone to hell
And love is going there, as well.
This helpless rage, this bitter ire,
Lights the spark, ignites the fire.
And from this useless bitter wrath
Comes a cold wind 'cross your path."

—*Light the Spark*, The One

CHAPTER 5

Light the Spark

10:45 p.m.
Monday, November 22, 2010
Airspace above Syria

Mosuma Hamad was angry. Intensely angry. He felt as though he might explode. Rage at his poor treatment at Isabella Bellwood's funeral, coupled with his already existing anti-American sentiments, had merged into an amalgam of pure and bitter bile-like wrath. He was, as Peter Finch screamed in *Network*, "mad as hell and not going to take it any more."

How dare they manhandle a member of the Syrian Royal Family at a funeral with the whole world watching.

Everyone had gawked when burly Secret Service men pinned Mosuma to the ground at the funeral, and then hustled him away. Although Mosuma and Isabella had been lovers for nearly a year, no one else knew of their relationship. As far as the Secret Service was concerned, a man fitting the profile of a terrorist was moving in on the President and his wife at the funeral of their youngest daughter. That was enough. Mosuma was gone in a flash.

The suspect the Secret Service had manhandled at the funeral was tall, thin, handsome, obviously Arabic. Mosuma had moved toward the funeral caisson with the natural grace of a jungle cat, the bearing of a gymnast. Now in handcuffs, Mosuma clenched his teeth bitterly at the irony of how close this was to the truth of the esteem the United States displayed towards the Arab world. He was just the latest casualty of American aggression towards the Arab states, a microcosm of the unrest and warfare destroying his beloved country.

The plane flight to Syria was turbulent, just like his life.

31

Just like his soul. He watched the lightning flash outside the plane's porthole window and pondered his past.

His love for the President's daughter, whom he'd met at Georgetown law, was not something either of them had made public. They had kept the world out. To let anyone else inside their private world of passion would have doomed their love. Keeping their trysts a secret from everyone had been part of the danger and part of the pleasure. It was intriguing. It was fun to outsmart the Secret Service. Although Isabella had a Secret Service detail assigned to protect her, the agents were not as attentive to Mouse One – her code name that distinguished her from Mouse Two, Kaley – as they were to the President or the First Lady. In deference to the fact that these were beautiful single young women who were free, white and twenty-one, the Secret Service tried to give them some leeway. If Lynda Byrd Johnson could show up on the arm of the very public ladies' man actor George Hamilton in the sixties, as she had done at one memorable Oscar ceremony, then Isabella Bellwood deserved a small measure of privacy when it came to her sex life. If the Bush daughters could regularly and routinely tie one on in the bars of Austin, why couldn't Isabella sip Chardonnay with a lover whose good looks she compared to busts of Alexander the Great?

Mosuma's looks were the antithesis of Bella's. His dark skin contrasted with the shell-like whiteness of her fair complexion. To see Mosuma and Isabella curled in one another's arms after sex, her Raphaelite auburn locks flowing across his well-muscled chest, was to look at fine art like that Michelangelo might sculpt. They were a gorgeous couple. Both of them were in the prime of their physical lives. Both of them glowed with feeling for the other. Isabella's lovemaking sessions with Zuma were the high point of her week. She would lower all the blinds, light all the candles, put on their favorite recording artists, chill the wine, dress as fetchingly as possible, listen for his signature knock – fingernails, drum-like, followed by two knocks on her door. She always felt flushed and giddy with excitement, listening for the sound. Sometimes, while waiting, she would lie on her opulent king-sized bed with the mirrored ceiling above it, listening to moody jazz (*Fourplay* was a favorite), sipping one glass of wine after another, thinking of the wonderful ways in which Zuma would please her and the ways in which she, in turn, would pleasure him. Those thoughts made her even giddier with excitement. At those times she felt as mellow as she had ever felt in her life. Afterwards, completely sated sexually, she slept soundly, always with a slight smile at the corners of her generous mouth.

In Isabella's case, she was aptly named. Bella was a natural beauty. Mosuma's eyes misted as he thought of her nearly translucent alabaster skin, her perfect breasts, her tousled auburn hair. Bella. Beautiful, beautiful Bella. She was passionate and compassionate. What a sex life theirs had been! In her Jacuzzi-equipped Georgian-style apartment penthouse, high above Washington Harbor on K Street, Bella and Zuma had a view of the canal that only the very wealthy enjoy. If it had been possible, they would have dined next door at Sequoia, their favorite restaurant, but it was imperative that they keep their romance secret. They never left the brick structure with the circular window that gave them a magnificent one-hundred-and-eighty degree view of the stippled water below and the expensive yachts moored there.

Mosuma and Isabella reached sybaritic heights of passion at 3000 K Street, passion that rivaled any experienced in Mosuma's twenty-two years on the planet. He'd had other lovers, but none for whom he had cared as much as he cared for Isabella Bellwood. She was beautiful and pure. He loved her deeply. He loved her with intense emotion. He hadn't even recognized the depth of his commitment to Isabella until she was gone. They had shared everything. They had made sacrifices for each other, done things for each other, that were complete acts of love. Isabella had been willing to do almost anything for Mosuma. He returned this devotion, although he had not been candid about his true identity. This was a decision his family had made for him. Mosuma must travel incognito for his own safety. He regretted having to tell Isabella a series of lies about his family and his background, but he knew that to reveal the truth was not possible.

Isabella had two parking spots in the garage. One was reserved for her sister Kaley's red Mazda Miata convertible when she visited. Mosuma was able to enter the building garage, park in Kaley's parking spot with an identical car, and escape detection by going directly to Bella's penthouse suite, on the top floor. Although there were guards assigned to watch the outside of Isabella's building, they were not stationed outside Isabella's door. To get to the top floor, a special key card was necessary. Isabella had been resourceful enough to secure both a second garage door opener and a second key card for her lover. The building management thought it was for Kaley Bellwood. Who was going to question the President's daughter when she made a very simple request? Since Kaley had not done much of her own driving in D.C., preferring to be chauffeured by limousine, the arrangement had worked perfectly. Usually, Kaley arrived on foot.

No one had known that Mosuma and Isabella were lovers, not even Kaley. There had been a point when Isabella was tempted to let Kaley in on the secret. Isabella hinted at a relationship with someone. Then, Bella thought better of revealing her secret to anyone. That was shortly after Mosuma made the request for the classified documents. While Bella would do anything for Mosuma, or Zuma, as she called him, stealing classified documents from her father's White House Oval Office was serious. If she had not been so blinded by passion, she would not have agreed to do it. But, God help her, she had taken the plans for a potential United States invasion of Syria, at Zuma's urging. Next, Zuma convinced her to take the plans for the new nuclear plant sites to be built on foreign soil, locations that were being considered by the Administration.

"Bella, I just want to make sure that my mother and my sister are safe. They live near the Syrian border with Jordan, near the Golan Heights. I have to make sure that they will remain safe. They are all I have left in life. I don't want my mother or my sister harmed. Surely you can understand this?"

Bella certainly could understand.

In the Arab-Israeli War in 1967 Syria lost the Golan Heights to Israel. Ever since 1976, Syrian troops had been stationed in Lebanon, just to the east of Damascus, for peacekeeping purposes. Of course, peacekeeping was about the furthest thing from the mind of the Syrian Royal Family. Syria plotted to take back the 1,295 square kilometers occupied by the Israelis and abolish the Israeli Golan Heights settlements.

Mosuma's father had said, time and time again. "We must make Syria whole again." When Syria was finally forced to leave Lebanon in the spring of 2004, it was a major blow to the Royal Family and the country.

There had been an increase in nuclear plants in the United States and elsewhere under William Bellwood's war-like administration. Bella was an anti-war activist, to her father's embarrassment. Hawk versus dove. Isabella disapproved of her father's policy supporting an increase in the number of nuclear plants, both in and out of the United States. It did no good to debate with someone as willful and stubborn as William Bellwood; he never listened to anyone about anything.

During their last conversation, Bella commented to her father, privately: "Dad, why didn't you support the Tokyo Protocol to stop global warming? Don't you care about the world? Don't you care about the world you'll leave to your grandchildren?"

Bucky Bellwood looked up, obviously amused, from behind his large carved mahogany desk in the Oval Office. "Are you telling me you're pregnant, Bella?"

Bella was exasperated. "No, Dad. I'm trying to tell you that it's wrong to allow the world to be ruined for future generations. Alaskan drilling in wildlife preserves. Ruining wildlife in Wyoming and the Southwest. Abstaining from trying to help curb emissions to stop the destruction of the ozone layer. Why don't you act in the best interests of the world, of all the peoples of the world?"

"Relax, little one. Don't get your panties in a bunch! Don't go worryin' your pretty little head about matters you don't know nothin' about. Your family is oil rich, Bella. Be glad about that, and realize that, if your family is oil-rich, your father is not going to help stop the world's dependence on oil. Capice?"

At first, Bella felt totally justified in playing a small part in helping her boyfriend Zuma. Both wanted to stop the spread of dangerous nuclear technology.

"It's not so much the technology," Bella said to Zuma, as

they talked in her condo far into the night. "It's the repercussions, if some nut-job gets hold of the makings of an atomic bomb, and the shit hits the fan. There are so many irresponsible leaders in so many Third World countries. What if they use weapons-grade plutonium to arm Korea? Or Iran? Or Pakistan? Or any of the countries of the world that would like to strike down freedom and democracy? What if terrorists send a car hurtling through safety barricades near a nuclear power plant? What then? How many will die? How would we stop it?"

Zuma hugged her close. "Yes, this was what the 9/11 terrorists did. They used American planes as weapons against the World Trade Center, and the Pentagon, and the White House. If not for the heroics of a few onboard the plane headed for the White House, your father and mother might have been killed."

Bella nodded. "Nuclear energy is like any other weapon. In and of itself, it's neither good nor bad. In fact, it has great potential for good. But will it be used for good?"

It had been hard for Zuma to maintain his cover story of being a law student with a deceased father, who had been a successful importer of Camels, Mercedes cars, to the US and Europe. When Zuma's fictional father died, the innocent victim of a terrorist bombing, Zuma told Isabella, it had made him more anti-war. His mother and sister had insisted that he leave the country and attend law school in the United States, so that he might return to run for elective office, perhaps as a member of the unicameral People's Council – Majilis al-Shaab – two-hundred-and-fifty members elected by popular vote to serve four-year terms. Elections had been held last in 2007 and would be held again in 2011.

Mosuma never mentioned the life-long vendetta of the Syrian royal family, the war in which he was a soldier because of an accident of birth. Mosuma was carrying out the directives of his father, King Musab Agil al-Hamad. Mosuma had shortened his name to Mosuma Hamad, in deference to western customs. Most of his friends and close acquaintances knew him as Zuma. Educated as a boy at boarding school in England, his British accent, coupled with his smoldering good looks and impeccable manners, made him a favorite of

Georgetown's females. But it was Isabella Bellwood, Bella Bellwood, on whom he had set his sights, for tactical reasons, at first.

If he could ingratiate himself into the good graces of the President's daughter, who knew what information she might have to share, what secrets she could access? For her part, Isabella, known as the quiet one, had been operating on instinct and chemical attraction, when she started to see Mosuma. She bumped in to him in one of their law classes.

"I'm sorry," she said, after dropping all her heavy books on the handsome fellow's foot. Little did she know that he had engineered the mishap.

"Don't worry about it." He'd helped her pick up her books. "In fact, let me demonstrate that my foot is perfectly fine, by walking you over to that Starbucks for a cup of coffee." He smiled a smile that few could resist. Bella certainly couldn't. They had coffee, Secret Service agents hovering nearby, but that was their first and last public outing, and it had seemed purely accidental to all, even to Bella.

Bella knew, instinctively, that going public with their relationship would put them both in jeopardy. It would lead to inquiries from her father, mother, sister and the world outside. Consider it Bella's act of rebellion that she suggested her penthouse apartment in Georgetown as a meeting place for their first study date. What a study date it had been! The animal magnetism between them had been so strong that neither of them had been able to resist it for the entire evening. Before she knew what was happening, they were kissing tenderly and teasing one another about their inability to keep their hands to themselves. Bella had finally found one act of rebellion that couldn't be stopped by her domineering father, or be cut short by the prying eyes of the Secret Service. If Zuma was willing to be just a friend from class to the outside world, he could become her entire world, her everything behind closed doors. What more could she ask? He was a wonderful lover, skillful, tender, and wise. He seemed to genuinely care for her, more and more as they met frequently.

This was the problem for Mosuma. He was to romance Bella, yes. Get close to her, yes. He was not supposed to fall in love with her. Yet, he had. He had loved her deeply and dearly, and he was inconsolable at her funeral, when he had approached the coffin and been unceremoniously thrown to the ground and handcuffed while the whole world watched. It was sheer luck and Secret Service incompetence that he had been released without any intense effort to determine his true background. The papers that identified him as a Georgetown student and the other fake documents provided him by his people were accepted without much scrutiny. After all, what had he really done? He had touched Bella's casket in a sad farewell. Once it was determined that he carried no weapons, and was a former classmate of the dead girl, the handcuffs were removed, and he was released.

"Someone will pay," he murmured to himself, as the Syrian Royal Family's private jet taxied to a landing at a small private airstrip in Latakia on the coast. Latakia was a seaport town, less well known than Damascus. This was the way Mosuma's contact, Musab Agil al-Khayal, told Zuma to handle his return to his homeland.

"Urgent matters await you," Musab said. "Do not fly into Damascus. It is too tainted with foreigners. Your father wants you to remain unrecognized as you re-enter Syria." By tainted with foreigners, Mosuma knew that Musab meant Americans. Americans were everywhere in the Middle East, desecrating the sacred ground and shrines of his country and those of Lebanon, Iraq, Turkey, Jordan and all of Syria's neighbors.

I loved Bella. She loved me. He felt utter desolation, as the plane's wheels bumped to earth on the rough tarmac. *She was my Juliet. What I do from now on, I do for her, to avenge her senseless death.*

Descending the staircase to the tarmac, Mosuma didn't recognize the security people waiting in the back of the black limo. Musab and Bashar, his childhood friends, were usually his guards and his escorts from the airport. These men were unfamiliar. He wondered for just one moment where his old friends were. A burlap sack was thrust roughly over his head, tied around his neck. The strangers forced him to the floor of the limousine.

"Don't make a move or you're dead."

Zuma felt the sharp blade, cold against his neck. He breathed shallowly, close to hyperventilating. He tried to calm himself. A hard blow to his temple brought unconsciousness

"I know that I shall never see
A love so real as you to me
I've tried to purge you from my mind
But caring's not my choice, I find."

—*Obsession*, The One

CHAPTER 6

Obsession

11:30 p.m.
Monday, November 22, 2010
Harrington Hotel
Washington D.C.

Dante Benedick, known to the world as The One, lounged in his hot tub in the penthouse suite overlooking Washington D.C. One hand held a flute glass of Dom Perignon champagne. He was reading text messages on his Blackberry. It was Thanksgiving, but Dante Benedick had no family, no kin with whom to spend this holiday. Thanksgiving was an American holiday. Boxing Day was for Dante Benedick.

"There is only one The One," *Mediatronic* said, in approaching Dante for an exclusive interview. He liked the sound of that. Jess Wilburne called him, directly. Also a compliment. Jess Wilburne was The Man of rock music publications.

"Dante," Jess said. "We'd really like to send Kaley Bellwood to interview you. You're our top pick for a cover story."

He agreed to the interview, on condition that *Mediatronic* quote him accurately. Often, he had been misquoted. He had not been allowed to disseminate his message. He felt that his message, if heard, could help heal the world. That was why he had agreed to interview with Kaley Bellwood, the President's oldest daughter. Kaley had been freelancing for *Mediatronic* for six months. However, it had been only one full day since her sister's funeral. Dante's brow wrinkled as he thought of that sad gathering. He wondered how Kaley was holding up.

41

His 30-year-old press liaison and personal assistant, Joshua Gottlieb, approached him. "I don't know if you want to do the *Mediatronic* interview, considering your opposition to her father's policies." Joshua's tone of voice was wry and sarcastic as he spoke. "Since you think her father is mad as a hatter and a real knob, perhaps you'd just as soon skip spending time with his daughter."

"No, the Bellwood women are nothing like William Bellwood. I met Kaley and the First Lady at the funeral, and Isabella briefly at a performance, last spring in New York City. The Bellwood women are nice people. Kaley might be too depressed to want to do the interview, though, but it's her choice. I'm in D.C. for a week."

Joshua jotted a few notes in his planner.

"I'll tell her yes, then, and set it up."

"Brilliant. Make it soon. Call her immediately. I'd like to help take her mind off her sister's death, if I can. I know that throwing yourself into your work is one of the best ways to try to take your mind off grief."

If Dante had only known the interview would set off a chain of events that would change the world. Nothing would ever be the same again.

"Accidents are bound to happen
And though at times it seems
When we're at our highest peak
The walls, then, tend to lean."

—*Broken Dreams*, The One

CHAPTER 7

Ignite the Fire

11:59 p.m.
Monday, November 22, 2010
Operating Room
Latakia, Syria
An operating room somewhere deep in the bowels of Latakia

Mosuma's head was in a steel halo, which was screwed to his skull. A huge drill, twisting bit grinding through bone, was making two burr holes on either side of his newly-shaven skull. Zuma had been given a local anesthetic; his brain had been targeted to millimeter precision by magnetic resonance imagery. Attached to Zuma's head was a stereotactic frame, providing his surgeons with precise coordinates and mapping imagery. Eight bilateral electrodes, four per hemisphere, were being implanted. They would emit an electrical current that would jam any brain circuits that might give Mosuma different marching orders than those his captives desired.

"Are you okay? Do you hurt? Can you feel this?" The surgeons continually interrogated him, while they operated.

"What is happening to me? Why are you doing this? Stop! Let me go." Brief, futile struggle. Restraints bind him.

Because of Mosuma's desperate pleas, his consciousness of the operation was terminated. No answer to his entreaties. He was put under general anesthetic.

* * * *

Surgeons threaded two 1.27 millimeter wires through the burr holes, wires on which platinum/iridium electrodes were strung. Next, the surgeons would lower the wires. They would

45

attempt to place them deep within the hippocampus, the thalamus and the tegmentum. These were the areas of Mosuma's brain where states of rage or fearlessness could be manipulated.

DBS – Deep Brain Stimulation – would make Mosuma a virtual slave to the hand that held the button. His objections to anything he would be asked to do would dissolve at the whim of his controllers.

Alim-Louis Benabid, a French neurosurgeon operating on a Parkinson's patient, resurrected deep Brain Stimulation almost single-handedly. Dr. Benabid had success in treating patients' shaking from Parkinson's disease by implanting an electrical probe into the patient's thalamus.

Before that, brain surgery took place with a leucotome, an ice-pick-shaped device with a retractable wire to whisk out gray matter. That method had fallen out of favor. Egas Moniz of Portugal won a Nobel Prize for his invention of lobotomy in 1936, but the operation had received very bad press since then. Very bad, indeed.

There was the specter of Elizabeth Taylor in *Suddenly, Last Summer*. *One Flew Over the Cuckoo's Nest* gave shock therapy a bad name, just as *Suddenly, Last Summer* gave lobotomies a bad reputation. JFK's youngest sister was shut away in an institution for the rest of her life after she underwent a lobotomy that left her a fuzzy but more manageable version of her young retarded self. By the late 1950's, thirty thousand patients had been lobotomized. Rosemary Kennedy, JFK's sister, was but one of them. Dr. Robert Heath at Tulane University School of Medicine had come along much later. He took the idea of DBS, Deep Brain Stimulation, into new and less barbaric territory. No more sawing and destroying portions of the brain via alcohol injections. No longer the primitive leucotome, thought Heath.

When Yale researcher Jose Delgado provoked an implanted bull with a red cape in a Spanish bullring, then clicked the button and turned the animal into a completely tame version of its enraged self, only then did the potential uses and abuses of neural implants become obvious.

By the late 1960's, implants were being considered for penal populations. In 1972 Dr. Louis Julyon West of the

University of California at Los Angeles formed the Center for the Study and Reduction of Violence. In 1968, officials at California's Vacaville State Prison performed electrode surgery on three inmates, one a minor, with the assistance of military doctors.

It was one of these military doctors, Dr. David Leibovitz, now operating on Mosuma's brain, implanting a device that assured Mosuma would go along with the plans laid out by his countrymen. True, only about fifty implantations had taken place for Obsessive-Compulsive disorder, added to another fifteen or so for depression, worldwide, up to this point. However, the technology was there, and it was definitely going to be used. Why not use it to change the world, not just change the topography of one man's mind?

Although Mosuma was devastated by the death of Isabella Bellwood and irate over his treatment at the hands of the Secret Service at her funeral, he was no religious fanatic. He would not willingly strap dynamite to his body and self-destruct, just to register his displeasure at being manhandled by the Secret Service. Zuma was a modern, rational, intelligent, well-educated young man. He loved his country and his family. Even threatening his family with harm might not tip a smart, sane man over the edge, and make him into the lead hijacker required for this mission. The DBS implants would guarantee Mosuma's complete cooperation. No matter what. Yes, there was a 5 percent chance of hemorrhage. There was a two to 25 percent chance of infection. What difference did that make when you were turning a member of the Syrian Royal Family into the next Mohammad Atta? The new Messiah?

Zuma did not have the suicide bomber's devotion to the cause. But they could give it to him. Dr. Leibovitz, who was being paid and paid handsomely for his efforts today, considered Mosuma a new and improved assassin.

"He'll be perfect for your plans," he said into the speakerphone, to. Mia Akaihane-Black, the Vice President of the United States, was a close personal friend of his. He liked the perks he would get for performing this surgery and keeping his mouth shut.

From now on, Mosuma would think his actions were all his

own idea. He would retain no memory of this surgery. He would still remember his grief at Isabella's death and his rage at his treatment by the Secret Service at her funeral. He would know that his father and mother and brothers and sisters could be harmed, if he did not do whatever was asked of him. Ultimately, the spark would be lit by a click of the control, connected to the chip buried deep within his brain.

"The world lay shattered at his feet.
Was its fate sealed? Would time repeat?
Our past will not our future be.
If eyes are not too blind to see."

—*Shattered at His Feet*, The One

CHAPTER 8

The Sand Pit

7:00 a.m.
Tuesday, November 23, 2010
The Sand Pit
Black Ops Detention Facility

Mosuma Hamad woke up in the Sand Pit, a secret Black Ops detention facility operated by the CIA deep within Syria. There were other such facilities operated by the United States government in at least eight other countries: Thailand, Saudi Arabia and, most famously, Guantanamo Bay in Cuba. The Hampton Corporation had built most. Both the Vice President and the Secretary of Defense owned stock in the Hampton Corporation, a very lucrative investment.

The existence of the bases had been concealed from the American people. The purpose of the camps was to use torture and other experimental means to question terrorists. The government called it "extraordinary rendition" - it was the United States outsourcing torture. The United States had decided that taking prisoners out of the U.S. for interrogation in Afghanistan, Cuba, Thailand and Central American countries would be much easier than facing scrutiny at home.

"I'm thirsty, very thirsty. Please, water."

These were Zuma's first words, after the DBS implantation procedure.

"Where am I? Was I in an accident? Where are my father and mother?" No answers. A silent nurse brought water to his bedside, flex-straw attached. She did not speak. She did not make eye contact. She wore a white surgical mask. All Zuma knew, for sure, was that her eyes were brown like his own.

In Mosuma's case, the DBS procedure allowed him to be

51

programmed for a Black Op about which even the President of the United States knew nothing. However, the nation's second-in-command, Mia Akaihane-Black, was *very* aware of the surgery Mosuma had endured. It was going forward on her orders.

Vice President Akiahane-Black was furious. Bitch Black bubbled to the surface. Twenty hours had passed. Still, she'd heard nothing from her operatives in the Sand Pit, the secret government facility concealed near Latakia in western Syria.

"Enough whining about rights," Mia said. "I'm sick and tired of hearing about the rights of killers."

No more pesky questions about human rights violations. It was so much simpler this way. Nobody bitching about wanting to contact his consulate. No pleas for defense counsel. No untidy explanations about bruises that appeared overnight on prisoners, held in cramped detention cells that resembled zoo cages. No problem if experimental surgeries were performed. No one the wiser, if a prisoner expired unexpectedly. Bush the Younger had established extraordinary rendition during his two terms in office.

Extraordinary rendition is a wonderful tool.

She lit a cigarette and inhaled deeply. *David will know what to do, and he will do it well. He is an excellent surgeon, and a respectable lover.* She smiled. Thoughts of their trysts when she was in Syria on a fact-finding mission lifted her mood. *Yes, David is definitely good in bed. He knows all the tricks.* Mia had enjoyed teaching him a few new ones.

Mosuma's neurosurgery, courtesy of Deep Op United States surgeon, Dr. David Leibovitz, had been state-of-the-art. It was so cutting edge that even Mosuma's memory of the surgery would be erased by a signal from the electrodes implanted deep within his brain.

Mia had plans for Mosuma. Plans that would propel her to the position she deserved. She had plans for David, too, but they were sexual and they would have to wait.

He's being paid well enough. He can wait for the frosting on the cake of the million he is pocketing. As long as the Syrians live up to their end of the bargain, this dog-and-pony show will put me in precisely the position I want to be in before the next Presidential election.

The smoke from her cigarette drifted lazily into the air of her office. *It's only right that I become President. Bucky is such a weak stick, in more ways than one. I will be so much better than him.* She smiled to herself at her own little double entendre joke.

Her aide, Rosita Perez, entered the smoky office. Mia looked up and scowled with impatience.

"Where is my briefing dossier on Hamad?"

"Father or son?" Rosa replied.

"Mosuma, the boy."

"He's resting comfortably. He's been informed only that he was in an accident. A fall. He's disoriented. We want to move him across country to his people in Damascus, but first we want to let him know what we expect of him. It's imperative that he be aware of the need for success. If he's aware of how high the stakes are for his family, I'm sure he'll cooperate, with or without the inducement of the implants."

"That better be correct," Mia said, stubbing out her cigarette in the ashtray, "or heads will roll!"

Heads were rolling, even as the Vice President uttered the threat. The momentum for destruction was building on the horizon. Dark clouds gathered. Doom awaited.

"Great men are they who see that the spiritual is stronger than any material force; that thoughts rule the world."

—Phi Beta Kappa Address, Victor Hugo

CHAPTER 9

The Interview

11:30 a.m.
Tuesday, November 23, 2010
Georgetown University

Kaley stepped from a black limousine to the interior of The One's white limo. She had been so glad to get the call to do this interview. The holiday didn't matter to her. In fact, the holiday was horrible, coming, as it did, one day after her sister's funeral. What was there to be thankful for? She leaped at the chance to interview The One, and, when he protested that he did not wish to ruin her family's holiday, she told him, honestly, "It's not much of a holiday. You'd be rescuing me from being part of the saddest trio of people imaginable."

Dante Benedick, alone, clad all in white. Shirt rolled up at the cuffs. Jeans. Puma tennis shoes. Suede jacket. A window between the passenger's side and the driver's side was lowered. There sat Davis, The One's driver, and, beside him, his publicist, Joshua Gottlieb. Gottlieb was a handsome young man from Chicago's Columbia College who had organized several fan clubs for Dante, earning his wings as The One's publicist because of his success.

"We met at your sister's funeral," Dante said. "Again, my condolences to your family. I understand loss. I lost my mother when I was young. It's very tough to deal with death at any age."

"Thank you," Kaley said. "And thanks for singing at her funeral. Bella would have enjoyed that. The looks from my father's fat cat, politician friends were priceless. Your songs meant a lot to Isabella, and they mean a lot to me. Even my mom likes your stuff."

She glanced up shyly at Dante, from beneath her long brown lashes, not daring to look directly into his tourmaline eyes. His eyes were movie star blue.

Davis closed his window in the front, and the luxurious car sped away.

"Do you want to do the interview here?" she asked.

"Why not?" said Dante. "We can talk while we drive."

Kaley started her tape recorder. "I suppose we should just dive into this."

"Dive into this?" Dante smiled.

Kaley began, nervously glancing at her notes as she spoke.

Mediatronics: What is your conception of God?

The One: Whoa! You're really starting with the easy ones then? (laughs) How about I throw in an answer to what is the meaning of life while I'm at it: two for the price of one? Seriously, I think that there is some force guiding us in this life. Don't know about beyond this life. I'm ambivalent there. But I think there is a force, call it karma, or, as the ancient Greeks did, call it *rhema,* which sort of means changing to fit the moment that we occupy here and now. Carpe Diem. Live in the moment. That's why I feel an obligation to try to help achieve, as we Brits have called it, "peace in our time." I view the Deity as being a bit like electricity, which I also don't understand, although my electrician will probably have a laugh at that explanation. I think of the Scriptures, which describe life and a deity as a clear reflecting pool. When we look in it, we see who we are, we see if we are enough, we see what needs to be done, what we have accomplished and where we need to improve, as people, as a race. Whatever is done to the least of my brethren is done to me. And whatever I do to the least of my brethren, I must be held accountable for. I've got to be willing to help relieve suffering; to help feed the hungry; to help keep the peace. I do think I should try to help. I *have* tried to help. Like a clear lake, whatever we do in this life radiates beyond one simple act, traveling outward in concentric circles. You might call it the circle of life, like that song in the "Lion King." And, as we go through life, those radiating rings intersect. I'm just a bloke from a small town in Kent, Chislehurst, but I left for the Big City, which, in my case, was London, and I have always felt that I was very lucky, and that the lucky have a sense of duty and an obligation to the less fortunate. Because of my celebrity, I'm in a unique position to improve our world a little bit. I could be wrong, but I'd like to try. I *am* trying.

M: Much of your music deals with love, with the search for love, with the angst that goes with that search? Do you have a significant other in your life at this time?

The One: Do I look like the kind of chap who would kiss and tell? But, as to the music being about love, I think that all of life is about love. When I wrote "Gold Above Dross" I made this clear.

(Recites lyric of stanza one) *"His work, he said, made relationships hard,*

Fleeting glimpses in the night, Many meetings in the day,

With travel and the rest of it, He never got the chance to say

Anything that really mattered, Anything that smacked of deep.

All he did was flirt and natter. Bed them well, then go to sleep.

He knew, in some remaining pocket, of what, at one time, was his soul,

That this was not what he was seeking, Not the thing to make him whole."

I think that pretty well sums up my position on

Michael McCarty and Connie Corcoran Wilson

casual sex. I know, in my soul, that that is not the thing to make me whole. I hope I don't disappoint any of my beautiful female fans by saying this. I could change my mind if I met the right woman, which I haven't, yet.

M: But, in the final stanza of that song, the lyrics say, 'What part of him was gone, was wanting? What quality did his heart lack? Was it hope or trust or honor? Could he ever get it back?' Can you explain those lyrics, in light of your own life?

The One: Well, I could, but then I'd have to kill you. (laughs)

M: You've been performing shows for over ten years now. What is your wildest road story?

The One: Early in my career, I played this small club in Manchester, England. There was this guy who had walked across this beam that was above the dance floor. It must have been thirty feet up.
We had just started our second set, when suddenly the guy fell through the roof and onto the stage with fiberboard splintering all over the place. He landed right in front of my saxophone player, who was on the side of the stage. We didn't miss a beat, we kept on playing. The show must go on, you know. And, at that moment, we were covering "The Doors." He fell through the ceiling right as we got to the lyric "Break on through to the other side."
I don't know who was more scared, this dude or the band. If he had landed on the drums, he'd have been one deceased fan. He was very lucky. He landed onstage where we had all thrown our jackets for the night. Anywhere else, he probably would have broken his neck.
M: Why does 'Gold Above Dross' seem to say that you had honor and trust and hope, but you

somehow, somewhere, lost it? Is that true?

The One: You ask the hard ones, don't you? I think that, to some extent, I felt that my own mentors - parents, teachers, others - sold me short, did not think I had what it takes to succeed as a singer and songwriter. My own dear dad, who was a laborer, a bricklayer, and later worked in a mill, used to tell me to get a real job, and that was pretty much why I left home at sixteen, bound for London. My mother was dead at that point. She died at her own mother's funeral, probably from a broken heart. I had no one at home to lift me up, no one to give me hope, and most of those I interacted with in that small town did not think I was going to amount to a pile of rubbish. But I knew I could soar. To show them, I worked, and I worked hard. I struggled to put myself in the position you see me in now, where I can encourage and help others who need that encouragement and that help. I owe my father this: if he had told me I could do it, I probably wouldn't have succeeded.

M: That explains your drive and ambition. If you can, explain something else for our readers: why do you go through so many drummers in your band?

The One: I'm hard on drummers. I think the rhythm section is the key to any rock or rhythm and blues band. I think all the great lead singers or lead guitarists in the world wouldn't be shit without a great rhythm section behind them, driving them.

M: After your trips to several Third World countries and your work to avert war, especially nuclear war, and your work to feed the hungry, you've developed an almost cult-like following. Do you think that's an accurate statement?

The One: It's true that I have a devoted fan base, to whom I am extremely grateful. But I don't think my fans are any more devoted than the Deadheads who followed Jerry Garcia or even those who, more recently, followed Phish, or those who follow the Dave Matthews Band. I'm just one man. I have a band that backs me, but the members don't remain constant. So, I think it's accurate to say I have very loyal and devoted fans. I humbly thank them for their support, and I hope that they'll continue to support me as I make more, and hopefully better, music.

M: Who were your musical influences as you were growing up?

The One: This is going to sound trite, but the Beatles were a tremendous influence on me, especially John Lennon. Lennon's "Imagine" really spoke to me, even though it was written years before I was even born. Styx. The Stones. Styx and Stones may break my bones, but they sure know how to rock 'n roll.

The Who. Jim Morrison and the Doors. All the classics. Plus, people like Howling Wolf, Bo Diddly, B.B. King. The blues, in general. Dave Matthews. I admire Dave's stand on the environment, but I'm glad it wasn't my tour bus that dumped a load of shit on a tourist boat in the Chicago River.

I really dig Lenny Kravitz' retro rock sound. I admire Bono of U2. I'm a big fan of bands like Green Day, the Red Hot Chili Peppers, and Fall-Out Boy - also from Chicago - because they know how to rock. Thoreau. Hemingway. Not musicians, but important influences. Sartre. Camus. The Nervous System, who brought out an amazing debut album last year. I've always liked that Peter Gabriel song, *In Your Eyes* from the old film *Say*

Anything. I admire anybody, any group willing to stand for something in art and in life.

M: Your parents are dead, you have no brothers or sisters, no pets and you are not married. Who do you turn to in times of trouble?

The One: In times of trouble?

M: Yes.

The One: Mother Mary speaks to me. (smiles)

M: Really?

The One: Really.

M: What will your next project be?

The One: I have a World Tour coming up to promote my new album, "Broken Soul." I'll be working to halt the spread of nuclear weapons, trying to help feed the hungry, helping achieve world peace wherever and whenever it is threatened. I'll do what I can, anyway. Just the usual stuff.

M: Can you give us a lyric or two from one of your new songs from Broken Soul? Will there be any free downloads available to fans prior to the start of the tour?

The One: Yes and yes. There's one song on it called *Reflections*, which goes like this.

(singing a cappella) *I took my heart down off the shelf, examined it for cracks.*
It seemed to have no major flaws, and so I put it back.

Michael McCarty and Connie Corcoran Wilson

It wasn't till much later, then, I realized it was torn,
that insults to its inner core had rendered it forlorn.
Where is the glue to heal such cracks,
To make it whole again?
Is there a formula somewhere
Residing with a friend?
What would you recommend to me
To fix my damaged soul?
Is there anything that one can buy
To really make it whole?
If you stumble on the answer
To this question I ask you,
Please let me know the remedy
So my spirit can be true.

M: Wonderful! Thank you so much for sharing that advance preview first with us, exclusively.

The One: No. Thank you for letting me ramble on. I hope I haven't bored you too much.

M: Not at all. We really appreciate your taking time to speak with us.

* * * *

Kaley turned off the tape recorder, her fingers nervously fiddling with the dials. This was only her third formal interview, and it was her first with a star of The One's magnitude. She had not planned on being so forcefully attracted to him. He was the most charismatic man she had ever met. She felt herself melting into the seat, wanting to make this moment last as long as possible. She was talking, but it was out of sheer nervous energy. She had no idea what she was saying. She feared she was babbling incoherently.

God, he must think I'm a complete ninny.

"Have you got what you need?" Dante asked.

No. I don't have what I need at all.

But a growing warm feeling told her what she needed was Dante Benedick. He was, indeed, The One.

"Passage, immediate passage! The blood burns in my veins! Away O soul! Hoist instantly the anchor!"

—*Darest Thou Now, O Soul*, Walt Whitman

CHAPTER 10

The Trip

12:11 p.m.
Tuesday, November 23, 2010
Inside The One's Limousine
Washington D.C.

The interview was over, but Kaley still showed no signs of leaving.

"Strictly off the record," The One said. "I think you'll love the new CD."

"Of course I will, but I have to wait until the beginning of next year to hear it. It seems like an eternity."

He smiled, cocked his head, and regarded her intently. The look a cat gives a bird. A look of interest and amusement. "Maybe you won't have to wait that long. I'll take you to England. You can hear the master tapes for yourself. My private jet is ready."

"Oh, my God. You're kidding, right? That would be ..." Kaley was flushed. "That would be so awesome. Do you know what that would do for the article? For my journalism career?"

"It would also be a bit irresponsible of me. You're only about a month away from finals. You probably have papers due. You're the daughter of the President of the United States. Can you set this up on your end to make it work? Be honest."

"Yes, I can. I just had my last class. I'm on Thanksgiving break right now."

"Good." Dante smiled.

The One thought about it for a moment. Intently. Musing inwardly. "Okay. We fly to England. Listen to the tapes. Do a bit of sightseeing. You fly back. That way you don't miss too much school. Deal?"

"Deal!" Her complexion took on a heightened rosy glow.

"I'll have the driver swing by your place so you can pick up a few things. Nothing fancy. It's a country estate. We won't be doing anything that requires lavish evening gowns. I don't go out that much. When I do, I try to remain as low-key and normal as possible. Get your things together. Davis will take us to the jet."

* * * *

Kaley could hardly believe what she was hearing. Her heart was pounding. She was ready to set sail on an adventure with the most handsome, the most amazing, man she had ever met in her life.

I've got to call Bella and tell her. Then she remembered, with a twinge of sadness that felt close to physical pain, she couldn't call her sister ever again.

"He took the gift and turned it over,
Shook it once and kicked it twice.
Read the words that told it purely,
Skimmed the story, caressed the dice.
All the while that he was reading,
Continuing to shake the dice."

—*Gold Above Dross,* The One

CHAPTER 11

Roll the Dice

7:45 p.m.
Tuesday, November 23, 2010
The White House

Just as Dante Benedick was arriving in England, sequestered in his private jet, chatting with Kaley Bellwood, the President's surviving daughter, the first earthquake hit San Francisco. It violently rocked the west coast of the United States, along the Hayward and San Andreas faults. The destruction rivaled that of the largest earthquake ever, the earthquake of 1906 that had nearly destroyed the entire city.

Hundreds of people were crushed. They emerged in the streets, dazed looks on their faces. The area bordered by Mission, 7th, Harrison and 4th was hardest hit. A temporary morgue was set up in Bill Graham Civic Auditorium. When the fires began, a hysterical tide of humanity surged through the streets, some with bones protruding from limbs. They desperately sought help. These were the lucky ones.

The cries of those trapped in burning buildings could be heard for blocks. Nothing could be done. The fires kept spreading – Market Street, Chinatown, Nob Hill. Everything was going up in flames. Explosions as flames reached car gas tanks.

Finally, Golden Gate Park was designated the last safe place to bring patients for treatment. At least there was less to burn in the green of the park. Triage. Screaming babies. Crying women. Sobbing men. Women clutching a picture, a memento, dazed, often still in their bedclothes.

The earthquake had struck in the evening, just as the theaters were letting out. Everyone was caught unaware. Many of those out on the town were killed by the collapsing theater structures. Vehicles scattered like matchsticks. Tombstones in nearby cemeteries were thrown about like confetti. Tombstones moved three to four inches to the right or left. Crypts gave up their contents in an obscene display of death.

In Chicago, meanwhile, a dirty bomb exploded.

It obliterated the top of the Sears Tower. The haze of the explosion drifted towards Soldier Field and Northerly Isle Pavilion, within what was known as the Chicago Station District. Residents within ten miles were warned to stay indoors.

"Do not leave your dwellings," WGN urged. "Stay inside."

The city had just concluded a huge party to celebrate the Chicago Cubs first World Series victory in over a hundred years. The Cubs hadn't made it to the big game since 1945; they hadn't actually won since 1908.

Getting Cubs fans out of the streets of the city, where they were taking part in a postponed ticker-tape parade and dedicated Cubs' Fans Day of Celebration, held late to coincide with the fans' being off for the Thanksgiving holiday, was impossible. The city would have celebrated immediately after the victory, in October, but the terrible October weather caused the event to be moved back an entire month. High winds. Rain pounding Lake Shore Drive daily. Grant Park was a sodden mess.

Days and days of inclement weather finally seemed to be over, when, on Thanksgiving Day, the terrorists took advantage of both the holiday period and the special celebration of what seemed like an impossible dream come true: a Cubs World Series victory! Confusion reigned supreme. The city was totally congested. The potential for nuclear contamination, with Chicago's famous wind factored into the explosion, had local experts scrambling for guidance from the Federal Government.

"What can we do?" Mayor Daley, of the FGDA, asked.

"Pray," was the response.

The Federal Government Disaster Agency was asked to help San Francisco deal with a crippling earthquake, just as the Midwest was reeling from the nuclear dirty bomb. Bucky

Bellwood's FGDA Director, Jimmy Fatone, was an old college buddy of his. They had been cheerleaders together at Texas A&M. The extent of Jimmy's disaster training was to argue with his wife on a weekly basis about what social event they should attend that weekend and whether he should wear the blue shirt or the pink one.

Just when it seemed that it couldn't get much worse, it did. News came that a much larger nuclear device had been detonated on the East Coast, in Virgina, near Langley Air Force Base and the Farm, where CIA operatives were trained. Terrorists had also flown a small bomb-laden plane into the spent-fuel cooling pool of WNP-2 in Richland, Washington and WNP-3 near Beaverton, Pennsylvania. Since the WNP-3 plant was near the Beaverton Steel Plant, the combined explosions were catastrophic. These irradiated pools near nuclear plants were elevated high off the ground, covered only by a lightweight canvas tarp. They were vulnerable from above, below and the side. The NRC (National Regularity Council) had made no provision for air attack. Their attitude was *"That's not our job."* They left the protection of such dangerous spent-fuel cooling pools to the agencies responsible for air security. And those agencies dropped the ball.

Mayor Daley, the fourth Daley to be Mayor, sighed. "Typical short-sightedness. What a way to run a country!" He knew about running things. He, and his father, grandfather, and great-grandfather had been Mayors of Chicago for the past eighty years.

This is typical of the Bush years. Regulations for Homeland Security right and left. All that was accomplished was to terrorize the populace into giving that incompetent boob two terms.

Homeland Security became a joke. With lax protection of nuclear spent-fuel cooling pools, open borders, unsearched cargo ships, the American people were the next big endangered species.

And now, as the piece de resistance, word came that an entire plane, filled primarily with US citizens, had been hijacked. It was sitting on the tarmac in Washington, D.C., at Dulles International Airport, while the hijackers made demands. Eight hundred passengers. Dulles was only twenty-six miles from the city.

God help them, the FGDA actually rejoiced because the plane wasn't at Ronald Reagan airport, only four miles from downtown D.C. If twenty-two miles is all that separates you from kissing your ass good-bye, you're in all-out disaster mode. What a bunch of fuck-ups!

The plane on the tarmac was an Airbus A380. It carried eight hundred passengers. The official United States policy was never to negotiate with terrorists. Knowing this, the relatives of the hijack victims were said to be hysterical in their anxiety. They were putting as much pressure as they could on the White House.

In the face of the government's refusal to talk to the hijackers, one irate caller managed to get through to FGDA headquarters. It was the husband of a woman passenger, and he now shouted at Jimmy Fatone's assistant.

"What, exactly, does FGDA stand for, anyway? Fucking Government Damned Arrogance?"

"I assure you," the assistant said, "that we're doing everything we can." Sweat stains soaking through his pink shirt belied this statement. "Please bear with us."

"Right," the caller said. "And I should do this why?" There was a *click* as the caller hung up.

* * * *

The last few weeks had been hell, and now this. Bucky Bellwood was furious.

"What the fuck is going on?" he bellowed at his staff. "How did the terrorists get control of the plane? Where were the Federal Air Marshals?"

"Remember when you vetoed the bill to reinforce the cockpit doors, Mr. President?"

Bucky felt uncomfortable at the blunt reminder.

"And then you cut the number of Air Marshals from two to one, per plane, to save one million dollars for the war effort? Then you cut the Homeland Security budget from $680 to $340 million, total?" The aide reminding him of all this was going to have a short career. Bucky made a mental note to fire him, soon.

"Yeah. So what?"

"Well, it seems that a particularly enterprising individual secreted himself aboard the Airbus A380, during the cleaning phase. He posed as a member of the clean-up crew. Later, he broke down the un-reinforced door to the cock-pit with an axe, and used that axe to kill both the pilot and the co-pilot."

"Jesus, Mary, and Joseph. Where-in-the-hell did he get an axe? Have you people never heard of metal detectors?"

Bucky's press secretary, Jimmy Johnson, looked uncomfortable. "He was really quite creative. He made it from materials already on the plane, during the night, while he was stowed away there. He apparently had some background in engineering such a tool out of available metals aboard the plane itself."

"How many passengers onboard?"

"Seven hundred and eighty U.S. citizens, sir, and twenty British tourists."

"My God!" Bucky looked green around the gills.

"What are they demanding? What do they want?"

"That's the odd thing, sir. There's just one hijacker, and he's not made contact with anyone yet. We don't know what he wants or where he might want to go. He wants the plane re-fueled. It had just arrived from London." Jimmy Johnson shuffled his feet nervously.

"Get Jimmy Fatone on the horn," Bucky said. After a brief wait, Jimmy's voice filled the Oval Office on the speakerphone. The Speaker of the House, Dean Howard, was present. So was Vice President Akaihane-Black.

"Jimmy, what-the-hell is happening in San Francisco and Chicago?"

"I'm trying to coordinate the triage units at Golden Gate Park, Mr. President. The fires are burning out of control. There was a huge explosion just to our north. Just huge." Sharp intake of breath. "There goes another one."

"What about Chicago? What's happening there?"

"It appears that the dirty bomb went off on the El. The elevated train, that is. The orange line. Just as people were getting off work. Absolutely the worst time of day. We've set up some medical tents in Grant Park."

"Are you stuttering?" Bucky was insensitive to the

infirmities of others.

"Yes, sir. I'm afraid I am. It's an old childhood habit. I haven't done it in years."

"Well you can shut the fuck up now, if you're going to keep sounding like Daffy Duck, for Chrissakes. I've heard enough. It's not like we don't have enough problems without a retard leading the relief effort." He slammed down the phone.

"There's just one other thing." This came from Dean Howard.

"What's that?"

"The hijacker. He claims he knew Isabella. He says that he's a member of the Syrian Royal Family."

"Great. Just fucking great." Bucky felt weary, as he sat in his brown leather desk chair.

"Things fall apart; the centre cannot hold…"

—*The Second Coming,* William Butler Yeats

CHAPTER 12

Whispers of Chaos

9:07 p.m.
Tuesday, November 23, 2010
Dulles International Airport
Washington, D.C.

Strange babble in Arabic, unintelligible to all passengers on the hi-jacked A380 plane, save one, Mosuma "Zuma" Hamad, filled the stagnant, cramped space. The voice belonged to the chief terrorist, demanding that Zuma denounce the United States "live," to be filmed on videotape.

The younger Syrian said, "Mosuma hasn't had enough time to recover yet."

Mosuma looked like he had been in an auto accident, and his head was covered in bandages.

"Time," the older Syrian said. "We no longer have any time left. Start taping now," as he shoved Mosuma into the aisle.

"I attended college at Georgetown," Zuma said, looking at the other two hijackers, submachine guns trained on him. "The United States is a country of greedy swine. These men do not understand or recognize anything good or true. Only one among them was both good and true – Isabella Bellwood. But, she is dead by her own hand. Her father, she despised, for the very reasons that the world despises him. I despise William Bellwood and others like him and all that they represent. Bellwood represents the infidel that we must annihilate. He represents the worst essence of greedy capitalism. He is an imperialistic opportunist. The Americans want to pillage and rob our homeland under false pretenses. For this, they must be punished. We must kill as many of them as we can, any way we can. God is good. Allah is great. Death to the infidels!"

Ali, the head hijacker and video operator, walked from the plane at Heathrow Airport to the limousine on the runway and threw the video camera towards the dignitary seated inside, the Syrian Prince funding this mission. The plan awaited only the arrival of the Prince's eldest son, Zacarias, to become fully operational. Bahar sat in the back seat of the limo. He would be calling the shots. Zuma was almost peripheral to the plan; he was useful only in that his years in the United States had rendered him extremely proficient in English.

Zuma was the translator: Arabic into English; English into Arabic. The Prince's older son, Zacarias, had grown up watching American westerns. He fancied himself a tough uncompromising gunslinger, like those he had idolized on film. Zacarias had only scorn for his younger brother, Zuma, whom he considered a weak pacifist.

When Zuma had told him of his romance with a young American woman, Zacarias had responded, "Why would you defile yourself with a filthy American whore? Find yourself a chaste and pure Arab female to bear your children."

Zuma's relationship with Isabella was not about bearing children. It was pure love. Zacarias, who had all the sensitivity of a pig, did not understand such emotion. He took women when he wished. He occasionally lusted after a type that most Arab men secretly desired: blonde, blue-eyed, full-breasted. But he was not tender when he made love. He certainly was not able to comprehend what Isabella's death had meant to his younger brother. As far as Zacarias was concerned, both Isabella and Zuma were expendable. In fact, it would be very good if Zacarias could somehow remain alive while his younger brother Mosuma was forever eliminated from contention for their father's throne, the throne of Syria. Zacarias' main concern was that he be remembered. He wanted history to remember him for something. Anything.

"I want the Americans to cringe when they hear my name. I want to become as famous as Mohammad Atta. I will carry out the will of my people, and I will go down in history as I do so. Allah will reward me with virgins in heaven after my death. My family will take my ashes and scatter them over the desert." In the tape Zacarias left behind prior to his potential suicide mission, he said "If I die, do not weep for me. I have secured my name and place in history. I have helped to punish the infidel invaders for their transgressions. My beloved mother, my father, I offer this sacrifice in your names."

The hijackers had planted three bombs on the plane, evenly distributed to do the most damage both to the terror-struck passengers and to the Airbus A380.

Zuma translated what Zacarias was shouting, in rapid-fire Arabic. Zacarias shot both the pilot and the co-pilot, fatal head wounds, as soon as he boarded the plane. The axe-wielding accomplice had given the terrorists access. It was not clear if the completely hysterical passengers comprehended what they were hearing from Mosuma, in translation. Chaos and whispers reigned.

"Americans, you must do what I command. I am your new leader; I am your new God. You must obey me."

Zacarias stopped, arbitrarily, next to a seat containing a family of three. The husband, David Anderson, was a man in his early thirties with short dark hair and a thin sleazy-looking mustache. The wife, Charlotte, a blonde, wore glasses and a light blue dress. She was in her late twenties. Their five-year old son Davy was coloring a picture of Spiderman when the commotion broke out; Davy had big blue eyes, like his mother's and a preternatural stillness.

Zacarias fired the semi-automatic weapon, first into the ceiling, to terrify the passengers and then into the chest of David Anderson. David Anderson fell to the floor, fatally wounded, bleeding profusely. Because the gun sprayed the general area where he was seated and was not target-specific, a bullet also hit Charlotte Anderson in the shoulder. She was alive, but moaning in pain. Only their son remained unharmed. He was so short in the seat that the bullets had gone completely over his head. Zacarias aimed the weapon at the small child's uncomprehending head and began babbling something in Arabic. Charlotte and Davy's blue eyes grew bigger and bigger.

For the weeping, wounded Charlotte, Zuma translated. "Do as you are told or your son will die next." This caused Charlotte to clutch Davy closely to her bosom, his fair hair was now drenched in her blood.

"Please don't hurt my baby," she blubbered, her eyes spilling tears. Davy was forcefully ripped from her arms, and thrust roughly into an empty nearby seat. He was alone.

Zacarias grabbed Charlotte by her injured right arm. He dragged her, protesting, screaming, and crying, down the narrow aisle. The effect on the other passengers was to spread abject terror among them. A few large men seated in interior seats far from the aisle, looked as though they might intervene, if they were strategically able to do so, but the hijackers had already re-arranged the passengers so that only women and frail elderly passengers sat in aisle seats.

The drink service cart was in the way of Charlotte's struggling form as she was dragged down the aisle. Zacarias shoved it roughly to the side. Charlotte rose to her knees in supplication, hands clasped, praying for mercy. This brought no compassion from Zacarias. He resumed dragging the wounded woman by her injured arm and her long blonde hair towards the back of the plane, where the lavatories were located. Davy, dazed, remained alone in the seat. In a high-pitched terrified child's voice, Davy screamed. "Mommy, Mommy! Help me!"

Zacarias shouted more commands in Arabic. Zuma, standing outside the lavatory door into which Zacarias savagely shoved Charlotte, shouted through the door. "Take off your dress!"

A few moments later the bloody, wounded woman emerged, clad only in her blood-soaked cream-colored bra and matching panties. She was crying so hard that she was incoherent. "Please! Please!" was the only part that Zuma could decipher. Her nose was running. She looked totally vulnerable. Hysterical.

Zacarias rattled off more commands in Arabic, most of them insulting comments about American women and their whore-like ways. Zuma was not translating verbatim. A shot rang out. Charlotte's nearly nude body fell halfway back into the lavatory, and came to rest, halfway in the aisle, halfway inside the lavatory. Zacarias kicked her corpse, waist-high. The sickening unmistakable sound of breaking ribs. She didn't move. She would never move again.

Mosuma leaned his head against the wall nearest the lavatory. He felt horrible. It felt as though the top of his head were in a vise. Every sound, every flash of the AK47 sub-machine gun echoed, reverberated like thunder inside his head. He felt nauseous, dizzy.

Zuma, completely ill now, operating on instinct alone, grabbed his own gun. He ran at the ruthless Zacarias, hitting him in the head with the butt of his sub-machine gun. Zacarias fell to the floor, bleeding.

The brothers had never had any love or affection for one another. After all, the Hamad family consisted of twenty-six children by many different mothers. In the cacophony of the moment, all Zuma could comprehend was that Zacarias was indiscriminately insulting all American women. His Bella had been an American woman. Zacarias had just killed an innocent, wounded American woman, a mother, in front of her small son's eyes. Zuma was appalled. *I must stop this!*
He was angry at his treatment at the hands of the American Secret Service, but he was not a schweinhundt – a German pig-dog, as the Hamburg cell would have called him.

Two of the hijackers, hearing the commotion, sprinted down the aisle. Zuma shot them both, aiming deliberately, his mind in a calm zone. Zuma raced towards the front of the plane from the back lavatory area, rapidly traversing the narrow aisle. Zuma pointed the gun for a third time at the third and final hijacker. The sub-machine gun didn't fire. The magazine was empty.

This gave the last hijacker, whose own submachine gun lay out of reach in a nearby empty passenger seat, time to pull a remote control device from his pocket. He glanced at Zuma, who stood there, dazed, clutching his useless weapon. His head pounded. He felt it was about to explode. With only a moment's hesitation, Hijacker Number Three pushed the red button.

Zuma's head did explode. The deep-brain implants worked exactly as they had been programmed. A pink spray of brain tissue and bone drifted over three rows of passengers. The job was done.

Obvious to the final hijacker, just before he pushed the button, was the fact that the mission had gone horribly awry.

The detonation of Zuma's implants, synched up with the bombs planted aboard the airliner, caused three bombs to explode simultaneously. The other hijackers in the plot knew about this "fail-safe" device. They had never completely trusted Zuma to do his job, royal family member or not. The DBI's – deep-brain implants – placed deep inside Zuma's brain were insurance against something like Zuma's hesitation. What if Zuma had second thoughts about his role in all this? All the hijackers were willing to pay with their lives. They expected to do so. They would be remembered: the thing that every man and woman in the world most wants.

But remembered for what?

It was clear that Zuma had decided he did not want to be remembered as a cold-blooded murderer of women and unarmed passengers. Belatedly, he had done what he could to stop the carnage. Before his death, he managed a final prayer.

The powers that be in Syria were in bed with the sitting Vice President of the United States, who had promised them many concessions when they helped her to gain power in the next election by casting her in the role of savior of the hostages they were to take. Knowing the affection that Mosuma had once held for America and Americans, his own people had cleverly calculated the odds that he might recant. Zuma might try to stop the simulated disaster they planned for this planeload of passengers. Betrayal of the plan by Zuma was to be avoided at all costs. Much rested on Mia Akaihane-Black's successful intervention in rescuing the hostages. The President she served would fail, but the Vice President, already pulling many of the strings of power, puppet-like, in the background, would move front and center. Her future as the first woman President would be assured by her successful negotiations to free the hostages.

As Zuma's pink brain tissue settled over the dying passengers, and chaos ruled, the moment proved one thing. Yeats was so right: *"Things fall apart; the centre cannot hold."* It was also true that the best-laid plans of mice and men could be fucked up, in a moment, by the mere push of a button.

"She softly touched the gift she'd sent him,
Tattered, battered, tossed aside,
Looked at the words, from deep within her,
Sad and hurt, with smarting pride."

—*Gold Above Dross*, The One

CHAPTER 13

In England

9:55 p.m.
November 23, Tuesday, 2010
The One's Manor (Potter Manor)
Chislehurst, Kent, England

The manor stood on five acres of wooded land near the tiny village of Chislehurst, in Kent. This was Dante's childhood home. The ability to build a gigantic, castle-like abode, on the outskirts of Chislehurst, was his way of saying to his old man, and to the town, *"Who has the last laugh now?"*

Of course, with his father dead for ten years, dead before Dante achieved stardom, the question was whether Dante had restored the old manor home for his peace of mind. Was it his way of dealing with the past? Dante was borne back ceaselessly into the past every time he revisited Chislehurst. Like F. Scott Fitzgerald before him, every time he crossed the threshold of Potter Manor he journeyed back in time.

He opened the ornately carved wooden door to the three-story castle-like edifice, surrounded by lush English gardens and ushered Kaley Bellwood into the immense living room.

"Can you see that gated entrance about a half-mile away? Stella McCartney spends a lot of her time at that big house down the lane. She keeps horses. Stella's a vegetarian like her mother. Rumor is that she didn't much care for her step-mum, but that marriage lasted about ten minutes." Dante shot Kaley a rueful look as he pulled the curtains back to improve her view of the manor house in the distance.

Dante also pointed toward a nearby turreted manor house. Horses were grazing in the pastures. Stables were nearby. The bucolic scene, the sun setting behind the fields,

85

made Kaley think of "Tess of d'Urbervilles" or any of Thomas Hardy's novels. Heather and gorse. The feeling was so pastoral. It was unbelievably picturesque. She couldn't believe she was really here.

I wish I had a camera.

"Of course," Dante said. "Stella's usually in London working on her collections. But we're quite close to the city here. Since her own baby was born, Stella spends more time here. That's one of the reasons I was willing to live here: proximity to the city. I used to live on the wrong side of the tracks, as you Americans like to call it. Now fine wines, great music, wonderful art surround me. Matisse, Renoir, Degas. The Impressionists. I hope I don't sound like I'm boasting. Their paintings just give me peace. They fill my soul. I love Monet's *Water Lilies*. Those paintings are just amazing. So peaceful. Come on. I'll give you the grand tour."

And grand it was.

Dante began slowly climbing the impressive staircase, hand resting lightly on the carved banister.

"This is the upstairs living room. See that white piano, near the balcony? Elton John gave me that after he used it on tour with Billy Joel. Actually, he lost it to me during a poker game," Dante added, laughing. "I don't think he was too happy about having to give it up, either. It was during his 'Songs for Dead Blondes' phase, as Keith Richards liked to call it. He was pretty affected by Princess Diana's death. I don't imagine he fancied losing his white piano to the likes of me, either, which only added insult to injury, I'm sure."

He continued down the long hallway. It was lined with framed originals by various artists: Degas, Toulouse Lautrec from his circus period, when he was incarcerated against his will in an asylum, and painted circus sights solely from memory, to prove his sanity.

Kaley was no expert on modern art, but she recognized that the art in the hallway, alone, was worth millions. Dante continued, like the good tour guide he was attempting to be. "I have three guest bedrooms upstairs. You're welcome to choose any one of them. They all have an attached private bath, a working fireplace, plus the modern things like a telly, of course."

"May I ask you a question?" she said.

"What?"

"Why isn't there much furniture? You've got the piano and plasma televisions. Yet the place seems bare."

Dante looked embarrassed. "I auctioned off all the Potter Manor antiques. Donated the proceeds to Feed The Children. Some of my friends like to call that charity YFF."

"What does YFF mean?"

"You're fucked for furniture," he added, laughing. "They know I haven't had time to replace the pieces. I'm rarely here long enough. Always touring."

"I don't remember reading anything about that in your press kit," Kaley said. She gazed at him, surprised.

Dante looked away, embarrassed.

"Well, I didn't do it for publicity. I did it because it was the right thing to do. I told my press agent, young Joshua, whom you've met, to keep it out of the press. Just say 'an anonymous donor.' Hey, it works for Streisand! She was sued by the buyer for a defect in one particular piece she auctioned off at Sotheby's. But she donates stuff like that to charity or your U.S. political causes all the time." Dante's eyes twinkled with amusement as he added this particular detail.

Kaley was astonished. The more she learned about the person behind the myth, the more she found she loved the mind behind the fame.

"I doubt if Babs would be donating to Dad. I don't think they see eye-to-eye, politically."

Dante laughed. "Is that so? Your father does seem to hold some fairly extreme views. He certainly thinks that he knows what is best for the rest of us. You're his daughter. You should know that better than anyone."

Dante walked downstairs. Kaley followed slowly. He turned down a hallway with no artwork on its bare stone walls. Opening another door, The One descended to yet another level. The entire lower level of the Manor house was a recording studio. Dante recorded all his albums in the privacy of his own home.

"It's pretty state-of-the-art," The One said. "A 64-track studio. I didn't bring you here to brag about my studio, though. I brought you so that you could hear the unmixed cut of 'Broken Soul.'"

He took a seat at the console. "Sit here; it's my favorite chair. In fact," he added, smiling, "it's my ONLY chair!"

Kaley sat in the black leather chair next to The One.

"Do you mind if I take notes?"

"Why would I mind? But remember: you're here to relax, not to work. You need to get your head on straight after all that's happened to you."

Dante went on. "This CD is going to be a lot different from anything I've ever done before. I'm doing it all myself, overdubbing the tracks. It'll be all acoustic, unplugged. The first song is called 'Everything'"

Dante turned a few knobs, pushed some console buttons. The music swelled, filling the room:

"I would give everything
Just to be with you
I wouldn't need anything
As long as I had you.
I would do everything
Just to have your love.
I wouldn't need anything
If I had your love
Everything
You're my everything
Everything
You're my everything."

Dante looked to Kaley for her reaction. "I know … it's kind of banal and repetitious, but that's what you need - a hook. It has a great lyrical hook. That's what'll sell it to my audience. Some of my songs have better lyrics. Maybe I should say, more complex lyrics."

"Everything" was followed by "Reflections," "Life," "Broken Soul," "No Longer Mine," "Calling All Angels," "The Storm," "All That Matters," "Sad Man Song," "Endless Rain," "The Key," "Embers in the Rain," and the last song, "Light the Spark."

As soon as the last song was finished, The One hit a red button, which shut the control board down.

"That was fantastic!" Kaley meant it. She was very impressed, and she didn't impress easily. "I like it more than the 'Gold Above Dross' CD, and that one's my favorite. I think this one is even better."

"Thanks."

"*Sad Man Song* is, well, sad." She blushed with embarrassment at the obviousness of the comment. Then she added, "And you said you were banal. How's that for a stupid statement?" They laughed together.

"People want to force happiness on us all the time. Nobody wants to be around someone who is sad. I wanted to say, through my music, that it's ok to be sad sometimes. Life is not all highs; we all have lows, as well. Other people need to be there for us when we're low."

"I really loved the piano in 'Reflections.'"

"I'm glad you liked it," Dante said. He seemed sincere and humble.

She looked at her notes. "The lyrics to *The Key* are kind of abstract. Did you mean for them to be so enigmatic?"

"Well, to me, they're not enigmatic at all. It all comes down to personal expression. The key to everything is the ability to elicit emotions. However, emotions destroy words. Feelings and words don't always go well together. When you try to actually express something that you are feeling in words, it comes out sounding trite or stupid. That's where music gives me the freedom to convey what I can't convey any other way. If it's a bit cryptic, well, maybe it's because I'm a bit cryptic, myself?" He gazed intently into Kaley's deep brown eyes. She felt herself blushing.

Recognizing her discomfort, he said "Let's celebrate." Then he paused. "Are you old enough to drink?"

Kaley was semi-offended. "I'll have you know I'm free, white, and twenty-one." She said this in a mocking tone that was meant to be humorous. She sounded as though she were only half in jest, though, and hoped she didn't come off rude.

"Well, then, let the champagne flow!"

He poured two glasses of Moet & Chandon Brut Imperial, 1997, a very firmly structured wine, packed with biscuit, citrus and honey notes. Delicious.

* * * *

For the next hour, the two drank champagne, talked, laughed and consumed more Moet & Chandon.

"And that is when I realized, I had just stolen Keith Richards' guitar," Dante finished his story.

Kaley laughed. "I hope you returned it?"

"The Stones were in the middle of their world tour. That night, Keith flew to Australia. So the next day I had to fly from Heathrow for twenty friggin' hours to return that guitar to Keith. Let's just say he never loaned me another one."

He looked at his watch. "It's getting late. Time for us to go to bed."

Kaley's heart was racing. Like girls the world over, she fantasized about The One. Sleeping with a rock star was the most basic fantasy of a teenaged girl. She was no exception. *"He really likes me. It's really going to happen,"*

Her palms were sweaty. Her mouth was dry.

Dante yawned and continued. "I have three guest bedrooms upstairs. Choose one. I'll see you in the morning. I'll have the staff make us breakfast or lunch, whichever you prefer. After that, a little sight-seeing and then we'll have you delivered back to your classes in the States."

Noting her puzzled expression, Dante added, "I don't sleep with my fans. I leave that stuff to Kid Rock."

"But, I thought you found me attractive?"

"Of course you're attractive," he quickly added. "You're drop dead gorgeous."

"I think I'm falling in love with you."

"Kaley, you really don't know me. You read interviews. You see my concerts; listen to my CDs. That's only a small part of me. I'm flattered that you like me, but I only brought you to England to try to cheer you up. I didn't think it would hurt for a budding journalist to have a private peek at a rock star's world. But I'm not going to sleep with you. Our friendship isn't that sort."

Kaley watched silently as Dante left the room. She was stunned.

In her room, later, she took her journal and wrote. "I am being torn apart from the inside. I feel that my heart and body are out of equilibrium. Why doesn't he desire me?"

As she wrote this, time passed. She lounged in the king-sized bed, tossing and turning, dressed in her sexiest negligee. At least an hour had passed since they retired. She could not get Dante out of her mind, nor could she easily give up the idea of holding him in her arms.

Slipping on the pale robe that matched her white peignoir, she slipped out of her room and tiptoed down the hall. She had seen Dante enter this bedroom. She quietly turned the doorknob. The door did not give. She pushed harder. There was no mistake this time; the door was locked. Locked against her.

Tears streaming down her face, she tiptoed back to her room and wrote:

It is the middle of the night. I lie in this large bed. I am cold and lonely. Then, you appear beside me, and you are naked, aroused. You lie down next to me. You hold me, like a circle being closed. It is a sense of completeness. Passion, but it is not a sexual moment. You softly whisper, "I love you with all my heart. You're so beautiful, so soft, so warm." These words change me from a scared and lonely girl to a warm, fulfilled woman. What is important is that you are next to me, holding me in your arms, telling me that you are mine. Then, you disappear; the magic is gone. You weren't meant to be in my arms. You were meant to be in someone else's arms, in someone else's life. I lie here, crying, desiring, longing. I think of this Egyptian Proverb: "The worst things: To be in bed and sleep not. To want for one who comes not. To try to please and please not."

Kaley's stifled sobs lulled her to sleep, near daybreak.

"Do I dare disturb the universe?
In a minute there is time
For decisions and revisions
Which a minute will reverse."

—*The Love Song of J. Alfred Prufrock*, T.S. Eliot

CHAPTER 14

Disturb the Universe

10:04 p.m.
Tuesday, November 23, 2010
The White House

The President, William Bellwood, and the Vice President, Mia Akaihane-Black, were seated in the President's study, drinking wine, holding hands, and laughing intimately. The intercom on the President's desk interrupted.

"Mr. President, I'm sorry to disturb you," It was secretary Anna Ferdinand's voice. "I know you gave strict orders not to bother you, but the Secret Service want to talk to you. They say it's urgent. They're concerned about the safety of your daughter."

The President released Mia's hand to push the intercom button. "The Vice President and I are in the middle of a very important meeting. Can't this wait?"

The Vice President put down her glass of wine. "Bucky, this sounds serious. We can do this some other time. There'll be other times." She started to re-button her blouse.

The President stood up from his chair and walked over to where Mia was seated. He began rubbing her neck. "There's no time like the present." With that comment, he started unzipping her black skirt.

He kissed the nape of her neck. Mia sighed, inwardly, *Shit!* It wasn't as if he hadn't felt her up about a million times before. She just wanted to get out of there. This was Bucky's daughter. His only surviving child.

If anything happens to Kaley while Bucky is fucking me, Renee Bellwood will take us both out. Talk about being screwed.

93

"I'm sorry, honey," Mia said, feigning an emotion she didn't feel. "This will have to wait. Your daughter's safety is much too important."

She was out of there.

* * * *

Two Secret Service men entered the office.

The first man, Lucas Nailer, was tall, muscular, black, in his late twenties. He had a Marine-style haircut and wore a jogging suit. He looked as though he might have been jogging recently, in fact, and appeared sweaty and out-of-breath. The other older man, Frank Racine, was in his fifties, nearing the mandatory retirement age of fifty-seven. Shorter, bald, with a well-trimmed sandy beard. He wore wire-rimmed glasses, a dark suit. He was carrying a black brief case and looked more like an accountant than a Secret Service agent.

"Mr. Nailer," The President said, eyeing the younger African American agent. "Mr. Racine," nodding towards the older man. "There's an urgent matter regarding my daughter, Kaley?" The President was testy, distracted.

Mr. Racine opened his brief case and removed a folder. He put on his glasses and read aloud. "At 11:30 this morning your daughter was interviewing Dante Benedick, the British singer they call The One."

"I hate that jerk," The President interrupted, face contorted. "My daughter loves his music. Goes to all his concerts. I'm not a big fan of rock and roll. Give me country music any day of the week. It's the only true American music."

"That limey bastard. He's been a thorn in my side for years. He constantly bad mouths me, and my policies, to the press at his concerts. The worst thing is he's not even an American. He's a British-born, Socialist piece-of-shit.

That song that he sang at Isabella's funeral should have been cleared. He insulted every politician there, singing it. That guy's got some nerve."

"Sir," Mr. Racine said, clearing his throat and continuing with his reading. "Your daughter and Mr. Benedick were riding in a limousine together, toward Ronald Reagan National

Airport. Our office cleared this. We had one of our men follow them, standard procedure. I believe it was Mr. Nailer."

"Yes, it was me, sir. I had to chase them through three terminals. I didn't have my badge on my person, since I was called to duty from my home rather suddenly. I was out jogging when I got the call. Security wouldn't let me through to stop what happened next."

"Why? What happened next?" Bucky said.

Nailer continued. "I'm afraid your daughter managed to take off with Benedick. They boarded the plane together."

Frank Racine chimed in. "Mr. Nailer reported the flight to the office at once. We checked the plane's flight plan with the airport officials. We also used one of our spy satellites. We were able to track them to Heathrow Airport, and, subsequently, to Mr. Benedick's manor house in Chislehurst, Potter Manor, outside London, in Kent, England." Having concluded briefing the President, the mousy accountant-type, Agent Frank Racine carefully placed the papers back inside the folder and started to place the folder inside his brief case.

"Do you want to see the report?" Racine asked Bucky.

The President was silent, ignoring the question. He drummed his fingers on the desk. Finally, he spoke. "Can we send some of our men over there to bring her back without her mother finding out that she's gone?"

"She *is* over twenty-one. She left the country of her own free will traveling on a valid United States passport. By all legal standards, she's an adult. We can make some discreet inquiries, but we can't just 'go get her.' And it's unlikely that we can even make the inquiries for a day or so, during which time I think her mother may hear that she is out of the country. Do you wish us to continue monitoring them?"

"Well, of course! I would have to have shit-for-brains to not want you to monitor them. We must try to keep this quiet. I especially do not want the First Lady apprised of this. I guess that's about all we can do," the President said morosely, as he gulped a last swallow of wine.

"You especially do not want the First Lady apprised of what?"

Bucky hadn't heard Renee enter the Oval office. She had a steely tone in her voice and had stopped by with some carpet

95

samples she was considering for her office refurbishing.

Hell hath no fury like a woman scorned.

He had a feeling that the next few moments of conversation with his wife were not going to be nearly as pleasant as the time he'd just spent with the Vice President.

"A lonely impulse of delight
Drove to this tumult in the clouds..."

—*An Irish Airman Foresees His Death,* William Butler Yeats

CHAPTER 15

Impulse of Delight

10:45 p.m.
Tuesday, November 23, 2010
The White House

"Renee, darlin'," Bucky Bellwood stammered. "What a pleasant surprise! I thought you were shopping for furniture for your office project?"

"I'm obviously not out shopping," Renee said. Often, it was necessary to explain the apparent to Bucky Bellwood. "I'm here, and I just overheard you tell these nice men to especially not apprise the First Lady of something. What?" Renee did not look like she was going to be satisfied with anything short of the truth.

"Ah, darlin' – it's not anything important, really."

"Gentlemen, will you excuse us?" Renee asked sweetly of the two Secret Service agents. Frank Racine and Lucas Nailer exited, stage left.

"What is it that I have to be kept in the dark about?"

"Kaley. It's about Kaley."

"What about Kaley?" Renee's voice echoed alarmed. She had just lost one daughter. She was feeling extremely protective of her remaining child.

"Well, she just took a little trip. That's all."

"Trip! Trip where?"

"Uh ... England?"

Renee looked extremely upset and angry. "England? What is our daughter doing in England?"

"Well, you know that rock star you gals like? The One."

"What about him?" Renee was growing less patient by the moment. You could almost hear the mental tapping of her foot, unless you were the extremely unobservant William Bellwood.

"He apparently took Kaley to London with him and landed at Heathrow Airport, and now they're at his country estate, Potter Manor, in Chislehurst in Kent." Bucky blurted this out as though he were a small boy confessing that he had stolen the last cookie.

Renee did not appear amused.

"She can't do that! We can't let her do that! She has school! She has finals! She has tests! I, for one, am not going to let my daughter become a groupie, following rock stars around the world."

Renee was pacing Bucky's office at this point. Her pacing grew faster as she learned more about her daughter's plight. Renee's furrowed brow made her look as desperate as a cornered mother wolf fighting for the survival of her offspring.

"The Secret Service does not think we have much of a case for storming over to London and kidnapping our own daughter," Bucky said. His tone was subdued, cowed.

Renee gave Bucky a final exasperated look and exited the Oval Office, a woman on a mission. Her angry heels clicked down the corridor towards her own space. The impulse she was feeling was not delight.

PART 2
Running Out of Time

"Heaven hath no rage like love to hatred turned
Nor hell a fury like a woman scorned."

—*The Mourning Bride,* William Congreve

CHAPTER 16

Hell Hath No Fury

10:47 p.m.
Tuesday, November 23, 2010
The White House

As Renee Bellwood stalked down the corridor of the White House, intent on the arrangements she must make to fly to England, what was going through her mind?

How can he be such a pitiful excuse for a father, a husband and a human being, all at the same time? A true triple-threat! Terrible at all three! What could I have been thinking?

But she knew what she had been thinking on that night, long ago, when she had conceived the twins. She'd been young, stupid, and drunk. She'd paid dearly for her poor judgment. Some would say she had been handsomely reimbursed. She was the First Lady of the land. The tradeoff was being married to a man who was a rutting pig. Bucky would screw anything with a pulse. Everyone knew it, including her. She was humiliated every day of her life simply because she was Mrs. William Bellwood, First Lady of the United States. Bucky had turned out to be one of the worst Presidents of the century. She was devastated daily by the stupidity and avarice of his decisions. These decisions affected the entire world. They were always designed to line Bucky's own pockets. Renee was completely out of patience with her greedy, self-centered, philandering husband.

Hearing Bucky minimize the importance of her only surviving child in his dismissive fashion illustrated, for her, the widening gap between them. Her children were her world. She and her husband no longer saw eye-to-eye on matters of world importance. That was a given. But he was also a parent who operated on a totally different wavelength than she did. Bucky did not see the damage that could be done to an impressionable young woman in the hands of an unscrupulous rock star. This was a young girl who had just lost her only sibling. She was vulnerable. She was his daughter and Bucky's only surviving child, unless one wanted to believe the rumors of bastard offspring from numerous mistresses. Although Renee enjoyed The One's music, she didn't know much about his character. The perversion possible in the greedy grasp of some unscrupulous musician was unimaginable, especially a rock star without a conscience who might gain power over a naïve, trusting girl at the most vulnerable moment in her life.

Kaley has just lost Isabella. She is vulnerable, psychologically and physically. She is certainly in danger of losing credit for all her hard work at the University if she misses her classes. Who knows if she made the necessary arrangements to be gone? She may have just ruined her entire semester!

Just thinking of how irresponsible all this was made Renee irate. She was feeling anger on top of anger.

She tried to prioritize her emotions, as she walked out of the office. "I don't know whether I'm more angry at Bucky, at Kaley, or at Dante Benedick!"

She had to put the anger out of her mind, compartmentalize her problems, prioritize them, and concentrate on securing Air Force One immediately. She must fly to her daughter's side. She must rescue her only child from the rock star who might, at this very moment, be preying on a distraught young girl reeling from the stress of the recent death of her sister.

Men only want one thing. Once they have it, you're only good for cooking, cleaning, bearing children, and being a trophy wife.

How well Renee had learned that lesson! *Not Kaley. Not with my daughter, you don't!*

The steam in her demeanor practically rose off her like a nuclear mushroom cloud. Anger kept her focused. Focused on what she must do. She must rescue her child!

To Renee, Kaley was still a child. Kaley's maturity was

not that of a full-grown woman. Renee, herself, had had to learn to grow up fast, after William Bellwood knocked her up that spring night twenty-one years ago in the back seat of his Mustang convertible. William Bellwood had promised her the world; he had delivered a world of grief. Renee had not had time to remain a child, herself. She was barely twenty-one. She had wanted to do so many things, to see so many places. All those hopes and dreams were cut short with the birth of the twins. She was suddenly responsible for two small, squalling infants.

Bucky was far too busy campaigning for public office, running the family oil business and playing Big Man to lend a hand. *Kaley just turned twenty-one!* Renee thought. *The same age I was when I threw away my life in one careless night.*

Renee was very proud of her daughters. She loved them both uncritically and unconditionally. She had poured her love and affection into the nurturing of those two small beings. Her love for the twins made submitting to Bucky's sexual demands slightly more bearable. Like any protective mother, if someone or something threatened her children, she would lay down her life to protect them. You didn't want to mess with Renee Bellwood, where her children were concerned.

Her protectiveness was running especially high right now. She had just lost Isabella. They had *all* just lost Bella. It had only been days.

She tried to shut down the pain that thought gave her.

No time for thoughts of poor Bella. Kaley was still very much alive; she might be in grave danger.

Renee walked towards the Secret Service escort, barking orders in an efficient manner. She had her cell phone out, contacting her aide, Rosita Perez. She was not acting like a wounded wife or a shrinking violet. She was in full battle mode. She looked capable of launching a crusade.

"Take me to the airport. Immediately!" the First Lady barked. She had no clothes with her. She must grab her passport from the credenza in the master bedroom before leaving. The mother hen had nothing other than a desire to be airborne, winging towards England to rescue her sole surviving daughter.

When Rosita returned her cell phone call, Renee ordered,

"Find the number for Dante Benedick's manor house in Chislehurst. Let me know within the hour. I think it's called Potter Manor."

"Who is Dante Benedick, Ma'am?" Rosita, she knew, was not much of a fan of rock music. "Potter what?"

"The rock star. You've heard his music. The girls played it all the time in the official residence. Potter Manor is his house in England. It's been a grand residence in the Chislehurst area, in Kent, for centuries. He bought it in 2000 and remodeled it."

"Oh. How would I get that number, Ma'am?"

"Call the FBI. Call the Secret Service. Here's the number for the Secretary of Defense. Call him if you have to, but get it! Do I have to do *everything* myself?"

Within forty-five minutes, Renee Bellwood had the private number of Dante Benedick's manor house phone. Five minutes after receiving it from Rosita Perez, while airborne flying towards England, she was dialing.

Dante and Kaley had turned in for the night. The One never answered the phone after midnight. He made sure that the phone was far enough away from the master bedroom that a message could be left, so that no late-night phone calls would awaken him. The press had awakened him in the wee hours of the morning after a late-night concert too many times to let calls come through directly after a certain hour.

Renee Bellwood, the First Lady of the United States, left one message:

"Kaley. This is Mom. I'm coming to get you. And you, Mr. Dante Benedick, I expected better behavior from you. You had better have a very good explanation for this, or you will be very sorry."

"Fading like dawn's early light
Embers blaze throughout the night
Like my desire, they do not die,
Our love will last, and that is why."

—*Embers in the Rain,* The One

CHAPTER 17

Smoldering Embers

5:00 p.m.
Wednesday, November 24, 2010
The One's Manor (Potter Manor)
Chislehurst, Kent, England

Renee's glare was livid with fury. Her only surviving child was in jeopardy. It was all Dante Benedick's fault. That is what she thought as the Secret Service cars, all black Navigators with darkened windows and bulletproof glass, slowly crawled up the winding circular driveway to The One's manor estate, Potter Manor.

The house sat back at least a quarter of an acre from the gated entry. A special two-way communications device allowed those in the house to allow or deny entry to intruders. When those seeking entry were the official envoys of the United States government, six cars strong, entry was allowed.

Kaley and Dante had spent the morning sightseeing. Dante had put her aboard his private jet bound for America well over an hour ago. This fact had escaped the attention of the U.S. authorities. When the government cars pulled up before Dante's mansion, The One had just finished a swim in his private heated pool. He wasn't expecting company.

His hired help, really just three gentlemen, Ellis VanDyke, who cooked and did light housework; Davis, his chauffeur; and Joshua Gottlieb, his personal assistant, were his only companions. The trio came to him, poolside.

"Dante, there's a large entourage demanding entry. They say they're from the United States Secret Service. They have badges and papers to prove it." This was all conveyed in an out-of-breath rush. Days in this part of Kent were usually

111

fairly uneventful. Dante had not bothered to check for messages after awakening. It had only taken a few hours to drive Kaley around the small village of Chislehurst. Mindful of her class commitments and her upcoming finals, he then escorted her to his jet and she had departed for the United States.

"I want to stay," Kaley said, at the airport.

"I'm sorry. You can't. Just give me a hug."

Dante wrapped his arms around her in a paternal bear hug.

"I wish this moment would last forever." Kaley still seemed star-struck and almost unable to believe where she was and who she was with.

"Time never stands still. The Earth circles the Sun, day becomes night, night becomes day. Then it starts all over again. Time is an impatient mistress."

She sighed, a wordless sound of regret that spoke volumes.

"Maybe we can do this again another time. Right now, you have your family, school and, of course, completing the interview, too." Dante smiled warmly at Kaley when he mentioned the interview, a smile she returned with brimming eyes.

The plane took off. Large, silver, languorous. It flew into the cloud-free sky, the silver speck dwindling as it met the horizon.

As the plane disappeared from sight, Dante drove back to Potter House, and resumed his morning exercise ritual: fifty laps in his private pool. It was this activity that was now being interrupted by the urgent voices of his staff.

"Dante, Renee Bellwood and six Secret Service cars full of armed men are demanding entry. What should we do?"

"Well, let them in, of course."

He sounded nonchalant, but he was secretly eager to once again meet the First Lady of the United States. Their only previous meetings had been under adverse circumstances: once, while playing a Command Performance for the Queen when the President and Mrs. Bellwood had been present, and once while playing for the President of Brazil, a huge fan. And, of course, at Isabella's funeral just two days ago. It was unlikely that Renee Bellwood remembered anything about the dreary November day of Bella's funeral when she was cloaked in intense grief.

The door opened. In stalked Renee Bellwood, booted heels clicking on the marble foyer. She wore brown suede boots with a two-inch heel, cut with a square toe and a short zipper on the side. She also had on matching brown suede slacks, cut perfectly to show off her size six figure. Underneath the matching brown suede jacket was a fetching gold sweater, set off with a single gold Omega chain. Renee believed in simplicity in all things. Her style was elegant, cool, rather youthful, and laid-back. She looked absolutely amazing to Dante, as he toweled off from the laps completed.

This morning, because he had taken Kaley sightseeing and then had sent her on her flight home, he had postponed the swimming pool ritual from start-of-day to mid-morning. The pool, itself, had a shell that was retractable. Automatic buoys, pool-skimming devices, helped keep the water clean. There was an eight-person hot tub set diagonally in the corner of the pool area. The pool had lane markers, so that competitive swimmers, like Dante, could mark the laps they had completed and time themselves.

Dante was wearing a white Speedo swimsuit. It showed off his well-muscled body. His chest and six-pack area of his toned thirty-one-year-old body were dripping wet. A white towel was thrown casually around his neck. He had just climbed from the water when Joshua, concerned, approached him.

"It's all right, Joshua," Dante said. "Show them in."

But there was no "showing in" of the Secret Service. They barged in wherever and whenever they wanted, ear pieces in place and generic Secret Service garb marking them as Special Agents more clearly than if they had worn large signs that said, "I am with the United States Secret Service." Their short crew cuts and their earnest demeanor marked them as men on a mission. Their mission was not music.

"Mrs. Bellwood," The One greeted Renee. "How nice to see you again!" Dante really meant it. He was so sincere that he hoped that neither his body nor his delighted facial expression would give him away. Just looking at Renee reconfirmed in his mind why he preferred mother to daughter.

Kaley was beautiful, a lovely girl. Renee was gorgeous and a mature woman. Renee was lush, intelligent, spirited. Kaley was putty in his hands. Renee was mad as hell and opinionated. Spirited. Renee would give any man trouble. There would be no controlling Renee.

"Mr. Benedick," Renee began, coming right to the point, "Where is my daughter?"

"I arranged for her to fly back to the United States. She left over an hour ago."

Renee was stunned by the news. "She's not here?"

"No. She's gone."

The news startled Renee, and Dante noticed how fatigued she appeared.

"I don't believe you," Renee blurted out, eyes wild. "I want to see for myself."

"Why don't you let Joshua show you around the estate. When you're done, I'll tell you all about her visit."

Renee allowed herself to be led away by Joshua Gottlieb, trailed by her two Secret Service agents, Jack Paskvan and Angel Savage.

* * * *

Ten minutes later, Joshua and Mrs. Bellwood returned.

"I'm sorry I didn't believe you," Renee said.

"I understand your concern," Dante said.

Renee was a little calmer now that she knew that her daughter had returned to the United States. Then she remembered her anger at the fact that Kaley had been here at all. Why had Kaley left United States soil? What had happened to her while she was a guest at Potter Manor?

"How dare you take my daughter out of the United States during the Thanksgiving holiday? She had commitments to her studies. She had commitments to her family. If she doesn't pass her finals, all of her hard work for the entire semester at Georgetown will be compromised." Renee's eyes were flinty, deep brown, the mahogany brown of intense anger.

Dante wondered if, when she was less angry and upset, her eyes would be the color of warm cocoa. Right now, her eyes were like dark burning coals. Dante realized he was becoming aroused standing in such close proximity to this remarkable woman.

"Mrs. Bellwood …"

"Please, call me Renee. It sounds formal and stuffy when anyone refers to me as Mrs. Bellwood."

"Renee, then, I am sorry that you think I would take Kaley from the country without making sure that she had made satisfactory arrangements with her school. She told me that she was on Thanksgiving break from the University. She felt she needed some time away because of recent sad events." Dante could not bring himself to actually say, aloud, anything referencing the recent death of Isabella. He knew the subject was too raw and painful. He must tread carefully before bringing it up.

Renee seemed to falter in mid-stride. She glanced at the half-naked dripping-wet man standing in front of her, clad only in the skimpiest of swimming trunks and a wet towel. She suddenly realized how incongruous this conversation was, under these circumstances. She remembered her position as an emissary of the United States of America and its First Lady and her good breeding and inherent good manners took over.

"Please, Mr. Benedick. Go put some clothes on. I'll wait in your study."

"As you wish, Ma'am, but I'll only call you Renee if you call me Dante. Mr. Benedick was my dad. I'll be right back. Meanwhile, my man Ellis will get you a drink, if you want one."

For the first time, he felt Renee thawing slightly. He thought he noticed the beginning of a smile at the corner of Renee's lush lips.

"Thank you, Mr. Benedick. I'll wait for you in your study. And I'll have a Canadian Club and 7-Up, if you have that on hand."

"No problem." He went to his bedroom, to put on something more suitable for a conversation with the First Lady of the United States. The Secret Service was patrolling the perimeter of his estate, checking all rooms, making sure that their charge, the most important woman in the United States, if not the world, remained safe.

Dante returned wearing his signature white jeans and a light sweater that was similar to an Irish Fisherman's sweater. The fabric was extremely lightweight and soft cashmere so that the weave appeared to be heavy and substantial. Upon touching the fabric, it felt as soft as a kitten's fur. Dante Benedick had chosen this particular sweater for its comfort. She blushed at her teenage moment of infatuation. Renee Bellwood didn't intend to be touching any part of The One during this visit. If anything, she might be ripping his limbs off, if he had harmed her daughter.

"Let's go out on the terrace," Dante suggested.

His study had a terrace with French doors just off to the right that overlooked the traditional English garden below. There were small café tables and chairs that added to the charm. The day was sunny with some wind. Although England is always chilly and damp, the terrace, like the pool, remained comfortable thanks to a removable overhead transparent glass top. It was cozy and very pleasant on the terrace, overlooking Dante's well-manicured grounds. Sunset was only fifteen minutes away.

Dante, flushed from his swim and from emotions that he couldn't quite identify, was eager to defend his actions with Kaley to Renee Bellwood. He had a feeling he was going to have to.

When he reached the terrace, his blue eyes were set off by the off-white cable-knit sweater, tousled, still-damp dark blonde hair falling fetchingly over his eyes. Renee Bellwood had had one cocktail. It was strong. She was feeling the drink, the effects of her long trans-Atlantic flight and the idea that she was in the presence of a man so well known, whose music she admired. However, she was still the angry mother hen.

She began interrogating. "Did you sleep with my daughter?"

Dante was taken by surprise. He almost laughed, but he could see that this wouldn't be smart or well received. He asked, "Is this the U.S. Inquisition? No, Ma'am. I did not shag your daughter."

"Shag?" Renee was puzzled.

"Sleep with, have sex with, shag …" Dante tried to be helpful in finding American terms that were the equivalent of

116

the British slang expression. He wanted to convey to Renee Bellwood that his relationship with Kaley was platonic.

"Kaley is a wonderful girl, but we're not lovers. We're friends. That's all. She slept in the last bedroom on the right, upstairs … her choice. I gave her the choice of rooms. That was it. I wouldn't take advantage of your daughter, Mrs. Bellwood – Renee. I wanted her to have a pleasant time and a weekend where she could try to put all the sadness your family has gone through recently out of her mind."

Hearing this, Renee's eyes misted. She turned her head, to keep Dante from seeing that she was about to cry. She had the presence of mind to ask the Secret Service men to leave them alone for a moment.

"Jack, Angel, would you mind waiting in Mr. Benedick's inner study a moment, so that we can talk privately?"

The Secret Service agents withdrew. They were now out of sight in the study connected to the terrace, awaiting the First Lady's next command.

Dante stood next to Renee, a glass of Chardonnay in a Baccarat crystal champagne flute. They both paused a moment to admire the sun, setting in a pink fury. The fiery blaze, sinking in the west behind the riot of colors in the rose garden, was impressive. It was also very romantic.

Renee turned to Dante Benedick, raised her cocktail, and choked out the words- "I'm sorry if I'm accusing you of things that didn't happen. I'm upset. I'm tired. I lost one daughter. That's why I'm so worried about my remaining-" Words failed her and she halted.

Dante, seeing the anguish clearly written on Renee's face, wanted to reassure her. He wanted to reach out to her.

"It's okay. I would have thought the same thing, if Kaley were my daughter. She's a wonderful, beautiful girl. But, without being out-of-line, she's your daughter and, to me, you're twice as beautiful. I know what pain you must be experiencing. I'd like to be able to do something to help you through it. I just wanted to do something to help Kaley in the same way. But the something wasn't sexual. Not at all. As God is my witness, I didn't touch your daughter. She wanted to hear the master tapes of my new CD; that was what inspired the trip in the first place. That, plus my instinct that she

117

needed safe haven after the death of her sister. And I have another instinct. I sense that you need passion in your life."

This time, Dante dared mention the unmentionable. This time, he felt he got the words right.

Renee looked deeply into Dante Benedick's eyes, searching them for signs of sincerity. Somehow, she knew that he was telling her the truth. She suddenly felt woozy, a combination of the long flight, the strong drink and emotion. She grabbed his right arm, the arm clad in the soft off-white cable-knit Fisherman sweater. She could feel his strength, warmth and goodness through the fabric. She was merely touching his forearm, but she was becoming light-headed.

Just then, operating more on instinct than from intellectual thought, Dante Benedick leaned towards the tear-stained face of Renee Bellwood. She looked so vulnerable, so unhappy, so in need of comforting. On his terrace, with the fiery sun sinking in the west and with the best of intentions, he softly kissed her full, warm lips.

"Lighting fires of desire,
Our impulse yields temptation.
Will our love end within the hour?
And bring complete damnation?"

—*Embers in the Rain,* The One

CHAPTER 18

On the Terrace

6:00 p.m.
Wednesday, November 24, 2010
The One's Manor (Potter Manor)
Chislehurst, Kent, England

High above Renee Bellwood drifted eyes in the sky. A United States spy satellite, miles above them in the atmosphere, watched Dante Benedick's estate, at the very moment that he and the First Lady of the United States ventured out on the terrace. As soon as it had been determined that Kaley Bellwood was at The One's estate, Bucky Bellwood had ordered the surveillance. The satellites were capable of taking amazingly detailed photographs from miles above the Earth.

The Skylab satellite recorded Dante and Renee's kiss, but not its aftermath.

"What are you doing?" Renee Bellwood pulled away. She was both frightened and intrigued. She hadn't received a passionate kiss in twenty years. Few dared approach the First Lady of the Land sexually. Her position as wife, mother, and public figure kept her in the public view and made anything of this sort off-limits. For that matter, if Dante Benedick were not one of the world's richest and most powerful men, he wouldn't have felt confident enough to hit on the most famous woman in America.

At first, Dante said nothing. He continued to gaze deeply into Renee's sad and frightened eyes. Her eyes were almond-shaped, warm coffee brown, sensitive, intelligent. When she was compared to other First Ladies, the one most often mentioned was Jacqueline Kennedy. However, Renee was far more curvaceous than the angular, tall, lean Jackie O. She was shorter, at 5ft 5in, and older, at forty-two. Her ample bosom put Jackie Kennedy's flat-chested elegance to shame in the sexuality department. Renee was not a clotheshorse, with a body best suited to wearing, not modeling, clothes. Renee was a real flesh-and-blood woman, with athletic interests: horseback riding, swimming, and tennis. She had played golf for a while, thinking it might bring her some contact with her husband. Bucky had refused to play together again after she beat him. From then on, Renee did not bother. The girls were small and she wanted to be a full-time Mom. Besides, hitting a small ball into a hole seemed stupid to her. What did men see in it? What did they get out of it?

Dante said nothing, but he kept gazing into the haunted eyes of the First Lady of the land.

Renee's initial pulling away, the slap, her standard rejection mode, began to break down. She dropped her guard. She still regarded Dante warily, but now she looked at him with inquisitive eyes, not angry ones.

"What … why did you kiss me like that?"

"I could say I was sorry, Renee, but the truth is, you looked like you needed kissing. I sense that you need passion in your life." Dante meant this, as he said it for the second time.

If this was a line, it was one of the best lines Renee had ever heard, because it was so true.

"Are you being cheeky, as you Brits like to say?" She was almost smiling, as she asked. It wasn't a flirtatious response, but it was close.

"No, ma'am," said Dante, pulling away slightly. He noticed that she kept her well-manicured hand on his right forearm. "I'm not being cheeky at all. I'm dead serious. I think you're one of the most fascinating people I've ever met, male or female. I just want to be your friend. I sense that you need a true friend right now. I would be honored if you'd allow me to be that friend. I would like to do for you what I did for Kaley. Provide safe haven in the chaos of your life right now."

Dante meant to say "safe haven." The Freudian slip in saying "heaven," instead, was not lost on him. From what he knew of Renee Bellwood, it wouldn't be lost on her, either. She didn't comment on his faux pas. He thought he saw the ghost of a fleeting smile cross her lips for a second.

"I'm just ... I'm very, very tired, right now. And I confess to being a little woozy. I probably shouldn't have had that drink," Renee said, hand to forehead. "It was a long trip from America and we have no accommodations arranged. The trip was the most important thing. Now that you've told me that Kaley is on her way back to Georgetown, I've accomplished my goal. I also may have misjudged your intentions, Mr. Benedick. Dante. I'll apologize when I'm more myself."

"I'll make the same deal with you that I made with Kaley. Go upstairs. Pick any room you like. All are equipped with the modern conveniences. All are user-friendly." He smiled at the computer terminology.

"Tomorrow, I'll take you for a tour of the countryside. We'll have a quiet dinner somewhere nearby or here in the Manor. Your call. I won't do anything that you don't want me to do. I give you my word."

Renee looked at him, lower lip quivering. Her eyes were deep, dark pools filled with unshed tears. She felt completely open, her emotions naked. At first, she said nothing.

"Thank you," she said. "I'll tell the Secret Service that we are your guests. They'll insist on checking all the rooms in the house." She almost smiled. Almost.

Dante's goal was going to be to forever re-kindle that smile on Renee Bellwood's gorgeously full lips. He would like nothing better than to once again feel their full firmness on his own. To caress her cheek. To whisper endearments in her ear. He hadn't felt this much for a woman in a long time, perhaps forever. And it had been just as long since Renee Bellwood had experienced any kind of tenderness or passion in her private life.

The One watched the President's wife walk slowly towards his study to give orders to the forces protecting her. She was in command, again, holding it together. He heard her voice, speaking without discernible emotion, instructing the bodyguards, telling them what was going to happen next. Jack Paskvan and Angel Savage nodded. In time, he hoped to become one of those whom she trusted to protect her from all harm. And perhaps more.

"It's dangerous to dream about you,
Dangerous, I know.
But with the stars shining bright,
And the hazy moonlight,
Dreaming is all I can do."

—*Dangerous,* The One

CHAPTER 19

Dangerous

8:00 p.m.
November 24, Wednesday, 2010
The One's Manor (Potter Manor)
Chislehurst, Kent, England

When Renee awoke in darkness in a strange bed, in a strange bedroom, she had no idea where she was or what time it was.

Moonlight was filtering through the slats in the Venetian blinds. She walked in that direction, pulled the cord, opened the blinds, and turned on the lamp. The light streaming in revealed the nightstand, now also bathed in the illuminating glow from a small Tiffany lamp. The room had no other furniture save for an antique four-poster canopy bed and a big wooden dresser. On the walls were framed celebrity photographs. Renee examined the photos; The One playing guitar with Willie Nelson and Keith Richards and Robert Cray, The One shaking hands with President Bill Clinton, The One kissing Bonnie Raitt on the cheek, Sting and The One giving a thumbs up salute. B.B. King. Bono.

She walked out of the bedroom and down the hallway following the sound of soft music coming from the room at the other end of the hallway. She followed the music as though she were a child mesmerized by the Pied Piper.

At the end of the hall, behind a wooden door, which she opened in search of the sound, she found and entered a room where Dante sat at the piano. When she entered, he stopped noodling on the keyboard.

"Don't stop," Renee said. "That was beautiful. Play it again."

"Sam?" Dante said, teasing, reciting the famous mythic

line from *Casablanca* never really spoken in the film. He began to sing, low and slow:

> *"The sun fades from sight*
> *Melting time's midnight*
> *We must stay The Path*
> *Path of light, cast darkness away,*
> *Illuminate the night, brighten my world today.*
> *Brighten my world today."*

Renee grew pale as she sank into a nearby chair. Her pallor made her appear frail, weak.

Dante noticed this and stopped.

"What's the matter?"

"That's the first song that Isabella ever played on the piano when she was five."

"I'm sorry," Dante said. "I didn't know."

Renee fought the emotion welling up within her, but the tears slowly leaked from her eyes. Dante got up, uncomfortable, unsure. He didn't know how to comfort her. He wanted to wrap his arms around her, but the memory of the kiss and the subsequent slap on the terrace lingered. Renee seemed so in need of comforting, so pathetically sad and desperate. She was like a whipped puppy, constantly kicked to the curb. He sensed deep unhappiness beneath the calm facade. Yet he didn't want to over-step his bounds.

"I'm so sorry for your loss. I know how much it hurts," he said. There was an awkward silence.

Renee stifled a sob.

When she was silent, Dante handed her a Kleenex.

"This isn't how I wanted the evening to go," Dante said.

"Speaking of going, I must go back to America. Tomorrow," Renee said. "This was all a mistake. I'm sorry that I got caught up in the moment on the terrace. I wasn't thinking straight. You shouldn't have kissed me. It was wrong."

"It was magical; it was special. It didn't feel wrong," Dante paused. "There are things I want to say, emotions I want to express, but first, I want you to learn who I am. I want you to know that you can trust me."

That took Renee by surprise. She had expected a lot of things from Dante Benedick, but not this.

"Forget it ever happened. It will remain our little secret." She rose to leave.

"Americans can't keep secrets," Dante said, smiling. "But I'm British. I'll keep our rendezvous a secret. You can trust me."

She looked at him from under long lashes. "I feel that I can. Thank you for that."

Renee had an instinctual feeling that in Dante Benedick's arms lay comfort, peace and the safe haven he had mistakenly called "safe heaven." She felt that his accidental use of the term might be correct. He seemed so kind, so sane, and so nice. He was everything that Bucky Bellwood was not: honorable, trustworthy, attentive to her needs and moods, respectful of her, solicitous of her welfare. But everything was happening too fast. She needed to learn more about this handsome, kind stranger. It was as though time had been condensed. She needed more time. Time was always the problem.

She mustered her courage to speak. "I really regret the slap on the terrace, but I was just so … so … surprised. I want to learn more about you. One way might be for us to travel back to the United States together on Air Force One. It would be my penance. Don't you have a benefit concert in New York City, on Thanksgiving Day? You need to be there for that, anyway."

"How did you know?" Dante was surprised that a woman as busy as Renee Bellwood would be aware of a rock star's concert schedule.

Renee smiled for the first time. "I'm a fan, like millions of others," she said, simply. "I'd very much like to try to make it up to you for misjudging you, barging in here, accusing you of all manner of things. That was impolite of me. It's not what I want you to take away from our meeting. Will you travel with me, back to the States? We can talk for eight hours, non-stop, if you can stand it." She laughed.

"It would be my honor," Dante said. "Brilliant! We'll leave at dawn. I think I can stand eight hours of learning more about you, Renee. I wish we had more time, in fact."

"Fear attacks from one side and desire from the other; from one side, anxiety; from the other, an empty and deceptive happiness; from one side, the agony of losing what one loved; from the other, the passion to acquire what one did not have..."

—On Free Choice of the Will, Chapter 11, Book One, St. Augustine

CHAPTER 20

Passion to Acquire

Wednesday, November 24, 2010
Aboard Air Force One at Dawn
Flying from London to Washington, D.C.

As The One and Renee stepped aboard Air Force One, a cool breeze whipped around Renee. Her shoulders shivered involuntarily. The breeze was not the only reason for Renee to hold her jacket closer. She wasn't going to waste a single moment of their shared time aboard Air Force One. Renee hungered for a real conversation. What made this man tick? She hoped she would find out, and that he would get to know her in the process and to know her well. No one had paid this much attention to the real Renee in years.

The two settled into two of the four swivel chairs around a small bolted-down table. The crew readied for take-off; seat belts were secured. Once airborne, the crew discreetly disappeared. Their much-anticipated conversation began.

Dante Benedick gazed intently into the eyes of the First Lady. His eyes were unusually blue. When asked about his eyes and his searching gaze in interviews, he attributed it to myopia. Renee seemed small and frail to Dante, but she had a larger-than-life aura. There was something indomitable about Renee Bellwood. Charisma. It was as though she would bend, but not break. He found her entire demeanor, the way she carried herself, her tone of voice, her very fragrance, enchanting. He regarded her now, as she raised a glass to her lips, and decided to simply say it.

"It's as though we're two shattered souls, sharing space and time, but only for a moment. I feel as though you're me, and I'm you. You're the female version of me." He smiled disarmingly.

Renee did not meet his gaze. She seemed nervous. Finally, she said, "What do you mean?"

It was a ploy to buy time to control her thoughts and emotions. Dante could see that Renee Bellwood was an exceptional woman, an extraordinary and intelligent woman. She had risen through the university ranks in record time to become a full professor of classics and philosophy at Stanford. Her education would not go to waste now, as she spoke with The One.

"Do you believe in autonomy, Mr. Benedick? Do you think we take control of our own destinies?" By sticking to an intellectual vein in their conversation, Renee felt she was protecting her fragile emotions.

"Call me Dante."

She nodded assent.

"Do you believe, like Immanuel Kant, that if we are our own bosses we are our own slaves? That we should be ruled only by the Truth? Kant believed that truth was superior to the individual. Augustine called it the eternal law: that the morally grown-up human being recognizes an immutable standard of divine authority. He felt that such a standard should bind us, regardless of what we desire or what we believe."

After she completed the last line about truth binding us, regardless of what we desire, a faint flush mottled Renee's neck. It made her eyes appear brighter, making her even more attractive.

Dante still gazed deeply into Renee's eyes. He searched for a flicker of happiness. None could be found.

"I believe in the pursuit of truth, yes. And I believe in what the Bible termed the Golden Rule. But I don't believe that God put us on Earth to be miserable serving some standard that was set in the eighteenth century. I don't believe that we have to bow to some antiquated moral standard, regardless of our desires or beliefs." Dante hesitated. "Let me ask you this: do you believe that you've done everything in your power to be a good wife and mother?"

Renee paused, briefly. She exhaled softly.

"Yes."

"Has that made you happy?" The One continued. "Be

honest."

"No," she admitted.

"We both would agree that you've been hard-working in your roles as wife, mother, and First Lady of the United States. I can tell without even asking that you've been a faithful wife and companion to your husband, the President. Has he repaid your devotion in kind?" The entire world had heard of the President's many affairs, his wandering eye. Much of his womanizing had been hushed-up, but not everything went unreported.

Renee's eyes misted. This was sensitive territory. She took another sip, attempting to regain her composure and looked away.

"I don't think my husband has been faithful to me, no."

"But you have been faithful to him despite his infidelity. For how long?"

"Twenty-one years. We married when I was twenty-one." Renee was uncomfortable when the topic of the conversation turned to the personal. It brought her grief and vulnerability too close to the surface. If they could continue to discuss philosophy and intellectual matters, she thought she could resist the urge she felt to seat herself closer to Dante Benedick. She wanted to reach out and touch his hand. She was controlling physical desires that she hadn't felt for anyone in years. And she was doing it by concentrating on intellectual issues, not the physical or personal.

"I'm not nearly as well-versed in philosophy as you are, Renee. But I do know that an arrangement where one gives all and the other gives nothing seems unfair and inequitable. I've done a little reading of my own. Augustine also said that someone who runs afoul of the laws of morality is violating the fundamental order of the universe. He said the result would be tremendous moral pain. But your husband seems to be the one violating the laws of morality and he seems to be suffering no such moral pain. It's YOU who seems to be suffering in your relationship. That brings me to ask, is Augustine right? Or is it more important to follow the truth and analyze the situation you find yourself in and do whatever you can to find a way to be happy?"

Renee paused. She couldn't believe that a rock star was

quoting Augustine to *her,* a professor of classics and philosophy. There was more to this man than met the eye. And Renee was surprised at the depth of his understanding, the logic of his arguments.

She responded with a quote of her own, "Fear attacks from one side, desire from the other. From one side anxiety. From the other, an empty and deceptive happiness. From one side, the agony of losing what we loved. From the other, the passion to acquire what we did not have. From one side, the pain of an injury received, from the other, the burning desire to avenge it.' That's Augustine, from "On Free Will and Choice." I used to teach that at Stanford. I didn't teach very long. I became pregnant with the twins and left to become a full-time mom, but I still remember. I still think about those words."

A long pause. Renee was wrestling inwardly with the desire to reach out and touch Dante's hand. She wanted to feel his hand, just to know that he was really here with her and that what she was feeling was not her imagination or a pleasant daydream after all the nightmares.

"I have an empty and deceptive happiness as the First Lady of the land, Dante. I just suffered the agony of losing what I loved most in the world. I'm struggling to gain the passion to acquire what I haven't had. I don't think I've ever had true love. Not true, passionate, faithful, intense love. Lust, yes. Love, no. I'm very lonely, right now, in my marriage and in my life."

Dante reached out and touched her hand. Her entire body tingled. "I know," he said simply. "I think most of the world suspects that you're a woman struggling to rise above your situation. Struggling to maintain dignity in an undignified world. I only wish that I'd met you a long time ago. Now that I have met you, I'd love to talk with you like this for hours every night." He laughed. "I mean, every night I'm not on the road. As I said back in England, I want you to get to *really* know me. I want to feel I really know you, as well. I want you to feel that you can trust me, can lean on me." Dante paused and removed his hand from Renee's smaller one. "I feel things for you that I can't explain." Dante paused. If he had been a smoker, he would have lit up by now, so that he had something to do with his hands.

He didn't want to take this conversation aboard Air Force One too far in what might be the wrong direction. He meant every word. He fantasized about just the two of them, alone, talking, becoming closer in every way.

The mention of being on the road reminded Dante of something else that had slipped his mind, as he held Renee's small, well-manicured hand. He noticed she wasn't pulling her hand from his grasp. Nor was she slapping him. There was an almost mystical electrical current running between them. Although they were sitting in chairs that were two feet apart, he wished that he could pull closer to her. He wanted to take her in his arms, comfort her, and tell her that everything was going to be all right.

Instead, he said, "The benefit concert is at Madison Square Garden tomorrow night. I want to give you three tickets, in case you and your family decide you'd like to come. I'll have the tickets and backstage passes waiting at the door for you."

"I'd like that." Renee sounded surprised and pleased.

The plane flew on into the night. Dante and Renee continued talking, trying to make their dream of complete knowledge of each other move closer to reality. But they were running out of time.

"I'd like to love
With all my heart
But it's much too difficult to start.
So I'll just feel this anger grow,
It's all that I'm allowed to know"

—*Ignite the Fire,* The One

CHAPTER 21

Forbidden Impulse

1:00 p.m.
Thursday, November 25, 2010
The Ronald Reagan National Airport
Washington, D.C.

As the long trip from Heathrow ended, Renee found herself weary, but content. She and Dante had talked non-stop about everything: politics, life, movies, music, his life, her life, the meaning of life. It was a non-stop session of sharing. Renee hadn't communicated her deepest thoughts and feelings to another adult in many years. In fact, she couldn't think of a time when her husband had ever talked to her like this. Theirs had always been a relationship based on lust and chemical attraction. William Bellwood had no desire to communicate deeply on any level, nor she with him, at this point in their lives. To actually be heard was such a refreshing change-of-pace. It has been said that your undivided attention was the sexiest gift you could give to another human being. Now, she believed this to be true.

Most of the time, Renee felt so alone. Even more so since the death of Isabella. As she descended the staircase from Air Force One, out of public view in a remote hanger, Renee felt mellow. Despite the long journey, she hadn't felt this refreshed in years. It was like the feeling you get after great sex. Endorphins of the mind? She didn't know all the reasons for her good mood, but she hoped that the mood would last.

Dante Benedick was thinking many of the same things. *What a woman. She's smart and funny and classy and nice.*

135

You can tell just by looking at her that she's real and genuine. I could fall in love with a woman like this.

Both of the famous public figures descended the airplane stairs in a fog. Neither wanted the trip to end. They both felt the chemistry. Now, it was coupled with intellectual attraction.

"I hope I'll see you at Madison Square Garden. Perhaps your husband and daughter can come? The money is for a good cause."

"Thanks, Dante. I appreciate your thinking of all of us."

They shook hands, awkwardly, formally. There were Secret Service men and others surrounding them. Their parting was stilted, nothing like the informal conversation they had shared for eight hours while airborne.

A limousine from the White House was waiting for the First Lady. She gave one last forlorn glance over her shoulder at Dante as it carried her away. He waved as he continued to wait for his own limo driver to load his bags into a white limo. Renee was whisked away, back to the White House, back to Bucky Bellwood and a world of sadness, grief and loss.

She had no thought that her return would be controversial. She went to England to rescue her daughter. She'd learned that her daughter didn't need rescuing, wasn't in danger, and was, in fact, not even in England any longer. And so she had returned. End of story.

Except that it was not the end of the story for William Buchwald 'Bucky' Bellwood.

When Bucky saw the satellite pictures of Renee's solitary kiss on The One's terrace, he went ballistic.

"What the fuck is this?"

He was viewing a still photo of The One and Renee, standing near one another on the glass-enclosed terrace in Chislehurst. The frame was frozen on what came to be known as The Kiss. Immediately after The Kiss, the satellite lost the feed. All was fuzz and white noise.

"That guy has some nerve, making moves on the First Lady of the United States! I hate that SOB. I've always hated him. I'll need a few private moments with my wife, when she returns." The throbbing veins at his temples foreshadowed a scene that wouldn't be pleasant.

Bucky's secretary, Anna Ferdinand, and the others in the

Oval Office obediently murmured, "Of course, Sir." They left him standing at his desk, eyes fixated on the picture of Renee and Dante, lips touching. The picture of Renee's slap of The One didn't make the cut. The true nature of The Kiss and Renee's reaction to it weren't revealed by the snippet of film that Bucky was avidly studying. The more William Bellwood studied the photo, the more irate he became, seething internally. *How dare he? How dare she? What does she take me for? A chump?*

Just as he was thinking such black hateful thoughts, Renee returned.

"Well, dear. Did you have a pleasant trip?" Sarcasm colored Bucky's tone.

"It was a pleasant trip," Renee said. She smiled. She didn't know that Bucky was angrier with her than he had ever been in his life.

"I found the countryside to be enchanting. And Mr. Benedick couldn't have been a nicer host or more of a gentleman."

"Oh? Is that so?"

Bucky threw the photos at Renee. They landed in a pile at her feet. "It doesn't look like he was *that* much of a gentleman. It looks like you were doing a little whoring around with The One." When Bucky said Dante's nickname, he made disparaging quotation marks in the air, a put-down.

Renee stooped to pick up the photos. She felt as though she were moving in slow motion. She was horror-struck to see the freeze-frame blow-up.

"Where did you get these?" she asked, stammering.

"Well, dear. In this day-and-age we have satellites. When you are the Leader of the Free World, which, as you may remember, I am, you can order one of those puppies to freeze frame just about anything anywhere, and that's exactly what I did. And just lookie here what it caught you up to, you cunt!"

Despite his crude and crass nature, Bucky had never actually used this word to insult Renee before now.

Bucky slammed his fist down on his desk as he hurled this extreme epithet.

"Bill, Bucky, nothing happened."

"What do you mean, nothing happened? It looks to me

like plenty happened. A little bit of extra-curricular activity, maybe? Something not on the tour itinerary? You thought you could get away with this and keep me in the dark? No wonder you said you had such a good time!" Bucky bellowed in obvious rage.

Renee flushed, half in embarrassment, half in shame. She began stammering out the truth, "Yes, he did kiss me, once, because I had begun to cry, thinking about Isabella."

"Oh, right. The kiss and all the rest were because of our daughter's death."

His tone dripped with self-righteous sarcasm. For a man who had been screwing his second-in-command only the night before, his hypocritical indignation was gargantuan.

"You're behaving like a whore. What a slut. I have to look out for Number One." Bucky was spitting out the words like bullets from a machine gun, each one finding and wounding its target. "I remember you used to be hot for me like that, when I had the Caddie convertible in college. At least you haven't forgotten how. Although you couldn't prove it by me!"

"I know it looks bad, Bill, but I can explain."

"Oh, I'm sure you can. Or I'm sure you *think* you can."

Bucky walked around from behind his desk and approached Renee, who was still clutching the photos she had picked up from the blue Presidential seal on the carpeting of the Oval Office. He grabbed her wrist.

"Don't *ever* think that you can cuckold me. Don't ever think that you can get away with anything without me knowing about it. Don't think that I will ever let you go. You are mine!"

His face was now within two inches of Renee's. He twisted her wrist painfully, before releasing it. She flinched, sure that he was going to strike her. She drew back, away from the towering rage of William Bellwood. The stink of alcohol and cigar smoke was on his breath.

Pulling herself up to her full height, she resumed the dignity she normally displayed.

"I'm sorry that you think that anything went on, Bill, because nothing did. And nothing went on between Dante and Kaley, either."

"Right. Good-looking rock star takes my twenty-one-year-old daughter halfway around the world, without permission, fucks her. Then, when my forty-two-year-old wife, who should know better, shows up why, he makes it a double!"

Bucky looked like his blood pressure had shot up by twenty points. He was red and flushed. The veins in his temples were throbbing. Renee was terrified. She and Bucky had had spats over the years, but never had she seen him so angry. He was drunk, the afternoon martinis with his Vice President adding to his anger and out-of-control behavior. He drew back his hand, as if to strike her. At the last minute, he stopped himself and, instead, grabbed the photos back from her grasp.

"For years you and the girls have been praising this guy and his music and his good Christian values." Bucky went off in a mincing high-pitched impression of Kaley, "But, Daddy, he raises money for all kinds of good causes. He flies to Africa to help the children dying of AIDS and malnutrition. He underwrites stem cell research because you won't. He fights hunger and poverty all over the world. He's like a missionary." He paused and took a long gulp of the glass of Jack Daniels sitting on his desk. "It looks, to me, like the only missionary work he's been doing has been done in the missionary position. With my wife!" As he shouted these last two words, he looked as though he could explode in violence at the slightest additional provocation.

Bucky continued. "I'm going to make sure that you never have anything to do with that son-of-a-bitch again. You're not to ever speak his name. You're not to ever see him. And that goes double for Kaley."

"But, William, that's an unreasonable request. Just a few moments ago he gave me three tickets for all of us to go see his benefit show in Madison Square Garden. I said that we'd come."

"R-iiii-ght. And I'd be going why?" Bucky was in prime sarcastic banter mode.

"All three of us would go, to support the charitable cause the benefit represents."

"I'm not going. You're not going. Kaley's not going. If

you ever are alone with that son-of-a-bitch again, I will send you far, far away and make sure that, when you come back, you are one whole hell-of-a-lot more docile. You CAN be sent packing, my dear, and I'm just the one to do it! I'M the one who gives the orders in this marriage and in this country. You're the one who takes them. Remember that, and we'll be fine. And don't think that you can sneak around behind my back. I have eyes everywhere, and you know it."

"Bucky, Bill, why would you accuse me like this? Why would you call me the worst names in the world? Have I given you any cause, in over twenty-one years of marriage?"

"No, dear," he said, with syrupy fake sweetness. "And you better not *ever* give me cause, if you know what's good for you."

Renee exited the room, sobbing.

"Lost in the lights
Lost on the stage
Lost is the message
And those it might save..."

—*Lights,* The One

CHAPTER 22

The Benefit Concert

7:00 p.m.
Thursday, November 25th, 2010
Thanksgiving, Madison Square Garden
New York City

After the confrontation with her husband, Renee drove to her daughter's condo near Georgetown University. She was dabbing at her eyes with a handkerchief that still smelled faintly of Chanel's Chance. The fragrance of the perfume took her back to the plane trip from England with The One. How dismal things were, now, compared to that magical trip.

Renee knocked several times before Kaley came to the door.

When Kaley finally opened the door, Renee hugged her, crying.

"What's the matter, Mom?" Kaley asked. She hadn't seen her mother cry very often. Not even at Isabella's funeral. There was alarm in Kaley's voice.

"Your father and I just had a huge fight. The worst ever."

Kaley hugged her mother, unsure what her response should be. "It'll be all right. It'll be all right." This mantra had become an ongoing joke between Renee and her daughters. No matter what the problem was, the family response from Renee was to hug the girls and repeat, "It'll be all right. It'll be all right." Usually, the problem was a small one: a skinned knee, a problem with a boyfriend. Sometimes the problem was bigger. But the response that Renee and the girls used, like a cure-all, was to hug each other and repeat, "It'll be all right." A pat on the back. A kiss on the cheek. The children would be back to their normal pursuits. Only, this time, the person who needed the hug was not the child but the parent. Kaley wasn't sure what else to do. She wasn't sure she wanted to know all the details of her parents' differences, so she reverted to tradition and continued hugging and patting her sobbing mother, repeating, "It'll be all right. It'll be all right."

When her tears subsided, Renee said, "I went to England to find you. I had a long conversation with Dante Benedick. In fact, we flew back here together on Air Force One."

"You flew back with The One? Cool!" Kaley smiled, hoping a cheerful façade and a change of topic would help.

"I have three tickets for The One's benefit show tonight in Madison Square Garden. Do you want to go?"

"Of course! Who's the other ticket for?"

"Your father. He doesn't want to go."

"Is that what you were fighting about?

"You shouldn't be worried about my differences with your father. Let's try to put it behind us. Let's go to this concert and have fun. "

"Can Skyler come along?" Kaley asked.

Skyler Bode was Kaley's roommate and best friend. The girls had known each other since grade school. Skyler was the reason Kaley was attending Georgetown University. When Skyler was accepted, it was a done deal that Kaley would apply, too.

Skyler had long strawberry blonde hair, blue eyes, a waifish figure, and she talked non-stop. She could talk for hours and hours without pausing. A very pretty girl, despite her Chatty Cathy tendencies, she was well liked by the entire Bellwood family. Kaley, who tended to be quieter, enjoyed being around Skyler, who had something to say on every topic. And, usually, Skyler said it well.

"Certainly Skyler can come. It'd be nice to listen to her." Both women laughed. The unspoken opinion was that Skyler tended to eagerly rattle on. Both women found this tendency endearing, because they appreciated Skyler's kind heart and zest for life.

Skyler, Renee and Kaley were driving a black Navigator, the Secret Service detail of Agents Savage and Paskvan following. Between D.C. and New York City, Skyler never shut up. Oddly, this helped, because so many things troubled

Renee, and Skyler carried the conversational load, allowing her to think about her problems. Skyler was a college freshman, taking a philosophy course, and Kaley and Renee heard a lot about Descartes and his opinion that animals don't have an immortal soul because they can't think.

"I mean, come on! Descartes used oysters and sponges for his argument that animals can't think. I guess Descartes never owned a dog, because dogs and cats are a lot smarter than oysters and sponges! I can't believe that someone as smart as Descartes would try to foist such a crummy argument off on us. I thought he was this 'I think, therefore I am' smart guy. He must not have been thinking very hard about THAT argument when he thought it up. Imagine trying to teach a sponge to play dead?" Skyler paused. "Actually, how would you know the difference, with a sponge?"

Renee and Kaley laughed. Skyler was spirited, intelligent, funny and opinionated. Renee enjoyed not having to think about recent events. Skyler was a much-needed distraction and filled any awkward silences with babble.

The benefit concert was a sold-out show. Madison Square Garden was packed. Dante walked onstage to tumultuous applause. He began playing the eight notes that were the well-known beginning of his hit song *Gold Above Dross.*

On the giant screen suspended above center stage and the four smaller screens to the sides of the stage, images of gold coins falling appeared. Strings of electric lights, similar to Christmas tree lights, hung from the ceiling. Different patterns were projected onto the brightly colored strings of lights. First, a Christian symbol appeared. Then, a Japanese rising sun. Next, a Jewish Star of David. Symbols of all countries and all faiths appeared, faded, and then re-appeared in the background, with the piles of coins gradually building into a huge pile of gold on the four flanking screens behind The One.

The bright spotlight turned gold as well. The curtain rose. Instead of just Dante, the solo artist, behind him on tiered platforms appeared an eight-piece rock band, as well as a forty-piece orchestra. The band, the musicians with whom he was playing currently, consisted of two guitarists, two keyboard players, a bass player, a saxophonist, a drummer and a percussionist. There were also three shapely female back-up singers in short skirts and high boots.

In a soft melodic voice, Dante began:

"His work, he said, made relationships hard,
Fleeting glimpses in the night,
With travel and the rest of it,
He never got the chance to say
Anything that really mattered,
Anything that smacked of "deep."
All he did was flirt and natter,
Bed them well; then go to sleep.
He knew, in some remaining pocket,
Of what, at one time, was his soul,
That this was not what he was seeking,
Not the thing to make him whole.
She saw, because her sight was special,
That she could change the dice for him –
Transcend time and past and distance,
Take the words and make them sing.
She could put her soul on paper:
Thoughts and hopes, dreams and feelings.
Risking all: courageous thing!
All it took was love and bravery,
Time and hope and tender heart.
It would be a risky venture,
"But," she thought, "it is a start."
So, she did it, in her spare time
And other times that weren't so "spare,"
Wrapped it in a veil of kindness,
Offered it, the lady fair,
There it was: a gift worth giving,
Labor of love, investment of time,
Offering things he said he looked for:
Body, heart, soul and spirit,
Passion, wit and first-rate mind.
He took the gift and turned it over,
Shook it once and kicked it twice,
Read the words that told it purely,
Skimmed the story, caressed the dice.

All the while that he was reading,
Continuing to shake the dice.
"Roll them!" he heard her say –
But dimly, Like a man within a trance.
She hoped he would waken –
Roll them quickly; seize the moment; join the
dance.
He almost did, but, 'for he knew it,
He'd forgotten how to be,
Remembering only "flirt and natter,"
No faith; no truth; no honesty.
She softly touched the gift she'd sent him,
Tattered, battered, tossed aside,
Looked at the words, from deep within her,
Sad and hurt, with smarting pride.
Part of her sobbed at the thought of betrayal,
That "boring" was all he could finally say.
But part of her knew that the fault was not hers,
Some piece of him long lost in the fray,
Some sort of obstacle blocking the way.
What part of him was gone, was wanting?
What quality did his heart lack?
Was it hope or trust or honor?
Could he ever get it back?
She knew that these she had and then some –
These she had, with much to spare,
But he had none; he was not tender –
He had no way to trust or share.
These she wished him for the future,
When he would realize his loss,
This she hoped he'd find forever
Choosing gold above the dross."

Dante's hands caressed the keys. The full, lush sound of the combined band and orchestra completed the effect. There were far more strings behind him than in the symphony orchestras of many major U.S. cities.

The music reached a crescendo, and then ceased. Dante repeated the same eight notes on the guitar that he had played at the beginning, more slowly and softly. He stopped. The crowd went wild. They whistled and shouted, stomping their feet in approval. Many took out their cell phones, opening them to light up the huge arena.

Dante stood and took a bow. While bowing, he expressed his thanks to the appreciative crowd. "Thank you, thank you." The applause slowly died out. Cell phone lights, held up in tribute, were put away – this generation's answer to the cigarette lighters. "Thank you, New York. That opening even got me excited! Thank you for sacrificing your turkey dinner to come out to help Feed the Children. How about this back-up band?" The crowd applauded appreciatively as Dante gestured to the large group backing him. "My next song is the title song from my soon-to-be-released CD *Broken Soul*."

For the next two hours, Dante rocked. Renee, Kaley, and Skyler rocked with him. At least for those one hundred and twenty minutes, Renee was not thinking of her problems, but was caught up in the enthusiasm of the Garden crowd.

"It's dangerous for you to stay,
It's dangerous for feelings to stray.
But, in the darkness of night
With your eyes oh so bright
It seems like the right thing to do."

—*Dangerous,* The One

CHAPTER 23

Backstage

9:30 p.m.
Thursday, November 25th, 2010
Thanksgiving
Backstage, Madison Square Garden

After the concert, Renee, Kaley, and Skyler waited for their car in the VIP room backstage at Madison Square Garden.

"The concert was fantastic!" Kaley said with enthusiasm.

For once, Skyler was silent.

"He's a great dancer, too. He really knows how to move!" Kaley added.

"Girls," Renee said. "I'm going to stay at the Harrington Hotel. After that long drive, I'm too tired for the drive back to D.C. If you girls want to stay there, too, Kaley, you can use the credit card your father gave you and charge a room on it, as well."

"Isn't the Harrington Hotel where The One and his band are staying?" Skyler asked.

"I'm not sure," Renee said. "It's nearby. Let's meet tomorrow around noon in the lobby."

"See you tomorrow, girls," Renee said. "Have fun."

"Thanks, Mrs. Bellwood," Skyler said, "and thanks again for inviting me! It was a great concert!"

"Yeah, thanks Mom," Kaley echoed, as Renee walked away.

Renee showed her backstage pass to at least five security guards on the way to Dante's dressing room. He had promised it would be waiting for her at Will Call, and it was. Each person she showed it to pointed to another checkpoint further down the hall. Each carefully studied her pass, to make sure it

151

wasn't counterfeit. The sweet smell of pot drifted from small groups of fans and musicians gathered in the hallways backstage. They looked at the Secret Service men uneasily, as if they might be busted at any moment, but they didn't seem to recognize Renee Bellwood. Dressed in blue jeans, blonde wig disguise, clad in dark glasses, she was certain that only her bodyguards would give away her true identity. She tried to distance herself slightly from her bodyguards, Jack Paskvan and Angel Savage, who were following discreetly.

When Renee finally made it backstage, the place was packed. Most were very young. A table laden with hors d'oeuvres and champagne flute glasses, with numerous bottles of champagne on ice nearby, had attracted a horde of freeloading fans and musicians alike. Champagne was flowing freely. Renee picked up a flute glass of champagne and, without breaking stride, kept walking towards Dante's dressing room.

The corridors were crowded. No sign of Dante. Finally, Renee saw him. He was standing with a few others, talking and laughing. She felt like a piece of metal attracted to a magnetic force. She could no more turn around and leave than she could deny magnetic north. The One was standing there, a towel draped around his neck, drenched in sweat, surrounded by at least twenty people, some of them celebrities in their own right. They were a sycophantic group. "You were SO great, Dante!" "It was awesome!"

Renee inched closer in the crowd that was becoming thicker the nearer it came to the leader of the pack. Her Secret Service guards moved others aside so that she was within three people of The One. When Dante finally made eye contact with Renee, over the heads of other hangers-on, he nodded and immediately dismissed the young blonde woman fawning all over him saying, politely, "One moment, please." He walked towards Renee.

"It's very good to see you," Dante said. He looked as though he meant it. "It's going to be crowded and noisy here. Come back to my dressing room, where we can hear ourselves over the madding crowd?"

Renee smiled. She followed Dante down the hall without argument. All along the route, adoring fans besieged him. He repeated, over and over, "Thank you. Thank you." Renee had not yet had a chance to tell him how much she had enjoyed his performance.

"My dressing room's at the end of the hall. There's a tall man outside with a long red beard, Mad Dog. He's the head of security. The sign on the door says White Room. I have to greet a few important record people, shake a few more hands, and pose for a few more photos. Wait for me there. I shouldn't be long."

Renee and her own entourage made their way towards the White Room. She went unrecognized in her disguise of wig, dark glasses, and youthful clothing.

Everything in Dante's dressing room was white. Two white sofas, a white dining table, a white refrigerator, a white stove, a white microwave, a white shower, a white whirlpool bathtub, a King-sized bed with a white fur bedspread, a stainless steel plasma TV on the wall, a white enamel glass-topped coffee table.

Renee was sitting at the dining table when Dante entered. He had given instructions to Mad Dog not to let anyone in, and the Secret Service men that Renee had with her were standing guard outside.

Dante had chilled Chateau Lafitte-Rothschild 1979 cooling in buckets of ice. They opened a bottle and Dante refilled the champagne flute that Renee still held in her hand.

"I think the excitement of the concert and the wine is having an effect on me. I feel really hot," Renee said.

"Really?" Dante said cocking an eyebrow. "Usually I have to serve two bottles to get that reaction." Their shared laughter was like that of friends who have known each other for years.

"Hot, temperature-wise," Renee said. She took off her dark blue jacket and hung it on the back of her chair. "My jacket's suede. I should have worn something cooler."

"I'm sorry, I don't have any lighter-weight women's clothes." Dante smiled.

"Really?" Renee sounded sweetly sarcastic as she made the remark.

"Do you mind if I take this off, too?" Renee asked, pointing to her blouse.

153

Dante flashed a smile. "Brilliant! Wish I'd thought of that."

"It's not like that. I'm wearing a camisole top beneath." She unbuttoned her blouse, her breasts momentarily straining at the fabric, which didn't fail to attract Dante's attention. She carefully placed her pale blue sweater on the chair back with her heavy suede jacket. Underneath, she wore a lacy white camisole top with thin spaghetti straps.

Dante dimmed the lights in the room. He led Renee to the larger of the two white sofas. Flickering candles on the table in a silver chandelier were now brighter than the dim electric lights in the room.

"You look tense. You look beat. Long drive?" Dante began to massage the back of Renee's neck. His touch was like a small electric shock.

"That feels great." She couldn't deny it; he was right. She was tired and tense. Shifting position, she inclined her head, so that Dante could reach the knotted neck muscles.

Dante seized the opportunity to impulsively kiss the nape of her neck, afterwards working his soft lips over to her ear and kissing her earlobes. He wrapped his arms around her waist from behind. Renee didn't resist, as she had at The One's estate in Chislehurst. She was tired and upset. She was falling in love. In the background, Norah Jones' "Come Away With Me" was playing softly.

He kissed her shoulders, her lips, and her neck. Her mouth slightly parted and his tongue touched hers in their first real kiss. Renee moaned softly. "Don't stop."

He slid his hands under her silky camisole top and felt her breasts.

Just then, the door to Dante's dressing room flew open. Two Secret Service men barged in without knocking and with every intention of interrupting. They weren't the agents who had accompanied Renee to Madison Square Garden. Agents Savage and Paskvan had been dismissed. These were Bucky's men, and they were in no mood for pleasantries.

"It's dangerous to love you
It's dangerous, it's true.
But with nobody home; the two of us alone
It seems like the right thing to do."

—*Dangerous,* The One

CHAPTER 24

Compromising Position

10:00 p.m.
Thursday, November 25th, 2010
Dante's Dressing Room Backstage

Renee was startled by the arrival of Bucky's Secret Service forces backstage in Dante's dressing room at Madison Square Garden. She hadn't felt this embarrassed since she was a naïve teen-ager, making out in her basement with Denny Fulton and her mother had come downstairs and caught them kissing. All those years ago, she had stammered out some lame excuse and had been grounded for two weeks.

The stakes were higher than that now, but the embarrassment was the same. Renee quickly re-buttoned her blouse and turned to face the Secret Service agents, hair mussed, cheeks red.

The penalty now, after twenty-one years of marriage to William Bellwood, would be negotiated in divorce court. However, she couldn't imagine twenty-one years of marriage ending because she was kissed a few times by a famous rock star. After all, she was the First Lady of the land. As that thought took hold, anger quickly trumped embarrassment in her demeanor.

What right does the Secret Service have to barge in on me like this? They're treating me like a criminal. I'm the First Lady and a consenting adult.

Renee had re-buttoned key buttons on her blouse, very casually, as though it were an accident that they were undone at all. Going on the offensive, she comported herself as though nothing at all out of the ordinary were happening.

"What is the meaning of this interruption? This is an

157

outrage." Renee was fuming.

Lucas Nailer and Frank Racine, the Secret Service agents Bucky had sent, remained neutral in expression, revealing nothing. They were plastic men.

"Where are my Secret Service agents? Mr. Paskvan and Mr. Savage?" Renee continued, rising to her full five foot five inch height. She appeared taller in her outrage.

"I must apologize for the interruption, but this is a matter of national security. We didn't mean to embarrass you or put you in a compromising position, Mrs. Bellwood. We are merely following orders." Mr. Racine's face displayed no emotion of any kind. "We have strict orders to return you to the White House immediately."

"Orders?" Renee said, "Orders from whom?"

"The President. Please, Mrs. Bellwood," Mr. Racine said, holding out his hands in a conciliatory gesture. "Cooperate and come with me. I don't want to have to use force."

"This must be some kind of mistake," Renee said. "Dante, I don't know what's going on, but I'll get to the bottom of this." From the look on her face, Dante believed her.

She rejected the hand Frank Racine extended toward her and stalked from the room.

The undivided attention of Lucas Nailer turned toward Dante. "Mr. Benedick," Nailer, the African-American agent said, "You have twenty-four hours to leave the country." He glared at Dante as he spoke, like a cat stalking a bird.

"What?" Dante was taken aback. "What-the-hell are you talking about?"

"Your Visa is invalid. If you don't leave within the next twenty-four hours, you'll be detained and deported."

"My Visa is good for another month. How-the-hell did it expire?"

"The United States government did it," Mr. Nailer replied. "On direct orders from the President of the United States. And President Bellwood has a personal message he wants me to deliver."

"And what would that be?" Dante asked with defiance. He wasn't sure he wanted to know.

"William Bellwood wants you to know, and this is a direct quote, that he won't let some 'good-for-nothing limey bastard fuck around with his wife.'" Mr. Nailer was standing nose-to-nose with Dante when, after throwing down the gauntlet with these words, he blind-sided Dante with a sucker punch to the gut.

Dante fell to the floor. Secret Service agent Nailer kicked him in the ribs, as he lay there helpless, and then slammed his knee into Dante's chest, knocking the wind out of the fallen man. All of Dante's security men had been instructed to stand guard outside his dressing room; he was on his own now.

The One gasped for air. He crawled to the sofa. Using the sofa, he pulled himself up and rose to his feet like an old person who has great difficulty in standing.

"Do you wanna take a swing at me?" Mr. Nailer asked. "Come on," he put his arms down. "Go for it. I'll give you a free shot."

Dante charged towards the Secret Service agent, knocking him against the wall. The impact dislodged a framed autographed photo of Mick Jagger. The glass shattered, flying in all directions. *Shattered,* the Stones song, played in the background.

How appropriate.

Lucas Nailer slammed his fist repeatedly into Dante's rib cage and face. The One staggered backward, fell a second time, this time atop the coffee table. He was unconscious, bleeding from several cuts to his head, neck and hands, his nose possibly broken.

* * * *

When Dante regained consciousness, he first felt his nose. He could feel that his nose wasn't broken, but it was bleeding profusely. His blurry, unfocused vision was like trying to watch a 3-D movie without 3-D glasses. His head throbbed and he felt as though someone wearing brass knuckles had hit him. Dante knew enough about the rough trade side of life to remember the sensation. When he regained consciousness sufficiently, he observed Mr. Nailer seated on his white sofa, sipping a bottled water.

Mr. Nailer stood up. "Do you want me to call an ambulance for you, Mr. Benedick?" The agent seemed unconcerned, as though his offer were mere lip service.

Dante shook his head. "No, but my stomach." He covered his mouth, clutched his abdomen and ran for the nearby bathroom, slamming the door behind him.

Nailer waited several minutes. He knocked on the bathroom door, hollering through the door, "Benedick, do you need medical attention?"

No answer.

The agent knocked again, this time more firmly. "Mr. Benedick, are you okay? The President had said rough Dante up, not kill him."

Nailer opened the bathroom door. Dante was clutching the sides of the toilet. Riding the porcelain bus.

Dante moaned. The agent walked towards Dante with a slight smile, to investigate further.

"Just help me up," Dante said, extending his hand towards Nailer.

Lucas Nailer reached for Dante's hand. At that moment, Dante pulled down with all his force. The Secret Service agent came crashing onto the bathroom floor. Dante smashed the agent's head against the side of the porcelain bowl two times, knocking Nailer unconscious.

Opening the bathroom door, Dante crept down the hallway as carefully as a cat, towards the side exit marked "Emergency Exit Only." The alarm, when he opened the door, assaulted the night air with raucous noise as Dante sprinted, under cover of darkness, for the safety of a copse of trees near a distant parking lot.

"I cannot glean the answer
Of riddles from the past
Nor see the future clearly
By the shadow that it casts.
But I can feel the future coming,
Feel its breath upon my cheek,
Whispering of the sameness
That makes me sick and weak."

—*Reflections,* The One

CHAPTER 25

Lost in the Shadows

11:04 p.m.
Thursday, November 25th, 2010
Silver Springs Asylum
Chevy Chase, Maryland

Renee wasn't sure where she was going, but she knew it wasn't to the White House.

Secret Service agent Frank Racine accompanied her on the private jet, flying out of JFK International Airport. Less than an hour later, the private jet landed at Ronald Reagan National Airport in Washington, DC and Renee was transferred to a waiting helicopter. Renee strained to see the Washington Monument disappearing beneath her as the helicopter took off in a direction that took it away from the Capitol.

"Where are we going?" Renee asked. "You aren't taking me to the White House? Where are you taking me?"

"We'll be there shortly, Mrs. Bellwood." Racine had a phony, reassuring smile that was as fake as his hairpiece.

The 'copter set down on a landing pad in a courtyard next to a shadowy mansion-like building. Agent Racine held Renee's arm, steadying her as she stepped from the helicopter. The wind from its blades blew her skirt. For one absurd moment, she thought of the famous Marilyn Monroe pose from *The Seven-Year Itch*. Her skirt, atop a manhole cover blast of air, held down by Marilyn's hand, Marilyn smiling her come hither smile. But Renee was not amused at being anywhere near this helicopter, and her reaction was anything but come hither.

"This is where I'm supposed to drop you off. I'm just

following orders." Racine's phony grimace served as his weak version of a smile. He opened the helicopter door, climbed back in and the silver copter flew towards the dark horizon.

Renee felt alone, abandoned. She regarded the spooky building in front of her. It was very gothic: gray stone veneer, French clay tile roof, and a three-story corner tower with side turrets. The place had a massive, brooding, hideous, monstrous quality. It was missing only gargoyles.

She felt lost, lost not only in the shadows the building cast, but lost as a person. Renee had no idea where she was and she didn't know why she had been brought here or what was going to happen to her.

The noise of a foot on gravel behind her caused Renee to turn, sensing someone standing behind her. William Bellwood was the source of the furtive noise, and the look he was giving Renee would be enough to bring a grown man to his knees. Bucky acted as though it was nothing out of the ordinary to be standing in a remote Gothic courtyard near midnight.

Behind the President was a middle-aged doctor. He was short and overweight and wore a ragged gray beard. The doctor, dressed in green scrubs, was smoking a cigar. Standing next to the white-coated physician were two large, young, well-muscled orderlies, a gurney between them.

"Bill, what am I doing here? What is this place?" Renee asked, confused. Her voice was beginning to reflect alarm and near-hysteria.

"Honey, calm down." William Bellwood spoke at last. "This is Doctor Garrett Shields, chief psychiatrist here at Silver Springs. He'll explain everything."

"Silver Springs?" Renee was disoriented. "Silver Springs is a lunatic asylum. What-the-hell am I doing at a mental hospital?"

"Silver Springs isn't really a mental hospital," Dr. Shields interrupted, apologetically. "We're a private mental health treatment facility. We're not really a hospital, per se." He sounded like a mouse or a rat, the high-pitched sound of a voice on helium.

"I'm not crazy," Renee said. Her voice rose in alarm.

"We don't use that term here." Dr. Shields looked down at the ground, speaking very softly. Renee could barely hear him.

"What do you want to call me, then? Nuts? Insane? Wacky? Loco? Mad? Loony tunes?"

"Please. Calm down, Mrs. Bellwood," Dr. Shields said. "Your husband just wants you to come in for observation. After the suicide of your daughter, well, it's understandable that you may have been acting a bit erratic or depressed."

Renee took a deep breath and, exhaling slowly, she paused. "This is some kind of a mistake, Dr. Shields."

Before she could finish the sentence, the doctor's goons leaped forward and forcibly administered an injection.

"Damn you, Bucky." Rene said, before losing consciousness. Whatever was in the shot, it took effect nearly immediately. Renee collapsed, but the orderlies caught her before she hit the ground, placed her on the gurney, and rolled her into the ghastly maw of the Silver Springs Mental Health Facility.

* * * *

"I gave her a strong sedative. She'll be out all night," Dr. Shields said to President Bellwood.

The President nodded.

"We should be able to schedule the lobotomy for tomorrow morning. Are you sure you want us to go ahead with the operation? There are newer therapies that might serve as well?"

"Not only do I want you to do it, I want you to step up the time-table. Can't you do the surgery tonight?"

"Mr. President, I'm not sure I can reschedule an operation that quickly. There's no surgeon here at this hour, especially on a holiday."

"There will be an extra one hundred thousand dollars in it for you *if* you get it done tonight." Bucky's intense eyes gleamed, ferret-like.

Dr. Shields smiled. "I'm sure it won't be a problem. Do you want me to give you a call when we're finished?"

"No need. As long as she's out of my hair and no problem when she comes back. I'm leaving for Miami with the Vice President tonight. I'll be back Monday morning."

"I look forward to your return Monday, then," Dr. Shields said. Shields seemed to want to add more; he hesitated and then said, "Bucky, I'm so glad you were elected President. Who would have thought that my old duck-hunting buddy would wind up President of the United States?"

William Bellwood smiled. "It's a strange world, Garrett, and getting stranger all the time. Just be glad I never mistook you for a quail on our hunting trips." Both men chuckled.

The President walked briskly to his waiting limousine.

"We didn't know that evil lived here
In the hearts of average men
We thought that all who lived here
Embraced peace, good will towards men
Now we know that all aren't like us
In this world, there are such things,
Now we know that steel cannot
Protect us from the lunatic fringe"

—*Burned Steel,* The One

CHAPTER 26

The Shadow Chasers

11:13 p.m.
Thursday, November 25th, 2010
Philadelphia, Society Hill

The townhouse sat twenty feet back from the narrow Philadelphia cobblestone street, in a ritzy section of Philadelphia known as Society Hill. Only the affluent could afford to live here now. Between 1950 and 1970, on the watch of Director of the City Planning Commission Edmund Bacon, one thousand poor families were dispossessed, their property and homes seized through eminent domain. Bacon even made the cover of 1964's *Time* magazine with his gentrification efforts in inner city Philadelphia. Once the riff-raff were expelled, I.M Pei designed grand townhouses and condo units only the wealthy could afford.

The area between Walnut, Lombard, Front and 8th street contained the largest concentration of 18th and early 19th century architecture in the entire United States. Cobblestone streets, bordered by brick row houses in Federal and Georgian style were Bacon's contribution to revitalizing this heart of the city. He succeeded magnificently. The neighboring identical-from-the-outside brick townhouses, with their red, green, black or white shutters visible from the street, were close to Independence Hall and Independence National Historic Park. Cross Walnut Street and enter Independence National Historic Park, to admire the sculpture of Robert Morris, one of the original signers of the Declaration of Independence. The Second Bank of the United States, now home to the National Portrait Gallery, a resplendent building in Greek Revival style, was also there, with welcoming park benches nearby.

There were a variety of other small pocket parks, like Three Bears Park. William Penn established his Free Traders Society here in the late 17th century. Other historic buildings were nearby: Old Pine Street Presbyterian Church at 4th and Pine; Washington Square at the intersection of 6th and Walnut Streets. That symbol of American freedom, the Liberty Bell, was located in a small park near Society Hill for years, then moved away and returned. Before 2003, tourists could see the bell in the park portico. Although urged not to touch it, the dull copper color of the brass was brightly polished along a one-foot space where tourist hands had reached out in defiance of the directions to rub the lip of this famous cracked icon of freedom.

Three steps to the heavy wooden door of 615 Lombard Street. The massive door had an ornate brass knocker, shaped like a roaring lion's head. Inside, a parquet floor with decorative brass inlay forming an attractive semi-circle. Above the semi-circle dangled a chandelier worthy of any Vegas casino, hanging from four floors up. Polished mahogany balustrades separated the stairwell from the foyer below.

The curving spiral staircase with its intricately carved wooden railing invited you to climb to the fourth floor, rising to the top of the city footprint of the townhouse. Thick pile carpeting in a soft neutral beige made the climb to the top floor silent.

First floor: an efficient kitchen with modern, gleaming appliances. A special wine refrigerator visible, each chilled hole filled with an expensive vintage wine.

One floor up, the second floor above the foyer, a pale lime green study and a powder room. The chair and footstool were well padded, comfortable. A standing lamp provided a soft reading light near the overstuffed chair. On the footstool lay a book, spine up, left open as if someone had been reading it and placed it there for just a moment. Bookshelves of attractive volumes lined the walls.

Third floor: one bedroom and another bathroom, in a pale orange sherbet shade. The king-sized bedspread in an opulent patterned damask, with matching drapes at the windows. The residents of this townhouse were wealthy.

The fourth and top floor housed the master bedroom and its attached bathroom. Walk-in shower, marble floor, a Jacuzzi tub large enough for four. The bathroom's marble floors were heated, a thermostat providing a constant read-out of the room's temperature.

The master bedroom was sunny yellow, the cheerful brightness in the room complemented by a large skylight, semi-circular in shape, the shape of a giant half-moon. The pastel shades and mirrored closet doors throughout gave an illusion of spaciousness, and the large walk-in closets confirmed the immense size of the townhouse.

Four floors of pampering for the city's wealthiest inhabitants. A residence for the city's elite. The President of International Airlines lived across the street. The CEO of Hopkins' Chocolates next door. This was a charming, quaint, historic town, and this particular part of Philadelphia---Society Hill--- was the most picturesque part of it all. Ironic that in this well-appointed residence two of the nation's most dangerous assassins lived in U.S. style comfort.

Faris and Bahar Hamad were occupying the townhouse instead of the royal palace in Damascus at their father's explicit request. They didn't question their father's orders; they just obeyed them. Cash paid for the townhouse and the Lexus parked outside. The Hamads had lots of cash.

Bahar, the younger brother, was a short man with a big belly and an even bigger bushier beard. He was praying on a Persian rug in the living room, listening to religious songs on the CD player; he had been at this since sunset. The older brother, Faris, taller and thinner with a thin mustache snaking along his sweaty upper lip, sat alone in his bedroom eating nachos.

Both brothers were on a mission from Allah and from their father. Their younger siblings, Mosuma and Zacarias, had died in the Airbus A380 failed hijacking in D.C. They vowed not to fuck up like their brothers, embarrassing the family name and shaming Syria.

The two brothers had been sent to live in America. Ironically, they were sent to Philadelphia, the seat of liberty and the City of Brotherly Love. Faris and Bahar had been given the task of flying a private plane into a cooling pool of spent fuel rods at the WNP-2 plant in Richland, Washington. That would cause an explosion in both the nuclear reactor and at the nearby steel plant in Beaverton, Pennsylvania. The resulting sequence of explosions would destroy the town of Beaverton, nearby Washington D.C., only twenty miles away, and most of the surrounding area.

Faris thought of himself as a "Shadow Chaser," from an old Arab poem: "Beware the Shadow Chasers, hiding in the darkness, stealing your soul, stealing the light, casting you into darkened shadows forever." The poem talked about devotion and what happens to those who lack it. It used to scare Faris, when he was a child, but now he could identify himself with the evil characters in the verse. If the mission went as planned, he and his brother would steal the light and America would be in the shadows for a very long time. *L'Amerique'a l'abysse: America on the edge of the abyss.* A French headline that appeared in Paris' *Daily Match* after the Watts racial riots of the sixties. Now, four decades later, it would be true.

Faris left the house shortly after sunset. His brother was still praying, bending forward from his prayer rug every so often to kiss the floor. Faris drove the Lexus to a strip club called Gentlemen's Row in North Philadelphia. The name was ironic. Nobody in this joint was a gentleman. On a holiday, the strip club would be extremely busy or it would be very dead. This Thanksgiving, business was slow with just a few regulars. Faris entered the club with a gun in the pocket of his jacket and a suitcase full of cash in his right hand.

Randy Blocker, the club bouncer, approached Faris. "Hey! Buddy! You can't bring a gun in here."

Faris opened the suitcase and began handing Randy hundred dollar bills, one at a time.

"I need bodyguard. For protection. And I need gun for this reason. Will you be my bodyguard?" After two thousand dollars had changed hands, Randy grunted in assent.

"I'm your man. Let me know if anybody bothers you. OK?" Randy tucked the money in his pants pockets, causing an unsightly bulge.

Faris sat at a table in the corner drinking a bottle of Budweiser and eyeing the strippers. He didn't like women with dyed or bleached hair or silicone breasts. All of the

172

strippers were heavily made up.

After the third beer, Faris was ready to leave. The music was too loud. He didn't see any stripper that caught his interest. But then Desiree entered the bar.

Desiree was one of the veteran strippers. Her brother owned the bar and she had been working the club for the last decade. She was over thirty-five, a little bit overweight, naturally blonde and she wore very little make-up. Normally, Desiree would be considered over-the-hill for nude stripping. Faris motioned to Randy.

"I want a private dance."

"No problem, Mister," Randy said, summoning Desiree. "But it's gonna' cost ya'."

"One hundred dollars a song, plus tips," Desiree said, cracking her gum as she spoke.

"This is not a problem."

"Then follow me."

* * * *

The sign on the door said "Private." The room had one wooden chair and a tape player.

Faris sat on the chair, his suitcase next to him. He opened it and handed Desiree a fistful of one hundred-dollar bills.

"Take off all your clothes," Faris said. His eyes narrowed and he was breathing heavily through his mouth.

"I have to keep my G-string on. City regulations," Desiree said. "I could get busted if we're raided and I'm not wearing my G-string."

"The bouncer will see that we're not disturbed."

Desiree quickly disrobed.

Faris unzipped his zipper. Desiree knew what to do. She wasn't as pretty as his wives in Syria, but his wives in Syria would not commit such unholy acts. He watched as she slid his organ in and out of her pink mouth. If he hadn't drunk so much whiskey, he probably would have been done by now. Faris thought of the seventy virgins awaiting him in Nirvana when his mission was accomplished and of the things he'd make them do. He emitted a small grunting noise and was finished.

Faris quickly zipped his pants, gave Desiree another handful of hundreds, and left the club. When he returned to the townhouse, the noise he made slamming the door and staggering drunkenly into the living room caused Bahar to momentarily stop in his marathon prayer session.

"Allah and our father will be very disappointed in you," Bahar said to his brother, who reeked of beer. "Giving into sin is not our way."

"We have to leave! We have to leave now! No argument," Faris said loudly in Arabic. His eyes glittered crazily in the dim chandelier light of the Society Hill townhouse entryway.

Bahar was going to object, but stopped himself. The brothers walked to the Lexus parked outside like men on a mission.

* * * *

Their plane was parked outside the hangar, already fueled. Bahar had been flying Syrian planes since his days as a teenager. Faris was still drinking, this time from a bottle of whiskey. Faris' job was to navigate, but Bahar was better at navigation, anyway. Faris had decided that his job was to stay drunk.

"Ever since we came to this wicked country, you haven't been the same. You used to be the smarter of the two of us," Bahar said sternly. "You are too much like our younger brother Mosuma: screwing America women, drinking alcohol. Maybe in Nirvana you will find redemption for your profligate ways."

Faris looked away. He took another drink and refused to make any further eye contact with his brother.

Bahar said nothing more as he started the plane. The ignition sputtered the small plane to bug-like life and the aircraft took off down the runaway, launching into the dark, moonless sky. The fate of America was sealed.

The scalpel lay there, cold and bright,
Reflecting the fluorescent light.
It screamed of fear and pain and crime
Was there a chance? Would there be time?

—*Damaged Soul,* The One

CHAPTER 27

Damaged Soul

11:43 p.m.
Thursday, November 25th, 2010
Silver Springs Mental Health Treatment Facility
Chevy Chase, Maryland

For the last half-hour, Doctor Garrett Shields had been on the phone, trying to get a neurosurgeon to perform an emergency lobotomy before midnight. None of the surgeons he contacted had returned his call. Garrett Shields was well known amongst neurosurgeons in the area. His reputation, as they say, preceded him, but not in a good way. Closet drug addict. Medicare cheat. Bellwood crony. Garrett had never been *caught* doing all the things that everyone knew he had done.

That's because I'm too smart, Garrett smirked to himself. He smiled, making sure that his yellow teeth didn't show. Garrett was very self-conscious about anyone seeing his ferret-like teeth.

Shields looked at the inert form on the gurney, Renee Bellwood, the First Lady of the land. *Too bad the Prez insists on a lobotomy. She's a pretty little piece of ass. Nice tits. I'd load her up on Prozac, if she were my wife. I'd have her so doped up that she wouldn't know if we'd done it ten times that day or ten thousand times.* Garrett smirked that squirrelly smile of his to no one in particular, head held at an odd angle, lascivious eyes on Renee's breasts.

Garrett Shields knew that Bucky Bellwood could be a headstrong guy. He knew from their college years sniffing cocaine together. Belligerent Bucky. Bellicose Bucky. Bad boy Bucky. The more he tooted, the louder he got. Garrett smiled at an old rhyme that had popped into his head when he thought of tooting coke with the future Prez, something he made up during their days of duck-hunting and camaraderie: "Snow, snow. A really good drug. The more you use; the bigger the thug." Garrett enjoyed his witticism silently. Nobody else there to enjoy it. Too bad.

It's a good thing he's given that up. I guess the only vices Bucky has left are whoring around and lying. Bucky's really the BEST liar ever! He always had the knack! But Bucky had always treated Garrett like shit. Garrett had been Bucky's lackey. *Get that lil' gal's number for me, Garrett. Send her on over to my room, willya' buddy?* There was never any consideration for all the scut work that Garrett had done for Bucky, even before he was Prez. Garrett shook his head, thinking of the many times he had pimped for the Prez, with no thanks from ol' Bucky. No "Good going, Garrett."

Since no reputable doctor on the east coast was answering his phone calls, that left only the disreputable Dr. Garrett Shields to perform the lobotomy on Renee Bellwood if he wanted the bonus money. And Garrett always wanted for money. His skeleton crew of medical personnel stood ready. To be accurate, most of them weren't really standing. They were bored and leaning up against the wall, smoking in the corridor. They thought it was weird to be asked to stay late, close to midnight now, to assist at an operation. They had no clue on whom they were operating and didn't really care. The white-coated assistants really did resemble skeletons. Ghouls, really. Thin. Malnourished. The whole lot of them couldn't get medical work anywhere else. But Garrett Shields had hired them. *A bunch of malcontents*, Garrett thought. *Not the cream of the crop, but they'll do; they'll have to.*

Garrett had performed many lobotomies over the years. Just not recently, and never very successfully. Lobotomizing a patient to achieve compliance was a pretty drastic procedure, even in its infancy, and with famous cases like Rosemary Kennedy's botched operation, the procedure had gone the way of World War I mustard gas.

Garrett had another clever literary thought: *I'd rather have a bottle in front of me than a frontal lobotomy.* Not original, but true. He laughed out loud at the old chestnut; to the boys in the hall, he just looked nuts. Garrett's offbeat actions didn't surprise any of his less-than-skillful crew.

Leave it to Bucky to come up with one of the oldest and crudest operations as a solution to his woman problems, Garrett thought to himself while washing his hands the requisite number of times to sterilize them. He was stalling, really, but chalked it up to being thorough. *Wouldn't do to give our First Lady an infection, on top of everything else, now, would it?*

She's going to have enough trouble, after this is over. Sure hate to make a pretty woman into a slobbering, drooling idiot, but money is money. An indifferent shrug, a motion to himself. This operation would make him rich. It would be the most lucrative operation he had ever performed.

Maybe I can even get that boat I've been wanting. Go boating on Chesapeake Bay or Washington Harbour. A dreamy smile flitted about the corners of Garrett's thin lips.

* * * *

While Dr. Garrett Shields prepped for surgery, Renee Bellwood drifted into heavy sedation. The anesthesia brought frightful thoughts and images, just before she lost her awareness.

Momma? Momma? Why was Momma frowning? Gramma ... Gramma Towlerton? But, you're both dead!

Renee, lay there, still as a corpse on the operating table, watching her parents and listening to them argue with her Grandmother.

"Renee can't go all the way off to California. She's too young."

That was her father.

"She's old enough to be screwing that miserable boyfriend Denny Fulton in our basement," her mother said. *"If she's old enough to fornicate, she's old enough to educate. She says she wants to go to California."*

"Where in California?" That was Gramma Towlerton, in a less-than-kindly tone. Sharp. Inquisitive.

"Stanford. Stanford has offered her a full scholarship."

"Well, then, what do you care? It won't cost you anything." Gramma always had a way of cutting to the chase.

179

She knew that Jim Towlerton and his wife, Davina, were concerned about shelling out real money to send their extremely bright daughter off to be educated. If it could be done inexpensively, fine. If not, well, there were chores to be done here at home. Renee could damn well do them. That was Jim Towlerton, always being practical.

"Well, we could use some help around this place, you know. A farm like this doesn't run itself. You're not getting any younger, Old Woman, and neither are we."

"Let the girl go. Let the bird fly. Time to cut the cord. She doesn't want anything to do with farming in Ohio," scoffed Gramma Towlerton.

Renee heard and saw all this as though she were the character in the play "Our Town," observing her entire family talking about her after her death.

Maybe it's true that your entire life flashes before your eyes just before you die, she thought.

Then, most horribly, Renee saw Isabella.

Isabella was clad in the same beautiful white dress in which she had been buried. But she was far from beautiful now. Her hair was disheveled. Her eyes, darkly circled, were closed in eternal slumber. Isabella was walking towards Renee. Her arms hung stiffly at her sides. The thick pancake make-up of death had run in the heat of the coffin.

How can she see where she's going? How can she be walking at all? Isabella's dead!

The expression on Isabella's face was unnatural. She had never looked like this in life. She resembled a ruined doll, mascara running down her pallid cheeks, lipstick the color of bright red blood.

My baby, my baby, my beautiful baby. Renee's heart broke.

Isabella approached five feet from Renee. She was close enough for Renee to smell the stench of death and decay. Eyes still firmly closed, Isabella opened her mouth and spat out an earthworm. That horrible act was followed by an inhuman noise that came from between Isabella's parched scabrous lips. The horrible noise was similar to a hissing sound, like a slow leak on a tire.

"You're coming to me. You will be here soon. It's so cold

here, Mother. It's so cold. So very cold."

"When will all the killing stop?
Save them from the bombs we drop.
Forgive us all our crimes, our deeds.
Show the path to which peace leads."

—*When Will All the Killing Stop?* The One

CHAPTER 28

When Will All the Killing Stop

11:52 p.m.
Thursday, November 25, 2010
Airspace over Beaverton Nuclear Power Plant
Beaverton, Pennsylvania

Bahar piloted the small plane laden with explosives, flying it towards the power plant. He was hyperventilating and his knuckles were white as he gripped the controls far tighter than necessary. All the while, his brother Faris lay in the seat beside him, drunk, semi-conscious, breathing heavily through his mouth.

Bahar intended to crash the plane into the irradiated spent-fuel cooling pools next to the plant. Since the pool had only a thin plastic covering, it was vulnerable from the top and the sides. No special security precautions were in place at the plant to prevent the catastrophe that would occur.

It's insane that they don't put this stuff underground, like in Iran. Bahar checked the dials of the small aircraft for the tenth time, nervously fidgeting with one dial after another. From the air, the target resembled an aboveground family swimming pool. The explosion that would occur when the small plane loaded with dynamite and nitroglycerine flew into the pool that held the spent fuel rods would create an immense radioactive cloud. In a causal chain reaction, the nuclear power plant explosion would trigger a second holocaust at the nearby steel company in Beaverton, Pennsylvania, where the furnaces would help contribute to a huge hydrogen-fueled explosion. A capitalist approach for terrorists: two disasters for the price of one. More bang for the buck. The fallout would destroy Washington, D.C. and the surrounding area.

Bahar thought about the legend of the sword of Damocles: a courier of ancient Syracuse was given a lesson in the perils of a ruler's life. As an object lesson, the king seated him under a giant scimitar, hanging above his head, secured only by a single hair.

It was time for the Sword of Damocles to fall; it would fall heavily on America.

Bahar wondered what his last words should be. His sense of humor dictated that it be something like, "Tell my countrymen that I said something profound." Perhaps his final words should be from the poem "The Shadow Chasers," which he had been discussing with his brother Faris during their last week of waiting for the signal to proceed with the attack. Bahar recited the last line aloud: "Be careful! Be very wary of the Shadow Chasers."

Bahar glanced over for Faris' reaction to all this drama. Faris appeared comatose. *Just my luck. The only person I have with me to hear my last words is dead to the world.* He smiled, realizing how true this statement would soon be for both of them. Bahar kicked at Faris's leg, sprawled near him in the co-pilot area of the plane. Nothing. Faris would never know what hit him.

The plane reached the target, crashing into the unprotected pool in a horrendous din of metal on concrete. Upon impact, the explosion could be heard and seen for miles; it could actually be felt twenty-five miles away, as both plants went up in sequence. A mushroom-shaped cloud spewing debris and radiation slowly spread over the land, a black shadow of doom.

Chaos ruled. The fate of America was sealed.

"When will all the killing stop?
When will tears no longer drop?
Can this world be saved, at last?
Or must we all repeat the past?"

—*When Will All the Killing Stop,* The One

CHAPTER 29

Burn, Baby, Burn

11:55 p.m.
Thursday, November 25, 2010
Beaverton Steel Plant
Beaverton, Pennsylvania

Carlos Peraza was taking a fifteen-minute cigarette break. He worked the graveyard shift at the Beaverton Steel Plant, from eleven at night until eleven the next morning. His job was to perform routine maintenance on the hydrogen furnaces at the steel plant. Although he wasn't supposed to take his fifteen-minute break until midnight, because it was a holiday, he had started his break early. Things were slow on a holiday.

For working on Thanksgiving, the employees would get triple time. Thanksgiving ended at midnight, so Carlos would only get one hour of triple time pay, plus eleven hours of regular pay. Carlos was pissed about that inequity. He had almost called in sick, in fact.

"Carlos, baby, we need the money. Go and do your job. You'll get triple-time for that one hour beyond your regular shift. Don't forget that!" Then Maria handed him his lunch pail like a dutiful wife, kissed him on the cheek, and Carlos Peraza walked from his home.

The fire resistant suit Carlos had to wear because of OSHA regulations was hot and sweaty. He removed his helmet to light a cigarette. He lit the cigarette, cupping his hand against the slight breeze, steadying the flame. Carlos was sitting on a bench outside the receiving area. Ironically, the Beaverton Steel Plant was a nonsmoking facility, so Carlos and all his co-workers were forced to smoke outside.

What a bitch! This gigantic furnace spews tons of fumes,

187

but we all have to freeze our butts off outside because of OSHA regulations. He flicked the spent match into some nearby bushes. Carlos hated rules and regulations and he hated his job at the plant.

That's when Carlos heard the noise, a noise so loud that it shook him. A huge explosion. He physically felt the vibrations. At first, he panicked.

Shit! Did one of the furnaces just blow?

If one of the oven-like furnaces in the plant exploded, it would cause a hydrogen explosion with the same impact as an H-bomb. As Carlos calmed down some, he realized that the explosion he had just heard was coming from further away, from the nearby Richmond nuclear power plant. Then he saw the light, lighting up the sky like a giant x-ray machine. A huge mushroom cloud followed this weird apparition.

Holy Shit! Carlos' lit cigarette fell from his fingers to the ground, forgotten in this moment of terror.

The fireball rising from the power plant mesmerized Carlos. Freakish gold yellow colors. Hypnotic colors that swirled in a circular motion, radiating out from the center of the explosion. The sound! It deafened him. It was the noise of twenty locomotives, louder than lift-off at Cape Canaveral.

Carlos Peraza wished, with what was left of his thought processes, that he had called in sick today. His wife wouldn't let him. Times were tough, and a little extra money came in handy.

Shit! Shit! Shit! Carlos' eyes were the size of saucers. He felt as though his head were about to explode.

Carlos felt a burning sensation over his entire body. It was as though he were in the middle of a frying pan, sizzling like a piece of bacon, his skin beginning to peel from his flesh. The pain was unbearable, excruciating. Carlos was screaming, but he couldn't hear himself over the din.

When a French prisoner named Languille went to the guillotine in Paris on June 28, 1905, he and his doctor, Dr. Beaurieux, decided to conduct an experiment on how long a severed head could think.

Just how long would a person who was dying be able to think? Would a head, severed from its body, immediately become unconscious? There were reports that Charlotte

Corday, when guillotined, had her severed face slapped. She reportedly gave a look of unmistakable indignation, even though her bloody head was now separated from its trunk and laying in a basket at the foot of the guillotine.

"I will continue to blink until I lose consciousness," Languille told Dr. Beaurieux. "I want you to take precise measurements of how long I am able to continue blinking, how long I can continue consciously thinking after my execution."

Carlos' last conscious thought in those thirty seconds, other than intense agony from the pain was, *Man! All this for one lousy hour of overtime! And I didn't even get to finish my cigarette.*

"Hate breeds hate and love yields love,
This a message from above
We must love or we shall die:
A cosmic order from on high.

—*Cosmic Crimes,* The One

CHAPTER 30

The Gray Wolf Coffee House

11:58 p.m.
Thursday, November 25, 2010
The Gray Wolf Coffee House
New York City

Dante had been running the back alleys of New York City for almost two hours. He was tired. There was a coffee shop, the Gray Wolf Coffee Shop, near East 56th Street under a bright green awning decorated with a drawing of a coffee cup and Dante needed rest. The café spelled everything with small letters: gray wolf coffee shop. It looked like a good place for Dante to stop and catch his breath, nestled inconspicuously next door to the Luscious Doughnut Shop at 455 East 56th Street.

He opened the door and entered. An Arab with a bandanna was furiously pounding away on his laptop in the small café and, when Dante entered, the Arab approached him.

"Go to the back room," he said in an urgent whisper. "Now. Alone."

Dante looked about the room from behind his mirrored sunglasses trying to determine exactly where the back room might be. He had just entered the place, which advertised sophisticated refreshments in an orange and brown slogan on the window. Trendy. Imported cigarettes. Despite the five red ceiling fans circulating air in the narrow room, Dante was nearly suffocating from the thick smoke. Smoking was illegal in New York City in the year 2010. The fans helped to conceal the true nature of this underground establishment. Bribes to the cops took care of the rest of the problem of the citywide smoking ban. Everyone here had a smoking habit that they

191

couldn't shake; the gray wolf was all about feeding that jones.

This must be the e.e. cummings of coffee shops.

After the Arab's urgent command and a quick check of the room, The One walked across the black-and-white linoleum checked floor towards an unusual door. His boots clicked on the flooring as he passed shelves filled with coffee cans, coffee containers, board games like checkers and chess. Machines filled with reddish-brown coffee beans gave off a pungent odor. Each wall of the café was painted red, beige, or black. The red wall on the right-hand side of the room contained an ornately decorated impressive door, mid-wall. It was one of many bizarre decorative touches in the small room.

Where does this door lead?

Overdressed in his usual white, he had waited in line a long time behind a man dressed in a black tee shirt and jeans before he followed the Arab's hissed command. The customer ahead of him had long gray hair pulled back in a ponytail. He wore a scruffy beard. T-shirt man gave him a surly look from above his unkempt beard. A girl with short hair and a shorter skirt stood behind the counter ready to take Dante's money. She gave The One a zombie-like stare.

The smoke was so thick that Dante couldn't tell if this was the waitress' normal look or if it was a look she reserved for over-dressed patrons who were out of their element. The thick smoke had helped Dante go unrecognized, behind his mirrored glasses and in his white tee shirt and nondescript off-white Chinos. Only his boots hinted at the rock star's normal stylish flair. White boots. Very dirty white boots. A putty color.

Dante had asked for a Diet Coke when he entered, and now waited.

Should that be spelled diet coke around here? I wonder what the grammar rules of the gray wolf are: abandon capitals, all ye who enter here? A smile at his private joke.

Behind the waitress, who was fumbling with his change, a wall of various cigarettes. Every imaginable brand. Walking towards the back room, he glanced at the menu of beverages posted high upon the wall, above the cigarettes. The drinks referred to were all coffees: Cappuccinos. Espressos.

Behind the counter, he saw a coffee machine and a soft

drink fountain. No alcohol was served, yet there was a bar. He slumped, briefly, on the cushioned black stool at the bar and waited for the waitress to figure the change for his $2.75 coffee from a $5 bill.

Ashtrays were everywhere, on every table, on every surface in the room. There was a two-seater table and other larger tables scattered throughout the room. Nearly every table was full. People were seated on sparkly red plastic-cushioned seats that resembled those in old-fashioned diners. No food. Only cigars or cigarettes. Leather settees sat low to the ground like ancient dogs waiting for their masters to take them for a run in the crisp night air.

An old-fashioned Coca-Cola sign hung wearily near the bar. Marlboro advertisements from the fifties were suspended to the right of the sign. On top of the cigar case in the center of the room sat a strange animal's skeleton. The skeleton was next to a cardboard model of the Taj Mahal. *What animal gave its life to provide a weird decoration for this place? Why is that mystery animal now forever linked to the Taj Mahal?*

The people behind Dante were playing cards and smoking. Everyone was withdrawn, introverted. Smokers came here to relax? *Let's go ingest massive quantities of nicotine and caffeine to relax! Wasn't that contradictory?* He smiled inwardly. This was no Starbucks. This place had the atmosphere and clientele of an opium den.

He drew near the eight-foot high wooden door set in the red wall. The carved top of the door approached the decorative molding at the apex of the ten-foot ceilings, ceilings of a pressed tin pattern popular at the turn of the century. This building was very, very old, almost as old as the mysterious skeleton serving as a decoration inside it. The door became a commanding presence as Dante stood before it, and also seemed ancient, a relic. It seemed to beckon, commanding Dante to enter.

Dante tugged at the massive weight of the door and crossed its threshold to the back room. Small. Only two tables. Sitting at one table was a man in his early fifties, who looked sixty. Dr. Charles Dunne. Thick black hair with streaks of gray. Glasses lenses that resembled old coke bottle bases. Dunne was dressed in a white lab coat and he, too, held a cigarette in his hand, one that was close to burning the fingers that absent-mindedly clutched it. Dr. Dunne could be an old surgeon or a decrepit veterinarian. He looked up at Dante, and asked, "Are you the man known as The One?"

Dante stared at the elderly man, intrigued.

"Yes. I'm The One. Call me Dante."

"You may call me Charles, Charles Dunne, or Dr. Dunne, if you prefer."

"You're a doctor?"

"No. A physicist. But I know enough medicine to dress the wound I see on your cheek. You're bleeding. Your nose looks broken, as well. Are you okay? Were you in a fight?"

"I'm okay. The bleeding's pretty much stopped." Dante had forgotten that he bore visible signs of his struggle with Agents Nailer and Racine.

"Come with me. I'll disinfect those cuts." Dr. Dunne rose and began walking.

Dante hesitated and then reluctantly followed the white-coated physicist through a second heavily carved door. Dr. Dunne fished a key ring with many keys from his pocket. He fumbled through the keys, inserted the proper key. The second door opened. Dante and Dunne began to descend the concrete stairs. Eight steps. Another door. This time, a steel door. More fumbling for the correct keys.

Another eight steps. Another door, this one of wire mesh.

"Quite a lot of doors just to clean two small cuts," Dante said, already regretting his decision to accompany Dunne, his apprehension rising. "What do you do down here, anyway?"

Momentarily, Dunne paused. Then, Dr. Dunne turned, gave his full attention to The One and said, "This is my laboratory, and only a select few know it exists. Listen to me carefully. Your life depends on what I tell you now. The lives of others depends on you paying careful attention."

"What?"

"I've been using this lab to experiment on accelerating and decelerating the aging process. Aging is a constellation of phenotypes that have escaped the force of natural selection. The organism becomes susceptible to epiphenomena, senescence, aging. I have been working on creating an effect that would defer reaching a deleterious phenotypic threshold."

"Talk English, Dr. Dunne. You're talking to someone who sings for a living."

Dunne appeared startled, then smiled and responded, "Never mind all that right now. The important thing is this: during my research in a completely different field, I stumbled on a method for time travel. I want you to go back in time to prevent Washington, D.C. from being annihilated."

What? Washington, D.C. is fine. I was just there. Washington STATE was having trouble with a Mount St. Helen eruption. Some terrorists blew up the Sears Tower. And there was a hijacked airliner in D.C. sitting on the tarmac awaiting the demands of Arab terrorists. I think they were having some quakes, as usual, in the Bay area, but D.C.? Definitely cool."

Dr. Dunne glanced at his wristwatch and clicked on a television set with the remote control.

"Take a look. That was then. This is now."

Dante and the doctor watched the live news alert, the footage of Washington, D.C., being destroyed in a horrific nuclear cloud was in living color from a New York station. The District of Columbia had been totally obliterated. Bethesda, North Bethesda, Baltimore, Chevy Chase, Friendship Heights, all of Fairfax County. Gone.

Dante had one thought: "Renee. I've lost Renee." He knew he should be feeling empathy for the thousands or millions of other casualties, but what mattered to him, right now, as he heard the news, was Renee Bellwood.

"My God. Doctor." He grabbed the elderly gentleman's coat sleeve. "Can you send me back? Can you send me back to save her, to save them all, to prevent this from happening?"

"I don't know, Dante. We're not even sure what happened, yet. As for the time traveling: the entire process is highly experimental. I think it will work. I think I have the method ready, but it will be extremely expensive. I'll need money. Your money. Lots of it."

"You've got it, Doc. You've got anything I have to give. I'll give my life, if necessary. I've got to try to save her, to save them all. Where do we start? When can we start?"

"Now, Dante. Now. Time and the world are ever in flight, so it must be now."

195

PART 3
Reverse the Universe

"Steel is thought to be impervious
Strong and resolute it is
So, we went on, all oblivious,
Never saw the lurking threat"

—*Burned Steel,* The One

CHAPTER 31

Burned Steel

3:14 p.m.
Saturday, May 24, 2025
HemiPark
Notting Hill, England

The pretty mother in the park with the two young girls knelt to tie one's shoe. The five-year-old wriggled and fussed, unwilling to stand still.

"Honey, Mommy needs to fix your shoes. Stand still." Kaley's voice smiled, even though she was exasperated.

"I can't want to, Mommy. Hurry up!"

"Isabella, don't drop your dolly on the ground. The ground is dirty." The second of the five-year-old twin girls dutifully picked up her doll and clutched it to her chest.

"OK. There you go. Keep your facemasks on. The air quality is poor today."

Each twin adjusted her white facemask and ran towards the jungle gym in the enclosed park.

The park had a large glass bubble overhead, but still the air was questionable.

I wonder if my children will ever know the freedom of breathing air without a mask?

Kaley thought back to her own childhood and the garden she and her sister Isabella had played in. The air had been fragrant with lilacs and redolent with other gorgeous floral scents, the names of which she did not know. Even if Kaley had been a better horticulturist, she couldn't have named all the fragrances in this British rose garden. Kaley wasn't a native of Great Britain, after all.

After the nuclear explosions in the United States fifteen

years ago, Kaley left the country to study abroad. While studying in London at Oxford, she renewed an old friendship with Dante Benedick. She had married Dante Benedick in 2020 and their twin daughters were born four months after the ceremony. She was five months pregnant at the small private wedding ceremony when she said I do, and life had changed dramatically, for both of them, from that moment on.

Dante Benedick lived near London now. When he encountered Kaley again in his home country, he felt a certain responsibility towards her. Maybe it was guilt at his inability, ultimately, to save her mother, Renee Bellwood. After Renee's death in the Great Destruction, Kaley was devastated. Always the sensitive one in the family, lacking her mother's inner strength, the deaths of her twin sister and her mother coming so close together had unnerved her to suicidal depths.

Her father lived through the Great Tragedy unscathed, as did Vice President Mia Akaihane-Black, the majority of Congress and the Senators. Although Mia went to prison for a long time for her role in conspiring with the terrorists, the terrorists' grand plan to topple American power and replace the President with an ally on whom they could rely backfired because it happened on Thanksgiving. Everyone of importance was out of town or out of state celebrating the holiday with relatives. Some high-ranking politicians died in the blast: the Speaker of the House, the Senate Minority Leader, a Supreme Court Judge, the Secretary of Education. The end result: it destroyed the location of power, but not the power hierarchy itself. Buildings were destroyed but the politicians lived on, like cockroaches. Cockroaches and politicians were able to survive any disaster. And not only survive it, but profit from it.

Kaley's father had had Kaley committed to a private asylum in the United States, briefly, citing a nervous breakdown, after her mother's death. It was true that Kaley's spirits were as low as they'd ever been in her life, even lower than when her twin sister Isabella committed suicide. In hindsight, she conceded that her father's precaution was probably a good one. But commitment to mental facilities in the Bellwood family was often punitive rather than therapeutic.

Some force of will had saved her then and had led her back to her journalism studies, which had to be continued elsewhere after Washington, D.C. was completely destroyed by the nuclear explosion. Georgetown was gone. The Capitol, the White House, and the Pentagon: all gone. William Bellwood sent his daughter to Britain to keep her further away from both the lingering devastation of the nuclear fall-out and from the disgrace associated with his now defunct Administration.

First, there had been the pathetic emergency response to the earthquakes in San Francisco by the FGDA, which could be summed up by the cliché, "Too little, too late." Hundreds of thousands died. Fires raged out of control. All bridges were destroyed, including the Golden Gate and Oakland Bay Bridges. It would be years before the bridges could be rebuilt and the city's transit system would return to normal. The underground public transportation system had been totally destroyed by the force of the earthquake. Hundreds drowned in the metal tubes under the Bay, trapped like rats in a flooding sewer. It was now very difficult to navigate the Bay Area. The main means of public transportation there in 2025 was boat or hovercraft.

Then, there was the public humiliation that Bucky suffered when it became public knowledge that his own Vice President was in league with Syria and behind the Airbus A380 hi-jacking. That scandal had rocked the country and the world. Mia Akaihane-Black had been prosecuted and sentenced to fifty years in prison. But, as usual, people with money buy their way out.

The Vice President had been able to cut a deal with the prosecution, giving up William 'Bucky' Bellwood in exchange for a lighter sentence served in the same cushy prison where Martha Stewart once did time. The public downfall of William Bellwood began.

Bucky had his finger in a million profit-making schemes, from the rigging of oil prices to sweetheart deals for the construction of facilities to detain and torture his enemies, both at home and abroad. On a personal level, there was ample evidence of his infidelity, which besmirched his already-sullied reputation. Topping all that off was the evidence that he had sent Renee Bellwood to her death, ordering a forced lobotomy on an unwilling victim. Bellwood was now the O.J. Simpson of ex-Presidents. He couldn't even command a decent speaking fee. Nobody wanted to know about Bucky Bellwood, including his only surviving child, who blamed her father for her mother's death.

That was another good reason to leave the country. Kaley left for Oxford as soon as she was finished with the therapy her father forced her to undergo, finished her journalism studies in England, and began writing for the London *Daily Dispatch*. Eventually, she was sent on assignment to once again interview the world's most famous rock star, just as she had been assigned to interview Dante Benedick when she was a young journalism student in Washington, D.C.

Kaley was more than happy to renew her acquaintance with the charming man who had come to her aid and helped her and her mother after her sister's death. This time, there was no Chislehurst country estate. Country estates were untenable in a world contaminated by radiation poisoning from numerous terrorist events. Survival was assured only in Eco-friendly domes, and Dante had moved to one in the city of London. It was the very same city where Kaley resided. Their friendship, rekindled by the repeat interview, grew as they began to see each other frequently. Now forty-six, The One still toured, but not constantly, as in 2010, when Kaley first met him. Dante was now composing a rock opera, Kaley's editors had heard, and they wanted the details. Rock star goes classical. A good story twist.

Every time she was with Dante, Kaley caught him gazing at her. She would find him watching her, quietly, not speaking. He would be lost in a reverie of some kind.

"What, Dante?"

"Nothing, Kaley. It's just that you look so much like your mother. She was a beautiful woman. You're also a beautiful young woman. You remind me of her more and more each day."

Kaley smiled. Far from being offended, she was flattered. "Thank you, Dante. I really miss Mom. I'm glad you think I look a little bit like her."

"Not a little bit like her, Kaley. I told you years ago that you were drop-dead gorgeous, and you're twice as beautiful now. As you've matured, you've grown from a budding rose to a mature English rose. All your petals are spread. To me, you are one of the Seven Wonders of the World." Dante smiled as he added this last bit.

"Really? So, what are the other six?" She knew she was blushing. It was one of the most romantic things anyone had ever said to her.

"Pizza, chocolate, coffee, blue jeans, rock music, and fresh air." When he said this, Kaley threw her napkin at him, realizing that he was mocking her, but also because she knew he was sincere in his compliment and she was embarrassed, unsure how to respond.

"Wasn't Rosebud the name of Citizen Kane's sled?" Kaley laughed. "I'm not sure I like being compared to a sled, or, for that matter, to a bud. I'm a rose all right, thorns and all. Don't forget it. You Brits just think you're so smart, so brilliant. Well, you're with a Yank. Don't forget that. How did that happen?"

The pair laughed in genuine enjoyment of each other's company. Their outings, first as friends and then as lovers, became more frequent and soon their relationship was tabloid fodder. It was the talk of London when they married, privately, in a midnight ceremony at the loveliest of the HemiParks, near Notting Hill. Only Kaley's best friend, Skyler Bode from the United States, and Dante's publicist, Joshua Gottlieb, were present. Kaley didn't invite her father. She strode down the short aisle an independent woman, giving herself away, freely, to her husband.

She'd begun confiding in The One as an old friend, but friendship had grown into something else. They'd been married for five years now. Her pregnancy with the twins had caused Dante Benedick to do something he thought he'd never do: marry and commit to one woman for life. Kaley's days now, fifteen years later, were so much different than her days in 2010.

Shrieks of girlish laughter, so reminiscent of Kaley and Isabella and their mother in their garden twenty-five years ago, drifted to her as she watched from a nearby park bench.

Kaley smiled sadly at the memory of the watering can and the flowers in another different park many years ago in the United States, remembering her mother and sister and herself clad in white-flowered sundresses made of the same white pique fabric.

Just then, she heard a commotion from the swing set area.

"No! No!" It was Renee, Isabella's twin. A strange boy was trying to take her facemask. Renee, like her namesake, was fighting back. Even though the boy was twice her size and outweighed her by a good thirty pounds, Renee wouldn't let him take her facemask without a fight.

Kaley waded in to restore domestic tranquility.

"Calm down, honey!" She led her daughter away from the bully. "When mean boys like that try to take your stuff, you're right to resist, but I'm here. I'll help you. Just call me."

"I want to do it myself, Mommy!" That was little Renee. The spitting image of her spirited grandmother. The five-year-old ran over to her sister, who was sitting on one end of a teeter-totter, with no one on the other end to make the playground apparatus operative.

Isabella, when they arrived, had grown very quiet. She had looked up in wonder at the bubble top of the dome. "Mommy, what's that thing up there?" she asked.

"Izzy, that's just to protect us from all the bad air that's outside. Plus, if it's a rainy day, we don't have to worry: we have a nice dry day in here." Kaley smiled a reassuring smile.

"But I wanna' go outside and see the real world." Isabella pouted.

"Well, honey. Some day you can do just that." Kaley gathered up the twins' toys and prepared to leave the HemiPark. She wondered if she had just told her girls a lie.

HemiParks had been put in place all over Britain in the days after the explosions in the United States. Any radiation could be filtered using special equipment that the British had been developing since World War II. Always resourceful, and aware of the effects of a war on a country, since the British Isles had actually suffered through the Blitz of World War II on their native soil, England had been light years ahead of the United States in putting response measures in place that would safeguard the British population from fallout. While the United States government was struggling to move the seat of power from Washington, D.C. to Philadelphia, and the senior senators and their families were slowly emerging from secret underground nuclear hidden bunkers, in various western states that the government had prepared exclusively for them, Britain had put Plan S, for Survival, into effect.

Special HemiParks were established to preserve nature and special HabitatParks were erected almost overnight to consolidate all citizens in safe areas. These areas were centered in or near large cities. In The One's case, he had had to give up his beautiful mansion in Chislehurst, but the trade-off was that he was in London full-time. Therefore, whenever possible, he recorded in London and traveled on tour much less than when a single thirty-one-year-old. Dante was now forty-six and the father of two. He was content to travel the world, or what was left of it, much less frequently. He went abroad to dangerous venues as little as possible.

China had emerged as a super power, but it was unsafe to travel to China. A united Korea was also dangerous. The various regime changes happened so quickly that it was impossible to know who was on first without a scorecard. The Middle East continued to be volatile. Israel had been wiped out by nuclear attacks from Iran and Syria. There was no Jewish State in 2025. Any Jewish survivors had fled to Europe, England or the United States. Christian vs. Muslim, Christian vs. Hindu in the Middle East. It had become the Fourth Crusade. The war spread from Iraq and Syria to Iran, Lebanon, Libya and everywhere in between.

As a destination, the United States was not as attractive as it once had been. The West Coast was blighted by the earthquake, which had caused damage as far south as San Diego. The Midwest was almost done rebuilding the very center of the Windy City, but it had taken fifteen years. The East Coast was completely different, in ruins, its largest cities shells of decay. New Orleans never recovered from hurricanes Katrina, Rita, and Wilma, coming one after another, so the picturesque French traditions had died with the city.

The detonation of the nuclear reactor in Richmond, Virginia and its chain reaction on the nearby steel plant in

Beaverton, Pennsylvania, caused fallout that had destroyed D.C. All officials not in the city were sent into hiding. The U.S. authorities, taking a cue from the British, were putting eco-friendly domes in place over the untouched Eastern seaboard cities, but the process was slow going and most of the cities were small ones, like Providence. Because of the incompetence of Bucky Bellwood and the red ink he left as his legacy to the country, the United States was unable to borrow enough funds from foreign countries to rebuild the damage to the infrastructure of the United States.

Canada was helping as much as its economy could tolerate, and certain European Union countries had stepped forward, but taxes had risen to levels so high that riots had taken places in the poorer cities, like Detroit and Newark and Gary. These riots had left even more cities in ruins. Only a few cities still looked "habitable" and it was these cities that were being domed: Chicago, Sacramento, New York City, St. Louis, Des Moines, Omaha and some Southern cities that were not considered high terrorist targets, like Nashville. Most cities to be domed were in the middle of the country, offsetting the water level increases from global warming on both coasts, which threatened to inundate New York City, San Francisco, Miami and other coastal metropolises.

Because of the nuclear silos in Omaha, the Midwest was hit-or-miss as to which cities would be selected to benefit from domes and which ones would not be granted the life-saving technology. Des Moines, for instance, was found worthy. It was central in location and located on Interstate 80, the main highway linking all the hubs that remained in the U.S. It caused Des Moines to swell to several million inhabitants.

On the downside, San Francisco was just barely alive, much of it was underwater, and any areas near Washington, D.C., were on life support. It was interesting what detonating a nuclear reactor in Beaverton, Pennsylvania had done to the eastern seaboard.

All the moneyed homes of the Newport, Rhode Island rich were gone. Entire cities had disappeared. Yet other areas sprang up and people re-located, just as they had fled to Texas and Baton Rouge, Louisiana, after the New Orleans flood of

2005. Like New Orleans, cities hit hard by the nuclear blast and the rising water levels never really recovered completely.

Life went on. For the Benedick family in London, Kaley and Dante Benedick and their twin girls, life was good.

"Steel is thought to be impervious
Strong and resolute it is
So, we went on, all oblivious,
Never saw the lurking threat
Steel is mighty; steel is strong;
Steel will hold great buildings up.
We did not know the aerodynamics
Of horror, hiding in our midst"

—*Burned Steel,* The One

CHAPTER 32

After the Fall

9:18 p.m.
Tuesday, December 30th, 2025
The One's Townhouse
Notting Hill, England

It had been over six months since the death of Dante's wife and twin daughters. The events of that day, burned into his brain, re-played like a film loop from an old horror movie, over and over. The hunger for celebrity news made sure of that.

Kaley had dropped the twins off at the Ashburnham School, an exclusive independent day school for children aged four to seven.

She was outside her idling car, just inside the school entrance, giving each small girl a hug as she did every morning. Moments after Kaley stepped from the still-idling car and accompanied the girls into the building, the school exploded in a paroxysm of violence. Glass and concrete and ash and paper flew everywhere within a five-block radius of the explosion.

One-third of Ashburnham Elementary School was leveled. Rescue workers, mainly parents, like Kaley, who had been dropping their children off for a routine day at school, frantically began pulling the wounded and dead from the wreckage. It was reminiscent of the horrible Oklahoma Federal Building explosion, a terrifying vision that had embedded itself in the American consciousness many years before the Great Destruction.

Lifeless body after lifeless body was carried from the carnage by shell-shocked fathers, while panicked mothers screamed and cried in horror. The faces of the victims were so innocent, so pale, bloodied by the senseless violence.

When things seemed as if they couldn't get any worse, a second explosion occurred, one-half hour after the first. A school bus parked outside the building exploded, killing the school's first grade teacher, who had been frantically trying to help save the victims. Also killed were a school board member, the local postmaster, who had come running from the post office to help, and another grief-stricken parent.

The terrorist bomb planted in Ashburnham killed one hundred and fifty children and twenty adults and injured two hundred more victims. Rescuers frantically searched through the portion of the school that was still standing. In doing so, they made another horrifying discovery that prompted them to call for everyone to evacuate the building.

The part of the school still standing was wired with over 500 lbs of unexploded dynamite, connected to a timing device and a battery. The dynamite might detonate at any moment.

"Get out of the building!" Headmaster Henry Ives yelled.

Kaley was clutching Izzy in her arms, sobbing wildly, and trying to locate little Renee.

"No! No! I can't find Renee. I can't find my little girl." Isabella's lifeless form draped from Kaley's weary arms, as she continued searching through the rubble for Renee. "She has to be here. She has to be okay."

Kaley, wild-eyed with horror and shock, was courageous and unyielding in her intent to find and save her daughters. In her frenzy, she ignored the warning of Headmaster Ives who was rushing for the nearest exit. She continued to search for the missing twin. Kaley didn't leave. She stood her ground. She hadn't left when the bus blew in the street, deafening her. Her ears were ringing. She was covered in soot and debris.

Kaley wouldn't leave now. "Not without my daughters!" The explosions in the school and the still-unexploded five hundred pounds of dynamite were the work of a terrorist posing as a janitor. He had planted the dynamite in the building over several months' time. Five minutes after Headmaster Henry Ives frantically warned those in the building to run for their lives, the remaining dynamite exploded, leveling what remained of the building, killing all trapped inside.

The blatant terrorist act, directed against innocents, received extensive press coverage all over the world. The fact that Dante Benedick's wife and children were among the casualties caused the story to linger on the front pages of newspapers around the world for days. Kaley, who had endured so much tragedy in her young life, lost her own life trying to rescue her children. She and the Benedick twins disappeared completely in the huge fireball that went up when the final five hundred pounds of dynamite detonated.

Blowing up schools was something that began happening more and more frequently after Washington, D.C. was destroyed. The media dubbed it "The Slaughter of the Innocents." The onslaught was bloody and cruel. It knew no class distinctions. It claimed the lives of Kaley Benedick and her daughters, Renee and Isabella.

Terrorists took the loves of Dante Benedick's life twice. Two different eras. Two different sets of circumstances. Both tragedies devastated him. He couldn't sleep for weeks, thinking about his darling girls, torn apart in the chaotic thunder of the explosions at the Ashburnham School. Every Muslim in the Middle East seemed bent upon destruction. Children were just collateral damage.

For six months, Dante sank into deep despair. He couldn't eat. He couldn't sleep. He kept seeing the image of his wife and daughters, dying horribly, screaming for his help.

Dante was six months behind on his CD "After the Fall." He hadn't been able to write music since the death of his wife and twins. He hadn't performed one live show. He hadn't been in the studio.

He spent most days lying in bed. Occasionally, he'd make it to the couch to do more of nothing. He didn't read or watch the news, which only reminded him of Kaley and Isabella and Renee. He accomplished absolutely nothing.

Dante stared at the white walls of the living room, lost in memories and grief. He saw the images of his life with Kaley and the girls swirling before his eyes:

The night they first made love in his manor, Dante had opened the curtains in the darkened room to allow the moonlight to filter in. He had tossed rose petals across the

211

pale blue silk bed sheets. Kaley had looked so beautiful in the moonlight. He was struck at that moment by how much she resembled her mother. She tilted her head sideways, and her hair, now a lighter shade of blonde, cascaded towards her shoulders. Kaley's shyness made her even more beautiful. Her doe-like brown eyes, so warm and full of love and passion, gazed deeply into his own.

When his two daughters were born and Dante first held the twins in his arms, he didn't think that he could feel love any more deeply than at that moment.

Izzy taking her first steps, balance a challenge, wobbling. When Izzy fell, she would knock her twin sister, Renee down as well and both girls would laugh merrily.

The night Dante sat at the piano with Kaley and the girls singing his old song "Kisses For Kitten," an unrecorded song he'd written when he was only sixteen:

> *"It's your eyes I'm missin'*
> *When you're a million miles away*
> *It's your lips I'm kissin'*
> *As night turns into day.*
> *We are long past forgettin'*
> *When so much love remains*
> *I'm cravin' kisses from you, kitt'n*
> *Your claws have me in chains"*

"Dante," Joshua Gottlieb said to his boss. Dante became more ghost-like in appearance with every passing day, lost in dreams, lost in the past.

The One kept staring at the blank wall.

"You have a phone call," Joshua said.

"Joshua," Dante said, with a far-away look. "No phone calls. Take care of it. I don't want to be disturbed. No phone calls – ever."

"It's a Doctor Charles Dunne in New York City. He says it's urgent."

"Dr. Dunne?" Dante said. "Dr. Dunne, I haven't heard from him or thought about him for years. How long since I've been to America?"

"You haven't been there since the destruction of D.C.,

fifteen years ago."

"Fifteen years. I can't believe it's been that long.

"Dante–"

"And I've been sending him a fortune to carry on his research ever since."

"Do you want to talk to the doctor?"

Dante paused. "Yes, I'll take it in the study."

The One walked down the hall, into his study, shut the door, and picked up the phone.

"Do you believe in God?" Dr. Dunne sounded excited.

Dante was puzzled. *What kind of question was that after fifteen years?*

"Yes of course, I do," Dante answered, annoyed.

"Then get down on your knees and thank whatever God you pray to, because I've made a miraculous discovery, a major break-through in science. Dante, this concept is incredible. It has implications for you. You must come to my lab in America. Come soon."

A long pause on Dante's end. "What kind of breakthrough?"

"One I've been working on for the last fifteen years and you've been funding for the past fifteen years. It's pay-off time. I don't want to say too much on the phone. Let's just say everything we were going to do before, we can now accomplish. Everything is ready. Now, I just need you, if you still want to do this."

It all came back to him: the plan, the speculative scheme to time travel. Could he go back in time to 2010 and save Renee Bellwood and much of the east coast? Even though Kaley's mother was dead fifteen years, dead in the explosion that leveled D.C., just the memory of her made Dante's heart beat faster. He was feeling dizzy, too, from the contagious excitement in Charles Dunne's voice.

"Yes, of course I still want to do this. I'll leave immediately."

Dante hung up the phone and began packing. He showed the first signs of life he'd displayed in months.

Renee had never left his heart. He had married Kaley, her daughter, and raised a family with her, but Renee Bellwood was entwined deeply in the emotions of his soul.

She was part of his psyche. He had loved Renee first. Perhaps he had always loved Renee best. Marriage to her look-alike daughter had kept his love for Renee flickering in his heart. That flame had never been extinguished.

If the time machine worked, as Dr. Dunne was cryptically hinting it did, could Dante go back in time and try to save Kaley and the twins? Or should he go back even further in time and save Renee Bellwood and the thousands who died in the Great Destruction?

Reality hit Dante like the explosion at the Ashburnham School. He began to think about these two times in his life and in the history of the world. A glimmer of hope became an acknowledgement of reality. Could he do both, or must he choose?

If Dante attempted to save Kaley and his daughters Renee and Isabella, lost in the terrorist explosion at their school, it would change nothing about their existence in this time and place. The world would still be the same: fucked up now and fucked up in the future. All of the survivors on the planet had been forced to take refuge in Habitatdomes. There was no real way to enjoy the world as it had existed in the time of Renee and William Bellwood, fifteen years ago in 2010.

Now, there was a never-ending war in the Middle East, throbbing like a dull toothache. The world's migraine headache. Today, terrorists blew things up at will. Nobody anywhere was safe, as they had been in the years before Renee Bellwood's death. The once great country of America lay in ruins. England wasn't far behind.

Dante felt that fate had given him a second chance to live in a normal world with the woman of his dreams. The choice was difficult, but he had to do this. He had to go back to the year 2010. Perhaps he could save Renee Bellwood and save her daughter, as well. Renee Bellwood: the woman he had never been able to forget. His soul mate. His first great love.

On a more humanitarian scale, perhaps he could save America. He might be able to preserve life on the planet, itself, as it had existed fifteen years earlier, when there had been clean air and fresh water and the quality of life and environment was more than just a distant memory.

He must try. Why? For love. For the undying love of the woman he had never been able to forget. For love of mankind. God help his immortal soul as he made this Sophie's choice. He knew he would be torn apart by the stark decision facing him.

He might never be able to forgive himself. Would he be sacrificing his family with Kaley to try and recapture what might have been with Renee?

He didn't know. He knew only that he had to go back, if he could. He was being true to himself. Wasn't that what Shakespeare urged in "Hamlet?" "This above all else: to thine own self be true, And it must follow as the night the day, thou canst not then be false to any man."

The power to change the planet. The power to recapture the world. To bring light from darkness. To bring calm from chaos. This power lay in his hands and in his hands alone.

"Time's wing'ed chariot hurries near
I gather strength to fight my fear,
If I should die before I wake
I pray the Lord my soul to take."

—Dante's Prayer

CHAPTER 33

Here, There, and Everywhere

8:15 p.m.
Wednesday, December 31st, 2025
Dr. Charles Dunne's Lab
New York City

Dante was trying to assimilate all the information he was hearing. He was going to go back in time. If this machine worked, that is. He would be transported back to the year 2010. The target date was November 18, 2010. His first mission would be to stop the President's daughter, Isabella Bellwood, from committing suicide.

If Dante could prevent Isabella Bellwood's suicide, that would prevent Mosuma Hamad's suicide mission aboard the Airbus A380. The Syrians wouldn't cause chaos by imploding the nuclear power plant near the steel plant in Beaverton, Pennsylvania. That explosion, if it occurred, would destroy most of the East Coast, killing millions, including the woman he loved, First Lady Renee Bellwood.

Dr. Dunne's hair had gone completely gray since the last time Dante had seen the scientist. He had liver spots on his hands.

"The most important thing to remember is this," Doctor Dunne said sternly. "You will only have a week to complete your mission."

"Why only a week?" Dante asked, surprise registering in his tone of voice.

"That is as long as the light-cycle will permit," Dr. Dunne explained. "If you don't get back to the time machine by then, the machine will automatically return to 2025. If you're not on board, you'll be left behind. It's imperative that you complete your mission and return to the time machine in time to be transported back, or you'll be marooned in the past, stuck in the year 2010 forever."

"I lived through 2010 once. I can do it again," Dante said, with a trace of humor.

"Don't even think such things," Dr. Dunne replied angrily. "Re-living a time you once lived violates space-time principles and creates many paradoxes."

"Violates what and what?" Dante asked, confused. "Do they give tickets for that? And, if they do, what's the fine?" Dante was not taking this as seriously as Dr. Dunne had hoped.

"Did you ever study physics, Mr. Benedick?" Dr. Dunne said, his tone of voice seeming strident.

"Me? Uh, no. I was never into science. I was into music and girls." Disapproval registered on Dr. Dunne's face.

"I don't have time to explain time-shifting and the different paradoxes this will cause. You don't understand the complexities of physics, so you won't understand the theories behind quantum mechanics. All you have to know is that it's extremely dangerous to extend your time in the year 2010 beyond one hundred sixty-eight hours. It could change everything in your life, everything in Renee Bellwood's life, everything in the future and the past of the planet. Not a minute more. Not one minute more, I say." Dr. Dunne was almost ranting.

"Chill, doc. I'll be prompt. I'll finish in a week or die trying. You have my word on it."

"One last thing, be careful, be very careful," the scientist said. "When you change the past, you change the future and we are the future."

Dante nodded.

"It's going to be a rough ride," Dr. Dunne said, with a stern face. "Those lasers burn."

"Sounds like I'm gonna' need a lotta balls," Dante said.

"No," Dr. Dunne said. "Any fool has balls. You're going to need courage, and the backbone to endure excruciating pain."

* * * *

The whole premise was like the domino effect, working in reverse. It was like a string, doubling back upon itself in time and space. Success in traveling through time was a long shot. Dante shrugged. *My whole life has been a long shot.* Thoughts and facts vanished as soon as the lasers began transforming him.

The smell was the worst, the odor of his own flesh burning. But the sound was just as unnerving: click, click, click. Directions were being shouted at the white-coated assistant turning the dials: "Left, two degrees ... down one notch. Right one degree." He half expected to hear someone yell, "Fire!" The sound, the shouted directions: it was like a bad submarine movie.

But this was not a movie, incredible as it all seemed. Time stood still. Dante could feel his heart pounding in his chest. He was seated in a chair like any you might see at your neighborhood barbershop or dentist's office, with one exception. His head was secured, immobilized, in a stereo-tactic frame. His arms were secured at the wrists, as though he were to be electrocuted. Likewise, his legs were immobilized. He was nude, his skin glistening with sweat as the laser beams found their mark and bit into his deeply tanned body. There wasn't an ounce of fat on his lean frame, bits of which were disappearing.

Dante Benedick was disintegrating, little-by-little, microscopically small piece by microscopically small piece. Ion by ion. The laser was aimed at his head. His eyes were propped open, wide, staring. He had been given directions not to move. If he moved any part of his body during the procedure, there could be no guarantees that he would remain intact. Like Humpty Dumpty, "All the king's horses and all the king's men" might not be able to put Dante Benedick back together again if he dared flinch or move involuntarily. His eyelids mustn't blink during the procedure, nor his fingers twitch. His toes or fingers mustn't move. Individual pieces of cotton batting had been inserted between his fingers and toes, as though he were going to be given the world's most expensive and unusual manicure. Each individual finger and each individual toe was taped to the chair, in order to assist Dante to remain immobilized. Breathing was the only movement that the machine would tolerate.

Short laser burst. Heat. Smell of smoke. Sound of murmured voices, consulting from behind the screen. The screen suggested that the procedure might contaminate those performing it, as X-rays contaminated X-ray technicians. As far as Dante knew, that might be the case. Who really knew what to expect? This was not a technology that had ever been tried on a living human being. Corpses had "come through" to the other side intact, but dead bodies didn't breathe or move. Dante was doing his best to cooperate fully. He would do his damnedest to be successful in the mission, but would his best be good enough? Dr. Dunne, the master theoretician in this end game, was supervising, directing the assistants, but his assistants seemed hesitant, unsure, and afraid.

All these adjectives applied to Dante Benedick, as well. He was being transported back in time using a highly experimental method of which the FDA almost certainly would never approve. Nor would they ever know about it. If the existence of the machine were ever to be made known, the military would co-opt it for its own devious purposes. This was a private lab, funded solely by private millions. Dante Benedick, the world's most famous rock star and one of the world's richest men had funded its existence. The laser technology employed was cutting-edge. The theories to support its efficacy had never been tested on a live subject, but they were essentially sound, in theory. Dante's very life was being put to the test of Dr. Charles Dunne's theories.

"Your arms full, your hair wet, I could not
Speak, and my eyes failed, I was neither
Living nor dead, and I knew nothing.
Looking into the heart of light, the silence."

—*The Wasteland,* T.S. Eliot

CHAPTER 34

Time and Time Again

8:38 p.m.
Wednesday, December 31st, 2025
Dr. Charles Dunne's Lab
New York City

Dante inhaled and exhaled. Slow, deep breaths. He was afraid to move, but attempting to calm himself with the only movement allowed. Deep breathing. Inhale. Hold eight counts. Exhale for four counts. He had been doing this for ten minutes now. The clock visible on the wall showed only ten minutes had elapsed. Those ten minutes seemed like an eternity. Dante wasn't sure what was happening to him, but he knew that everything on this plane seemed to be growing less and less sharp, less and less acute. It was as though he were watching a television set playing in black-and-white from the next room, with the sound off. Black was white. White was black. Everything was fuzzy. He was only half-aware of what was appearing on the screen. He was only vaguely conscious of what was happening to him, in this room, at this moment in time. At one point, he had a vision of himself trapped inside something that resembled a storefront, peering out through shattered glass. Then, it was gone. But the smell, the godawful smell of burning flesh, of *his* burning flesh, remained.

The laser worked, bit-by-bit, to de-materialize The One's DNA and to re-materialize it on the other side. Dante would be transported back through time, from the year 2025 to the year 2010. He would be thirty-one years old again instead of forty-six. If he lived, that is, if the experiment worked.

Time. Time was such an unforgiving concept. He who controls time controls everything. Dante remembered a talk he once had had with his father. His dad was nagging him about getting a real job for the hundredth time and Dante, as usual, was arguing that writing and singing songs *were* his "real jobs."

"You're just wasting your time," scoffed Jack Benedick. "You'll never amount to anything unless you use your time wisely. Get a job at the mill, like me. Become a bricklayer, a plumber, a house painter. Save your money. Get married. Settle down."

"Dad, who controls your time? Doesn't your boss control your time? Don't you have to clock in when someone else says, and clock out when someone else dictates? Isn't your life totally controlled by outside forces? Do you think your boss or your supervisor controls it 'wisely' If you work for The Man, you're at the mercy of The Man. He who controls your time controls you."

Dante stalked out of the small row house in Chislehurst. He never looked back and he never returned. At first, Birmingham beckoned, with its polyglot culture of ethnic types and its label of most modern city, a debatable claim. The city was working on modern technology: sidewalks that moved, escalators, like those once found in airport terminals. Somehow, they thought this made them modern. Dante learned better fast. Birmingham did expose him to a variety of ethnic types, though, and he met a few mates there.

But Birmingham didn't hold his attention for long. The real action was in London, closer to Dante's original home in Chislehurst. London was where groups were hooking up and starting out. It was the city to be. He met up with a few other musicians who were into doing what he was doing: writing songs and making music. Some of these musicians would accompany Dante as he re-located to London. They would aid Dante in his task of making great music. And, in Dante's case, as members of his band, ultimately, they would aid him in doing good in the world. Always the idealist, Dante wanted to help those less fortunate than himself.

"Time is on my side," he thought to himself. "I'll never let time rule me; I will rule time."

Now, with this daring experiment, designed to save the past from the future, Dante was, indeed, ruling time.

Dante's consciousness of his surroundings waxed and waned. His impressions of the experience were like a fragmented dream, sounds heard from afar. It was as though he were seeing through a glass darkly, as the expression goes.

Sounds. Children laughing. Children at the beach. Were these sounds real, or were they memories from his cerebral cortex, his cerebellum, being transported through time? Dante's eyes, propped open Clockwork Orange-style, were curiously tearless. Special eye-drops had been applied. His neck hurt from being immobilized in the stereotactic frame for almost one full hour.

The procedure for de-materialization and re-materialization of DNA would take 90 minutes. Near the end, there was very little to do in the year 2010, except turn off the machines and pray. Walk away and pray.

Dante was praying throughout the procedure. He wanted to help mankind. He wanted to be a good person in a bad world. He was willing to risk his life to help mankind and two very special women.

With that thought in what remained of his cerebral cortex, he ceased to exist in the future. He was terrified. He was hot. He was tired. He was thirsty. He was uncomfortable. Was he dead? Was he alive? Where was he? What would happen to him in time?

Time, and again, time. Creeping until the end of recorded time. Moving backwards from the year 2025 to the year 2010. He was able to keep going because he knew that one person, in particular, one person for whom he would lay down his life, needed him now more than ever.

Why would the World's Most Successful Rock Star, the personality of this or any other decade, take such an extreme risk? For love. For the love of a woman. For the love of Renee Bellwood. He hadn't seen her since the explosion on the East coast on that fateful day fifteen years ago, but she had never left his heart. For love of mankind. For love of the world. Time and time again, the answer came back, for love.

"Between the idea
And the reality
Between the motion
And the act
Falls the Shadow"

—*The Hollow Men,* T.S. Eliot

CHAPTER 35

Twisted Fate

10:10 p.m.
Wednesday, November 17, 2010
Dr. Charles Dunne's Lab

Breathe. Dante gasped for air. He was suffocating. One deep breath. Another. Then another. His heart rate slowed. Simultaneously, he felt nauseous and his head ached. His entire body ached. It took a long time for his eyes to adjust to the gloom of the room, but the lab now looked threatening in the darkness.

"Doc, lights! I can't see a thing." Dante's plea went unanswered. The laboratory remained dark.

Only then did Dante realize that he was alone in the lab. This was starting to make sense. He wouldn't meet Dr. Dunne for another week.

He had to get out of this black box. He had to get out of New York City, return to Washington D.C. *before* Isabella Bellwood committed suicide. He must stop her. Isabella's suicide had set everything else in motion. She must not kill herself. Stop Isabella from committing suicide and all would be different.

He tried to remember what he had been doing in New York City fifteen years earlier. He had flown in to do a photo shoot for his new release, *Broken Soul*. All he'd have to do would be to call his personal assistant Joshua Gottlieb. Joshua would bring him fresh clothes, arrange passage to D.C., and make it possible for him to save Isabella. First he must make the phone call that might save Bella's life.

Dante rose from the chair, naked, cold. In the darkness, he bumped into a piece of furniture, striking his kneecap and causing a tingling pain.

"Damn it." The lingering sensation of his bruised kneecap reassured him that he was alive, even if uncomfortable. Naked, cold and hungry were never comfortable.

He searched for a wall with outstretched hands. Finally, he stumbled over something on the floor and it threw him towards a solid wall. He ran his hands over the rough bricks of the unfamiliar space, trying to locate a light switch.

Bricks. Nothing else. *Wait, a switch.* He flipped it up, and light bathed a small room, a lab with unrecognizable scientific equipment. To his left, an apparatus he could not identify. To his right, a dentist's chair. Clocks everywhere. Next to the computer, a phone. Next to the phone, a clock. The digital read-out said 10:30 p.m. Dante rushed towards the phone, shivering in his nakedness.

I don't have much time, Dante thought to himself. *Less than ninety minutes before Isabella dies.*

Dante picked up the phone, dialed Joshua Gottlieb's cell phone number. The phone rang a long time before the familiar voice of Joshua Gottlieb came on the other end.

"Joshua, this is Dante."

"Dante, where are you? After dinner you disappeared. I looked for you everywhere. I called your cell several times. Are you still going to Miami on holiday tomorrow? Did you leave for Florida without me?"

Dante remembered now. After the photo shoot he and Joshua were to have a week's vacation. A well-deserved break from work. A trip to Miami for a brief holiday. However, all that had been canceled when he was summoned by the White House to sing at Isabella Bellwood's funeral services.

"I'm still in New York," Dante said. "Pack some of my clothes. Meet me at the Gray Wolf Coffee Shop. It's a coffee shop next to a Luscious Doughnuts shop. East 56th Street, in the four hundred block, on the corner. You can't miss it."

* * * *

It was only two minutes after eleven o'clock, but Dante was worried that he was already too late.

Money can buy you many things: power, privilege, a life of luxury. One thing money can't buy is time. Time is distributed randomly amongst rich and poor. Time keeps ticking relentlessly, aging the world and its inhabitants. Some get more time than others, which seems intrinsically unfair. But who said life was fair?

Joshua arrived at the Gray Wolf Coffee Shop, as requested, bringing fresh clothes for Dante, a cell phone, Dante's wallet and cash. Josh didn't ask why Dante was naked and shivering in a small café over what looked like a laboratory on East 56th Street. He'd found Dante Benedick in other unusual situations. Part of his job was not to ask too many questions that Dante didn't want to answer.

"Josh, thanks for bringing the stuff. I'll call you just as soon as I'm able. Don't mention this, okay?"

"Whatever you say, boss. Your jet's waiting at LaGuardia. A limo is outside with a driver."

"Yes. We'll drive to the plane, but I have to call first." Dante dialed Kaley Bellwood's cell phone number, still programmed into his phone from their interview date.

* * * *

Dante's private Lear jet landed at Ronald Reagan National Airport in D.C. By the time the limousine was parked outside the condo where Isabella Bellwood lived, it was shortly after midnight. Dante had already called 911 in D.C. and had alerted them to a possible overdose at Isabella Bellwood's address.

Dante bolted from the car, ran to the door on that side of the brick building. Locked.

Dante dialed Kaley's cell phone number again.

"Kaley, please. This is Dante Benedick. Come to Isabella's now, before it's too late. She's taken some pills. I called from New York, but I only got your machine. I hope the first call I made to the cops has brought help, but I don't know."

Dante had no time. He had miles to go before he slept. He hung up. Isabella's bedroom window was dark.

If the police came immediately after my call, Isabella is

in the hospital by now, having her stomach pumped. Her room should be dark.

What Dante did not know, as he was breathing a sigh of relief at the thought of Isabella receiving medical attention at the hospital was that, at the four street intersection - only two blocks away from the hospital - the ambulance ran a red light and was involved in an accident. A semi-trailer truck crossing the intersection at the time (what they call an articulated lorry in England) collided with the ambulance. There was a sickening sound of breaking glass and crashing metal. The ambulance flipped on its side. Broken glass, gasoline, diesel fuel everywhere.

Reaching the intersection, Dante jumped from his car and opened the back of the ambulance at the scene. There was blood everywhere, but all bodies had been removed. The engine of the semi-trailer truck had crushed the paramedics, along with their patient, Isabella.

Fate was indeed cruel. Dante had heard the expression "a twist of fate." This seemed more like twisted fate. Fate had a sick sense of humor. Fate was laughing all the way to the cemetery.

Kaley joined Dante, following his phoned directions. She was horror-struck. She'd only been half-awake when he first called and left the terrible message about her sister's overdose.

Dante walked towards Kaley. He folded her in his arms. "It'll be all right," he said, patting her back in his loose embrace. "I'm sorry. It'll be all right."

She was going to push him away. Who was this man? This must be some surreal nightmare. She recognized Dante Benedick, The One. She thought she was having a dream. Maybe an out-of-body experience. Nothing was real.

They stood holding each other, Dante patting her on the back and repeating, "It'll be all right." Ambulance and police sirens blared in the distance, growing nearer.

"Whene'er I see you in despair,
I feel as though it's me that's there.
We are as one; a gift to give
Please, God: let my sister live."

—*Kaley's Prayer"* Kaley

CHAPTER 36

Kaley's Prayer

12:08 a.m.
November 18, 2010
Our Lady of Mercy Hospital
Washington, DC

The distance between the crossroads where the accident occurred and Our Lady of Mercy Hospital couldn't have been more than five miles. It seemed like a hundred miles. Each block stretched for an eternity as they sped towards the hospital. Dante drove Kaley's Jeep Grand Cherokee at such high speeds that they were in jeopardy of ending up like Isabella, now lying in the emergency room, fighting for her life.

"Where's the accident victim you brought in a few minutes ago? A young girl – twenty-one? She was in the ambulance. A truck collided with the ambulance about five miles from here. This is her sister." Dante sounded authoritative, like someone whose questions should be answered and whose orders should be obeyed.

There was no mistaking the urgency in Dante's voice. The emergency room nurse quickly pointed towards a triage unit with curtains drawn.

The pair rushed in the direction pointed, even as the nurse's voice called after them. "Are you both immediate family? No one should be in there who isn't immediate family."

Dante had to think fast. "We're both family," Dante said. He wasn't sure the nurse was buying this lie or not; he could only hope that she was.

The nurse seemed to make a decision to suspend

disbelief. "Go through those doors straight ahead, then take a left."

The usual bureaucratic rules and regulations didn't stop them, even though there were even more hurdles to navigate, more obstacles to surmount to get to Isabella.

Isabella lay on a gurney, tubes connected everywhere. Her clothing had been cut from her body. Doctors were frantically working to save her life. Isabella's breathing was coming in short gasps, the oxygen mask on her face useless. Bella's struggle to fill her damaged lungs with air was so painful that it made anyone observing feel uncomfortable.

Behind the curtain to her right, a large black man was shackled to a gurney. He was screaming, "Fool shot me! He's supposed to be my friend! Fuckin' fool shot me in the stomach!" The prisoner was agitated and handcuffed. "What's you lookin' at? You be lookin' at me, fool?"

When Isabella saw them, she seemed to struggle to raise her arm and remove her oxygen mask. The doctors cautioned her to lie still.

"Miss Bellwood. Try not to tear out any of the tubes or remove any of the equipment. We're trying to stabilize your vital signs." Behind her, on a heart monitor, Dante and Kaley could see that Isabella's pulse and heartbeat were erratic. Isabella was wild-eyed with fear, like a gazelle in the wild. She was fighting frantically to speak, to communicate.

"Doctor," said Kaley. "I'm her sister. Maybe if we let her tell us whatever she wants to say, she'll be more at peace?"

The chief attending physician hesitated, and then relented. He assisted Kaley in removing the oxygen mask, but, as he did so, he pulled Kaley aside.

"She's very badly injured. Massive internal bleeding and the oxygen are not helping because of the crushing nature of the injuries to her lungs. We've done everything we can. You should prepare yourselves for the worst. Are your parents here?"

The doctor didn't seem to recognize the celebrity of the young girl he was trying to save, her equally famous sister, or the rock star accompanying her. He was relating to Kaley and Dante assuming them to be brother and sister.

"We've called my parents, Doctor," Kaley said. "They're

on the way. But, right now, it's just us. We want to reassure Isabella and try to calm her down."

"All right, Miss, but only for a moment. We're prepping her for surgery. If we don't stop the internal hemorrhaging…" The doctor trailed off with that statement, but the sense of foreboding remained, hanging heavy and unspoken, casting a pall over the mood of the room.

With the mask now removed, Isabella struggled valiantly. Against pain. Against fear. Against overwhelming odds. Kaley held her hand as Bella gasped, "Please, take care of my sister. Tell my folks I loved them, and I'm sorry. I only gave the plans to Zuma because I thought I was doing the right thing. I was trying to help."

Kaley felt faint. The emotional nature of Isabella's plea to Dante, which clearly showed that Isabella knew how badly she was injured, amped the emotional volume of this exchange. Kaley's ears rang. She felt leaden. She started to say the usual, reassuring things. *What do you say to someone who is dying?* She was confused by what Bella had just said. *What plans? Who or what was Zuma?*

"Isabella, the doctors are going to fix you up. They are taking you in to surgery."

"No, Kaley. I think it's too late. I want you to be sure to tell Mom and Dad that I loved them and that I'm sorry. I didn't know." Isabella's voice trailed off as she winced in pain. The attending physician interrupted.

"I'm sorry. But we have the operating room open now. Your sister has to go. Right now. We'll ask you to sign some documents at the front desk. After that, you can wait in the waiting room."

The attendants rushed the pale, broken bird from the emergency room and into surgery.

*"Grief crawled inside the empty husk of her heart
And began to gnaw upon her soul."*

—*Broken Soul,* The One

CHAPTER 37

Broken Soul

12:28 a.m.
November 18, 2010
Our Lady of Mercy Hospital
Washington, DC

The young girl hooked to tubes in Intensive Care was as pale as paste. Her pallor underscored the seriousness of her injuries. She had been crushed beneath the truck as it jackknifed into the ambulance. Tethered on a gurney at the time, she'd been thrown about the inside of the siren-blaring doomed vehicle. Seat belts might have prevented some of her injuries, but seat belts had not been possible. Bella was barely alive. An oxygen mask covered her mouth, tubes snaking everywhere. As Dante and Kaley entered, she was unconscious. Medics worked over her.

It looked like a bad television medical show, the difference being that this was real. Dante exhaled deeply. Instinctively, he moved towards Kaley, who had burst into sobs at the sight of her mortally wounded sister.

"It's all right, Kaley. It's ok. Let it out." Dante put a reassuring arm around her shoulder. He was overwhelmed to actually be holding Kaley again, warm, vibrant, alive.

"I … Is she going to be Okay?"

Dante didn't speak, and none of the attendants had the time for useless reassurances. They were too busy trying to save the patient. Doctors stepped in and out of the green-draped area, giving orders for her care. Many of them moved to the head of the bed and, using a small pen-sized flashlight, shone the small light into Isabella's pupils. None said anything to Dante or Kaley. They were battling the Grim Reaper, and his scythe was mightier than their puny swords.

As Dante put a protective arm around Kaley's shuddering shoulders, the curtains around Isabella's cubicle parted and Renee Bellwood entered. She appeared frail and distraught, but, unlike Kaley, she did not immediately break down in tears. She went to the head of Isabella's bed, touched her daughter's forehead, looked at Bella's now-closed eyes, took her hand. Renee would do anything in her power to save either of her girls. Now was not the time for weeping, moaning and gnashing of teeth. Now was the time for action. If ever there was a time to try to save the life of one of those nearest and dearest to her in the entire world, it was now. She wouldn't hold back or waste valuable time in useless tears. Plenty of time for sobbing and regrets when every possible avenue for survival was explored. Renee hoped with all her being that she could help save her daughter through sheer force of will.

Seeing Renee again like this, Dante felt overcome with emotions too complicated to describe.

"Please, doctor," Renee said to the young attendant who had just entered through the ICU curtain, "how is my daughter?"

The question was a simple one, but the answer was not. "Ma'am, we're doing everything we can. The prognosis isn't good."

To Dante Benedick, who'd heard many euphemisms, the message was this: Isabella is dying.

Renee interpreted what she had heard differently, more hopefully, the way any mother would.

"But you can save her?"

The young doctor looked away and wouldn't meet Renee's gaze. "We're trying, Ma'am." That was all he said before he quickly exited. When he returned, later, he used Princess Diana's crushing injuries as an example of what sort of trauma Isabella's frail form had endured. Only one lung was intact; the other was crushed. Her sternum and clavicle and ribs were broken. Crushed, really. She had massive internal bleeding from multiple sources. The shadow of the Grim Reaper's hooded cowl grew blacker with each labored breath the injured girl took.

Isabella's breathing was very shallow. Her one healthy lung was intubated. IVs with plasma. They were attempting to replace the blood Bella had lost, but she continued to hemorrhage, internally. The emergency room personnel had tried to pump Isabella' stomach to remove the Seconal she had ingested during her suicide attempt, but much of what they pumped out was crimson with blood.

Had Isabella reached the hospital in time, without incident, her stomach could have been pumped, the Seconal countered by medical means, and she would now be lying in a bed in the hospital recuperating from nothing more serious than a sore throat from the tube forced down her throat. She wouldn't be fighting for her life and losing the battle. If only the truck and the ambulance hadn't entered the intersection at the same time. If only the trucker had taken a different route. If only the truck had been five minutes earlier, or the ambulance five minutes later. If only, if only, if only. The outcome of all these "what ifs" were the same: Isabella would die.

Isabella's beautiful blue eyes opened slightly. For the first time since Renee's arrival on the scene, the patient was semi-conscious. She wanted to communicate with her mother and sister, but the oxygen mask and tubes were preventing her from speaking.

"Can't you remove her mask for just a moment?" Renee asked.

The young doctor, recognizing the inevitability of Isabella's situation, and realizing that the fact that she had regained consciousness at all was a small miracle, nodded assent to his team. For the second time the mask and tubes were removed, allowing Isabella the opportunity to speak to her mother and sister for just a moment.

"Not for long," the young doctor had said. "We're still trying to save her. She can't be off the oxygen for long,"

"I understand, doctor. I just want to speak to her and I want to let her speak to us for just a moment. We want her to know that we're here with her."

"Where is Dad?" Kaley asked.

"He's in Beijing at the environmental conference. He's been notified of Isabella's accident, but he won't arrive for some hours."

Renee didn't say what else was on her mind. *Where had Bucky been when the twins had their tonsillectomies? Where was Bucky when Kaley and Isabella both got the measles at the same time? Where was Bucky when Kaley had her emergency appendectomy?*

Just then, Isabella half-moaned, half-whispered a few words. "Mom, I'm so sorry. I didn't mean it. I'm scared. And I'm cold. So cold."

"Don't worry, honey. We'll take care of you. I know you're hurting, but you're in the hospital. The doctors are doing everything they can. Kaley and I are here. We're here for you; we're here with you. We'll always be here with you. We love you."

"Who is he?"

Isabella's stare was fixed on the unfamiliar face of Dante Benedick. It was at this point, for the first time, that Renee actually looked at the stranger in their midst. As she did so, there was a momentary delayed shock of recognition. She knew this man! *He was famous! This was Dante Benedick, whose songs delighted her daughters. What was he doing here?*

Rather than go into a long explanation, Renee responded, "Don't worry about that now. Rest and save your strength. He's here to help."

Renee didn't know how right she was. She did know, however, that his comforting hand on Kaley's shoulder when she had entered, had given testimony to a concerned and sympathetic soul.

"Mom, Kaley, please tell Dad I'm sorry. I didn't know what I was doing. I was confused. I hope he can forgive me. Please remember me. Remember me for the good things in my life, not the bad ones."

Isabella lapsed into unconsciousness for the last time.

Renee murmured encouraging things to the now-unconscious girl lying there, still and battered. "Don't worry. We're with you. We love you. We'll take care of you. Everything's going to be all right. Nobody is ever going to forget you. We love you. We're all here."

These words may have been as much for Renee as for

Isabella. Isabella seemed far, far away. She was losing the battle for her life.

Renee turned from the comatose form of her oldest twin and hugged Kaley. She held Kaley in silent sorrow, struggling to control her emotions, still trying to save her darling daughter.

"Darkness in the aftermath.
A gaze blank and pitiless from the hooded man
Passionate intensity cannot forestall his shadow.
The world crashes in; the bloody tide is loosed"

—*Darkness in the Aftermath,* The One

CHAPTER 38

Darkness in the Aftermath

12:47 a.m.
November 18, 2010
Our Lady of Mercy Hospital
Washington, DC

Renee remembered only fragments of what she was told. Whispered lies. *This can't be happening. This can't be real.*

"No real hope of saving her ... injuries were too serious. We are deeply sorry. We did everything we could ... autopsy her remains ... massive internal hemorrhaging ... massive organ failure." None of the explanations meant anything to her. She was in a fog.

All she had absorbed was one grim fact: Isabella was dead. Her baby was dead. Renee was just barely holding it together. Still trying to remain in control. She knew she must. Now, she had to plan a funeral. She had a task and a duty as Isabella's mother and as the First Lady to stand tall and stay strong. She wished that she had a willing helpmate in this time of need. William Bellwood was halfway around the world. Even if he had been here, how much comfort would he have been? Renee had been through painful and sorrowful events before with only Bucky by her side.

There had been the time that her mother lay dying, but Bucky had a much more important golf game. There had been the time that her father had suffered his heart attack. Bucky couldn't be found. Renee went to the hospital alone that time, too. Bucky was only Governor of Texas then. When his bodyguards found Bucky, he was shacked up with a stripper. They told Renee that Bucky had been "delayed by urgent matters of state." William Bellwood missed the deaths of both of Renee's parents, and he had provided precious little emotional support at their funeral services.

When Renee brought these details up in conversation, Bucky responded in a surly manner, "I went to visit your old man. I went more than once to that nursing home where your mother was, too. How was I supposed to know that she would die *THAT* day? Besides, she was batty as hell. I don't think she even knew who I was, at the end."

The nursing home had provided many signals that the end was near. "We're giving her oxygen now, but her pulse rate is dropping. Her breathing is labored." None of these signals had been emphatic enough for Bucky Bellwood to miss his 10:00 a.m. tee time. After all, Jack Nicklaus was in his foursome. How could Renee expect him to miss playing golf with a superstar of the game just to pay yet another boring visit to his cranky old mother-in-law? But it was not "just another visit." It was the final visit.

Renee made it alone, tears streaming down her face, speeding down the interstate and getting stopped by a state trooper young enough to be her child. In those days in Texas, when Bucky was Governor, she and Bucky often drove themselves. Renee remembered saying, "Please. My mother is dying. Just hurry up and give me the ticket." When she couldn't get her license out of her billfold's clear plastic slot, tears streaming down her face, she had simply handed the entire billfold to the young trooper, who had left her momentarily and then returned, saying, gruffly, "Try to hold it together, okay? And slow down." She had gone on her way to sit deathbed vigil for her mother.

She sat there, holding her mother's cold hand, trying to communicate with her as best she could. At one point, she asked her mother, "Mom, what was your favorite city in the world?"

Her mother smiled and said, "Why, whatever city you and your father were in."

Renee smiled at the thought of her mother's response.

Now, as she stood with her surviving daughter and a compassionate stranger who had barely known her dead daughter, she felt more supported emotionally than she had ever felt while in William Bellwood's presence. That fact, alone, may have been what was making it possible for her to hang on to the control needed to preserve her sanity in the face of this calamity. This was the worst blow of many blows in her life. Tragedy seemed too small a word to encompass the grief she felt. And yet she knew this scene played out every day for many, many people the world over.

Renee turned to the tall, handsome, silent stranger and addressed him, "Mr. Benedick."

"Please, call me Dante."

"Dante, Isabella loved your songs. We all admire your music. You are here. Why, I don't yet know, but I know that it would be an honor to have you take part in the celebration of Isabella's life. I have perhaps twelve hours before I totally collapse. It could be longer than that before the girls' father arrives from China. Can you help me plan a service for Isabella in which you will be involved, while I can still think cogently?"

Dante was struck at how calm Renee seemed. *The calm before the storm*, he thought. He understood what she was saying. He, too, had suffered a delayed reaction to the deaths of his parents. At first he functioned well, if somewhat robotically. Three days after the service, he was a mess, emotionally.

"Is there somewhere the three of us can go and talk about a memorial service for Isabella? I hope we can convince you to participate. I just need to change my clothes back at the White House. Then, I can meet with you anywhere you say. Kaley will come, too, of course."

Dante spoke with sincere empathy. "Of course, Mrs. Bellwood – Renee. To avoid the difficulty of getting past security, I would suggest that you and Kaley come to my suite at the Harrington Hotel on Embassy Row. I'm in the penthouse. I'll leave orders for you to be escorted up by my security man, Fitzgerald. We can talk there."

"Good. Kaley and I will fill out the necessary paperwork here at the hospital, stop so that I can change, and then we'll be there. We'll call first. And we'll have our own security, of course, but I have ways of making the security appear unobtrusive, so that we won't be mobbed. In two hours, then?" Renee extended her hand. Dante marveled at her composure in the face of the most awful thing a parent can face.

Twelve hours of lucid thought. During that time, she would be able to function in a controlled fashion. After that, all bets were off.

* * * *

Upon reaching the private quarters of the White House, Renee gave some thought to her disguise, for a disguise was what she used when she wanted to go out and about with minimum press coverage. The news of Isabella's attempted suicide, subsequent accident, and recent death had not yet reached the wire services. Renee knew that, when it did, all hell would break loose. It would be a media feeding frenzy. Nothing and no one would be sacred. She thought, ruefully, that Bucky would probably catch the brunt of it as he debarked at Dulles from his trip to China. *It will serve him right.* As usual, he would be unprepared to help his family in time of need. At least Bucky would have a full complement of Secret Service agents to provide a buffer zone to ward off the press. She and Kaley, on the other hand, would have only two agents.

She decided to give explicit instructions that the agents dress as inconspicuously as possible, Secret Service regulations be damned. She wanted them in blue jeans and windbreakers, a casual look. Nothing made an agent stand out more than the standard gray flannel suit and tie, coupled with the earpiece. Very conspicuous. Renee had often wondered how an agency as supposedly sophisticated as the FBI or the Secret Service couldn't figure out that any idiot could pick out agents in a crowd, just by their attire. She would wear the long blonde wig she sometimes used as a disguise, sunglasses, something very casual and low-key. Kaley would do the same.

Just before leaving the quarters, the private area of the White House, she examined her outfit in the mirror briefly. Boots. Blue jeans. Western-style shirt with pearl buttons. Long blonde hair. Sun glasses. She looked nothing like First Lady Renee Bellwood, nor like the woman clad in the gray business suit who had given the address to the Women's Empowerment Society earlier today. She had been called from the WES speech to her daughter's bedside with no time to change.

She thought of Jackie Kennedy in the bloodstained pink dress with the pillbox hat on Air Force One as they returned Jack Kennedy's body back to Washington from Texas. When urged to change, Jackie had refused, saying, "Let them see what they have done." Renee, however, wanted to avoid the press and the public for as long as possible.

Kaley always dressed casually for her life as a student at Georgetown; her profile in the press was much lower than the First Lady's. Although the twins certainly made headlines more than once, and had been photographed whenever they went out, their pictures were not worth as much as a photograph of the President's wife.

Kaley already owned the wardrobe for disappearing into the crowd. It was Kaley, in fact, who had provided her slim and youthful-looking mother, who wore the same small size, with some suggestions to help her blend in. At first, the two had gone out in public disguised like this for fun. But now, as the overbearing press attention deepened well into Bucky's second term, Renee had paid much closer attention to her daughter's suggestions.

She had picked up a trick or two from superstars such as Madonna and Michael Jackson. Renee had learned that a different hair color, courtesy of a good wig, and a baseball cap and dark glasses went a long way towards concealing her identity. Her chestnut hair disguised in this fashion, with youthful clothing styles and blue jeans, rather than stylish French couture, she was often able to jog or take solitary walks, the Secret Service contingent trailing discreetly behind, clothed as Renee dictated. If they were jogging, jogging suits. If they were going to a concert, concert attire, but never the standard business issue of the Men in Black variety. Too obvious.

When her gray business suit was hanging in the closet and the down-home country look was in place, Renee easily looked ten or twenty years younger than her chronological age. She was forty-two. She looked no more than thirty-two. Her complexion had always been amazingly wrinkle-free, a genetic gift. With the figure of a woman half her age and the right clothes, she fit right in.

She picked up the phone in the White House private

quarters to call Dante's suite prior to departure. Then, remembering that all phone calls to and from the White House were carefully monitored, she used her cell phone, instead.

When she heard Dante Benedick's voice on the other end, she marveled at how much his speaking voice sounded like the voice that sold millions of CDs

"Dante – Mr. Benedick – we're ready. We're leaving in a few minutes. We'll be arriving in a black four-door Ford Taurus. We don't want to attract attention. We'll have two Secret Service men with us, but they have been given explicit instructions to look normal. With any luck, nobody will recognize us and we won't be a burden to you or to ourselves. Which entrance do you recommend that we use, front or back? Is there a password or a pseudonym that you have registered under?"

Dante found himself marveling at how cool, calm and collected this distraught mother was under pressure. A steel butterfly. He knew she had to be breaking apart, inside, but she was holding it together.

"Come to the front desk. Ask for Mr. Yeats. My security man, Fitzgerald, will accompany you up in the private elevator. If you are hungry, I can order in some sandwiches while we talk."

"I don't feel like I'll ever be hungry again, Dante, but go ahead and order something for Kaley and yourself. We'll see you in approximately one-half hour."

"Your husband? President Bellwood? Will he be able to come?"

"No. He still hasn't returned from the conference in China, but he would leave most of these arrangements to me, anyway. We'll start without him." She didn't feel it necessary to let Dante in on the knowledge of how little William Bellwood ever seemed involved in the personal lives of his wife and daughters.

Kaley and her mother walked to the private exit where a very ordinary car awaited them. The black Taurus, in fact, was actually the private vehicle belonging to one of the Secret Service men, Jack Paskvan. Jack had been assigned to Renee for most of the Bellwoods' years in the White House. This was not the first time that the First Lady had asked him to use his own automobile – which was really his sixteen-year-old son's car – in order to avoid attention. When she did duty at the soup kitchen in the poorer part of D.C., she did so out of a genuine sense of compassion. She wanted no publicity for her actions. No media coverage. Therefore, Jack's son's black 2002 Taurus was the perfect car to drive. It was perfect for this run, too.

Arriving at the Harrington Hotel, agent Angel Savage, a Hispanic who held the record for excellent marksmanship in his graduating class, got out and opened the door for the women, while Jack gave the keys to the parking attendant. He was secretly glad that the door of a standard Taurus wasn't ungodly heavy, as the reinforced doors of a Presidential limousine would have been. The quartet walked unobtrusively into the building, heading for the desk. Renee asked them to ring "Mr. Yeats' room." No hesitation or emotion in her voice. It was done immediately.

As the elevator door opened at the Penthouse level, the Secret Service men immediately checked the hallway and perimeter, as they had been trained to do. The women then left the relative safety of the elevator. The group continued down a long hallway that led to the first set of double doors, complete with doorbell. Rather than ringing the doorbell, however, a Security agent of Dante Benedick's awaited the group. He swung open the doors with a word of deferential welcome.

"Mrs. Bellwood, Miss Bellwood, gentlemen, go right on in. Mr. Benedick is expecting you."

The quartet, now a quintet with the addition of Dante's private Chief of Security, Fitzgerald, entered the sumptuous suite. The first thing they saw was a 52-inch plasma TV, decorating a wall as though it were a painting. In fact, multi-colored fish were swimming on the large screen that dominated the semi-circular room. There were two semi-circular love seats flanking the screen, forming a circle. In front of the couches, which were covered in a striped damask watermarked fabric, sat small marble coffee tables. Off to the right, a wet bar with refrigerator and various bottles of wine and whiskey. The refrigerator was hidden from sight beneath the bar. A thermostat on the wall behind the bar. As Renee crossed the room, she saw that there were three separate thermostats, five couches, three bathrooms, a Jacuzzi tub that had a semi-circular retractable door so that the large plasma television could be watched from the privacy and comfort of the tub, and a panoramic view of the city through porthole shaped specially lighted windows.

Since this was quite near the tourist area of Washington D.C., on Embassy Row, the Washington Monument was visible from the window. The room was decorated exquisitely. There were two other rooms that Renee did not enter. She assumed that one was the master bedroom. Through the door of the other she could see a glimpse of a desk and computer. Lying on a couch in that room was a white guitar. A baby grand Yamaha piano, also white, dominated the main room where they were. All of the furniture and carpeting was white, with blue as the accent color of the damask watermarked furniture. *This room is as elegant as the White House*, thought Renee.

Renee started in with plans for Isabella's funeral eulogies immediately. Two hours had elapsed and she had predicted no more than twelve good hours for herself before collapse. She still needed to get to the funeral home and select a coffin, a task she dreaded and was putting off, hoping that William Bellwood would have returned before she needed to undertake that gruesome duty. She wanted to get this done. She wanted to get the eulogy and music planning part done before Bucky returned and began butting in. He had an annoying way of always opposing every good idea that Renee or Kaley presented.

He would raise objections to the sun coming up, if he could. It was just his way of being in control. He didn't really want the work of making decisions like this himself; he just wanted to second-guess anything and everything that Renee had done. Often, the suggestions Renee and the girls had made he would co-opt, later, claiming they were his own. "Wasn't that a good idea I had?" he would say, acting like it was a great joke. It wasn't. It was one of his annoying little habits. She was in no mood. She wanted this done, done now, and done right. After she had the eulogy, music and flower plans firmly fixed in her mind, she would meet with the funeral director and, God help him, Bucky would have to go with her to help pick out a casket for their oldest daughter. Just the thought made her mind crumble.

"Dante, I want to thank you for what you did today. What you tried to do, to help. I also want to ask for your help in planning the service. And then I have some questions for you. Is that okay?"

I hope the questions don't involve how I happened to be in the right place at the right time. How I even knew that Isabella had taken a drug overdose.

To Renee, he responded, "Of course. Anything I can do to help."

"First, I want Kaley's input on the song or songs that Isabella would most want sung at her funeral ..." Renee glanced at Kaley, seated to her right. Kaley was already in mourning. She looked as though she could collapse at any moment. Renee would not allow herself this luxury for at least three days. She must remain strong, for now.

With her mother and Dante both focused on her, however, Kaley, by a great effort of will, managed to wrap her mind around the horrible reality that they were planning her twin sister's funeral. Kaley had given the choice of songs to be sung some thought as they drove to Dante's hotel. There was one song, above all, that Bella thought summed up the Washington experience. It was entitled simply "Words," and Bella had liked the cynical view of D.C. life that the song encapsulated. Kaley could think of nothing more apropos than to send a message from the grave that would have her sister smiling down from heaven above. This song would accomplish that.

"Mr. Benedick, you know that song 'Words' from your very first album?"

"Know it?" Dante smiled sadly. "Know it? I wrote it. When I was sixteen, I might add. Almost nobody remembers that song. I'm surprised you do. That was before I had a hit record. It was only released in the United Kingdom. I'm impressed that you know it at all."

"Well, as Mom has said, Isabella and I are huge fans of your music, all of it. Mom has become a fan, too, in the last couple years." Kaley even managed a polite smile, despite her grief. "I think that Isabella would really love it if you would sing 'Words.'"

Renee was a little left out of this discussion. She would have deferred to Kaley's greater knowledge of Dante's early work. She, herself, had become a fan, but not until "Burned Soul" came out, which was one of Dante's more recent works. Of course, she had always known the song "Path of Light" that the girls picked out, by ear, on the piano when they were just toddlers. Renee had been too busy with affairs of state to listen to all of Dante's early work. The girls grew up with The One's songs, however, and were true aficionados of his work. If Kaley selected this particular song, that was good enough for the grieving mother.

"So, that's settled, then, Dante," said Renee, seeming relieved to have one small detail out of the way. "I can't say how many people will eulogize Bella or how long the service will last, but I think it would be best if you could sing at the cemetery, itself. It would provide a fitting end to the service. I want the last thoughts we have of Isabella's funeral to provide a small shred of happiness. How excited she would have been to have you singing to her." Renee teared up.

This seemed to be all the strength that Renee could muster for one day. Her eyes misted. She said nothing further, which allowed Dante to study her features under the long blonde wig. He had been startled by her appearance when she entered. *Why, she looks like she's my age.* He couldn't see her eyes behind the dark glasses, but, once inside, Renee removed them, and he was struck once again by the kindness in her eyes. Kaley had an almost catatonic expression on her face. She had to be in shock. Renee, although pale, radiated warmth and empathy and compassion and kindness. Once again, he felt attracted to her, however inappropriate the timing.

Kaley had finished the club sandwich that Dante had room service bring to the suite, eating it mechanically. Renee had eaten nothing. She seemed intent on discussing matters at hand, but, now that the song selection and Dante's availability, which had previously been in doubt due to his busy touring schedule, were confirmed, Renee turned to Dante, seated on the half-moon shaped couch across from her and asked the question he was waiting for. And fearing.

"Tell me, Dante. How did it happen that you were aware

of Isabella's desperate situation? Kaley tells me that you called her to tell her to go immediately to Bella's condo, and then you both discovered the aftermath of the horrible ambulance truck accident at the intersection. Why were you there? How did you know?"

He took a deep breath. *Where do I begin?*

"The pebble is thrown; the circle begins.
Where does it start? Where will it end?
Can man undo the harm he's done?
Can the father continue to parent the son?"

—*Lagrimas de Luna (Tears of the Moon),* The One

CHAPTER 39

Tears of the Moon

2:30 a.m.
November 18, 2010
The Harrington Hotel, Suite 1700
Washington, DC

Dante paused. What he was about to reveal to Renee and Kaley would either convince them to help him or make them think that he was a complete lunatic.

He began his story.

"Do you believe in reincarnation? In the concept that a man can live in more than one time?"

Renee said nothing. Kaley responded, dubiously, "Maybe. Like Buddhists and reincarnation, right?"

"The concept is accepted by Buddhists, yes, and by other religions, as well. And I'm sure you've all heard or read about those who say they can remember past lives."

The two women nodded assent.

"What if the 'past lives' concept merely meant that these individuals were able to travel back and forth through time? What if there were a formula or a method for time travel?"

Renee met his gaze. "Go on." Her voice sounded level, impassive.

"Ever since time began, man has been fascinated with the idea of exploring other cultures and other times, sometimes for personal gain, but, other times, simply to forge a new frontier. There are writings from Bernal Diaz del Castillo, a Spanish soldier with Cortez. When Cortez set out on his Conquest of the New World in 1519, his writings suggested that Hernan Cortez, himself, might have been a time traveler. He may have come to the coast of Veracruz on his expedition that year because he knew that this was the place to start, because he was from the future. The natives were so in awe of Cortez that Emperor Montezuma's envoys presented him with a gold disc as big as a cartwheel, shaped like the sun. Back in the 1950s or 1960s there was a book about how "gods" had visited the Earth. *Chariots of the Gods*, it was called. Those gods may have been nothing more than time traveling humans, revisiting times and places that some of them lived through, before."

"I remember seeing a film about that in school," Kaley said. "It was cool. It was all about Machu Pichu and crop circles and stuff like that."

"Yes. That's part of the legend. The reasons someone from the future might travel back through time were probably as varied as those of explorers from Europe setting off on various exploratory sea voyages. Some did it to get rich and fatten the coffers of wealthy benefactors like Ferdinand and Isabella of Spain. Some wanted to do good deeds, even change the course of history, if time would allow that to occur, which is still subject to debate."

"Why open to debate?" asked Kaley. She had many questions about what she was hearing.

"I'll answer that in a minute. Let me go on." Dante took a breath and glanced at Kaley and Renee, to see if they were still with him, or if they were ready to holler, "Guards!" and have him carted away in a straitjacket. He saw no indication that they were not going to hear him out. He plunged ahead.

"Aztecs believed that silver and gold were divine gifts from the gods. Silver was *iztac tcocuitlatl,* tears of the moon, and gold was called *cuztic tcocuitlatl,* tears of the sun. Perhaps they were right. Maybe these precious metals *were* gifts from gods who were really no more than time travelers. The Mayan people, too, possessed a superior knowledge of astronomy and science, as anyone who has ever visited Chichen Itza and toured the ruins of the ancient Mayan observatory there can tell you. If these peoples were so advanced in so many ways, centuries ago, is it that difficult for us to believe that modern-day man has built his own Chichen Itza, his own Great Pyramid?"

Dante paused, to see if either woman commented. He

was holding their interest, so he continued.

"But, like so many things in this century, modern man's accomplishment is not an edifice that can be pointed to, many centuries later, when it lies in ruins. It's not a bricks-and-mortar thing. It's something more, well, modern. Think Silicon Valley, Bill Gates, the computer age. The internet. High-tech accomplishments like cell phone technology. Is it so hard to believe that a talented scientist, using ancient knowledge and lore blended with modern technology, could invent a successful time travel technique? Can you accept this if I tell you that it is absolutely true? Right here and right now?"

Renee looked into Dante's incredibly blue eyes, and, without hesitation, said, "Yes. I can believe it."

Kaley said nothing. Her expression was like that of an intelligent bird, waiting for the person to offer her something more, waiting for an intellectual cracker. She cocked her head to the side, further fostering the impression in Dante's mind of a beautiful cockatoo.

"The new frontier of 2025 is time travel. I want you both to know that I come to you, today, from the year 2025, fifteen years in the future"

Dante stopped to let that statement sink in. There was a gasp, and then silence in the room. He watched as Kaley looked towards her mother, questioningly. But Renee did not return Kaley's gaze. She was mesmerized by Dante's expression, by his message, hanging on his every word. Then, she spoke.

"You don't look fifteen years older," Renee said.

"When you travel back in time, you resume once again the age you were at that time. Dr. Dunne said that age reverses with time. If he patented that as a beauty aide, he'd make a fortune." Dante smiled.

"Do you have any proof of this, Dante? I'm trying to believe you, but this all sounds like something out of a Dean Koontz novel."

"I haven't read his books," Dante said.

Kaley smiled. "I have. I love Dean Koontz. I also love Stephen King and Ray Bradbury and Frederik Pohl and Richard Matheson and William F. Nolan."

"Suddenly this has become a science fiction book club," Dante smiled. "Returning to the topic: my strongest proof of time travel is that I knew what was going to happen to Isabella before it happened. You can call me the Amazing Dante, namesake of the Amazing Kreskin, who often accurately predicted the future."

"Is there no other object you could bring back from the future, to prove to others that what you say is true?" When she asked, Renee did not seem confrontational. She just seemed curious.

"I am allowed to bring nothing with me in my time travel, not even clothing. Which can make things on the other side pretty interesting upon arrival."

Dante paused. He offered a small smile, and then continued. "Only carbon-based living organisms can make it through the process, using lasers and, yes, somehow, a formula involving gold, silver, carbon, and other sci-fi stuff that I don't pretend to understand and wouldn't even attempt to explain. I'm a musician, not a scientist. But I paid the best mind in the field very generous sums for many long years to do extensive research and development. He only recently contacted me to tell me that the technology now exists, in 2025, to send me back in time. When he contacted me, Dr. Dunne warned me that there are rules for time travel, that the cosmos will not allow you to violate its basic tenets. One of those tenets is that when you change the past, you also change the future. When I go back to 2025, it will no longer be the same 2025 because the past in 2010 has been changed. There's always the risk of creating a rip in time that could prove disastrous."

Kaley, an avid reader as a child, piped up, "Is that anything like *A Wrinkle in Time*, by Madeline L'Engle?" She smiled wanly. The book had been one of the girls' favorite bedtime stories. The twins had also loved Maurice Sendak's *Where the Wild Things Are.*

"I'm sorry. I'm afraid I'm not familiar with that book, either," Dante replied.

"You need to go to a library some time," Kaley teased. "Never mind. I'm just being a smart-ass. But you're scaring me, and when I'm scared, I make bad jokes. Are you saying that you're from the future?" she asked. Renee was just as anxious to hear Dante's answer to this question as Kaley.

"Well, yes and no. You know me from the year 2010 and before. I was born, after all, in 1979, so I'm thirty-one years old in 2010. In 2025, I'm fifteen years older, of course, which makes me…." Dante had to stop and think a moment. "Forty-six when I began my return to 2010. When you travel back through time, though, it reverses your age. I'm thirty-one again. I was thirty-one when I sang at Bella's funeral the first time, the very same song you asked me to sing at her funeral today. Her death set off a chain of events. Those events threaten the world. I hoped to be able to travel back in time to save Isabella and, by saving Isabella's life, avert that catastrophe. It's a bit like my song 'Time Kaleidoscope,' which I recorded in 2012. That was about the time Dr. Dunne began making progress in his research: "Time turns back upon itself, collapsing in concentric circles. Kaleidoscopic intersections of time and space reversed. Will the future or the past be worse?" Dante stopped singing the melody of a song he wouldn't record for at least another two years.

"No," Kaley spoke up, "finish it. I'd like to hear a sneak preview from two years in the future." She smiled.

Dante obliged, in a low, soft baritone, a cappella.

"Time is power; time's the dance.
All we are depends on chance.
All our life we're powerless here.
The future threatens those held dear."

He stopped. He looked intently into Renee's uncomprehending eyes.

"I'm sorry. I hoped I'd be able to save Isabella, but time and fate are funny that way. They collapse back upon one another. The same things happen, only in different ways. We all like to think about historical events turning out differently: what if JFK had not been killed in Dallas? What if Hitler had died during the unsuccessful assassination attempt, rather than surviving it? But time has its way. Kennedy's plane would have gone down. Or his health would have given out. JFK sensed that he would die young, and he was right. Hitler was still destroyed. It just took a while longer. And Bella, beautiful Bella, still died, even though I tried. I really tried, with all my might."

His voice crackled with emotion. He fell silent, a brooding look crossing his face.

"Mom?" Kaley's tone sounded skeptical. She was looking towards her mother to affirm or deny what Dante was saying. It all sounded so radical, so implausible.

Renee, however, continued questioning Dante in a calm voice.

"What does your crystal ball tell you about Kaley and me?"

"You're in grave danger, Renee." He hoped the look he was giving her didn't scare her, but that it held her attention.

Renee's eyes seemed riveted to his by this news. She was fascinated. "In what way? How am I in danger, Mr. Benedick?"

Dante noticed that, the crazier he sounded, the more formal Renee became in her speech. He had gone from being addressed as just Dante to Mr. Benedick.

"Your husband, President Bellwood, he will be behind it."

"Dad?" Kaley looked confused. "How is that possible? What's he going to do?"

"Your father has become a power-mad megalomaniac. He has very nearly ruined your country, already. If left unchecked, his actions will ruin your life and very possibly ruin the lives of everyone on the planet." These words from Dante were delivered in the gravest manner possible. There was a solemn silence.

From Renee came only a sharp intake of breath and an expression that hinted of deeply repressed emotions, followed by a rueful laugh, "He's already ruined my life," she said grimly, "and I can well believe that if his self-interest conflicts with mine, he'll do whatever suits him, without a thought for me or Kaley."

"You must believe me. You're in danger." Dante clasped his hands together. Without thinking, he reached out and took one of Renee's hands in his own strong hands. As he did so, an almost electric charge passed between them again. "I'm not trying to scare you; I'm trying to help you both."

Renee spoke again, in a muted voice. "Strangely enough, I do believe you. Otherwise, how could you have known about Isabella's suicide attempt? How could you have called Kaley when you did? And I can easily believe that my dear husband might find me in his way, at some point in time, and then who knows what he is capable of? Can you tell me more? Can you tell me about Kaley? Can you be more specific?"

The questions were coming too fast. Dante realized that he would have to be very selective in exactly what he revealed about what he knew. Best to stick to the bare bones of the story.

"I can tell you only if both of you promise not to tell another living soul. And be very clear on this point: that most certainly includes William Bellwood, first and foremost."

"Hate breeds hate and love yields love,
This a message from above
We must love or we shall die.
A cosmic order from on high."

—*Cosmic Crimes,* The One

CHAPTER 40

Back From Beijing

4:32 p.m.
Sunday, November 21, 2010
The White House
Washington, D.C.

William Bellwood left the environmental conference in Beijing early because of his daughter's attempted suicide. The President only attended to stifle the criticism that he wasn't very environmentally friendly. He had no plans of changing his policies for some damn tree-huggers. He had big business to protect, not some loud-mouthed aging hippies. But the death of his daughter changed everything.

When he arrived at the White House the place was swarming with press. Cards and flowers were arriving from all over the world. People on Pennsylvania Avenue had begun a makeshift altar, with pictures of Isabella from news clippings and flowers and personal messages of grief at her passing. This always happened with the rich and famous when they died young. It had happened with Princess Diana. It had happened with JFK, Jr. both outside his apartment in Tribeca and outside his publishing house, Hachette Filipacchi Media U.S. in New York City. Employees of Hachette Filipacchi Media had been sent outside to remove the candles and pictures within an hour of their placement. *What a nuisance!* was Bucky's first and only thought when he saw the sentimental displays.

The President's chief of staff and his staff members awaited him in a conference room.

"Thanks for your support. I think I need to be with my family right now," said William Bellwood gruffly. "Where is

263

Mrs. Bellwood? Where is Kaley?" He had tried to call each on their cell phones. Neither answered. Neither had returned his calls.

Vice President Black approached the President. "President Bellwood, I'm so sorry," Mia said. Tears had streaked her make-up. If it was an act, it was a good one.

"Thank you," the President said simply. "Isabella always liked you. She often said you were a great boss and a terrific friend." Isabella had worked as an aide to the Vice President during her summers off from Georgetown, as other interns in the Capitol worked for Senators from their home states.

"I gave Bella her first job. She had such a promising career ahead of her," Mia said wiping the last of her tears away. "Is there anything I can do?"

"We have some important Xerox-ing to do. Lots of it."

"Now? But your daughter is dead. Shouldn't you be spending time with your family?"

"Kaley and Renee are gone. I have no idea where they are. They aren't returning my calls. So the answer to your question is yes. Now. I have some free time right now. Meet me in the Oval Office in five minutes."

The Vice President sighed. *What's the matter with this guy? He's about a quart high on testosterone. Does he ever give it a rest?* Bucky, however, was still her superior. Best she comply, for now. "Xerox-ing" was their code word. It meant that Bucky was horny. *As usual*, thought Mia, as she headed towards the Oval office. Their sex sessions always left her feeling like her jaw muscles had been injected with Novocain. It numbed her tongue. The man was an animal, an insatiable beast.

With their tryst in the Oval Office over, the President lay napping on the couch in the Oval Office, pants unzipped. A thin stream of drool hung from his lips. The corners of his lips were faintly smiling. Endorphins loosed by wanton sex tranquilized him into deep slumber.

Mia Akaihane-Black. That woman's really something. Asian women. Wonder if they all know how to give such good head? She could give lessons.

Bucky dreamed.

He was standing outside a dilapidated house. Whose

house is this? He had never seen it before. The house was a dump: greasy gray walls, windowsills clinging weakly to windows shored up with badly nailed supports. A downward-sloping porch, dusty boards, thin, creaky steps. Its shingles resembled teeth with a bad case of plaque. The house looked like it was bleeding, oozing drops of blood.

Five broken steps led upwards to the porch and the front door. The door hung crookedly on the doorframe. He walked past the untended lilac bushes. Faint smell of lilac from the overgrown flowering bushes. The bushes ripped Bucky's arm as he brushed past, leaving bloody scratches.

A rusty mailbox out front by the road, leaning like a tired soldier. Whose house is this? Bucky walked to the mailbox to look at the names on the box. No name. No address. He heard a steady drip-drip-drip. Something rusty that smelled like blood and tasted like a wet copper penny was in his dry, parched mouth. Something putrid had pooled beneath the old-fashioned rural delivery-style mailbox. Mingled with the smell of hot copper, of blood, a smell like day-old vomit and cat piss. Bucky moved away quickly, the chlorine burning his eyes.

He walked to the side of the house. The side door was wide open, as though the place were inviting him in. Bucky Bellwood entered the dilapidated structure tentatively, through the gaping side entrance. A few stairs leading up; more stairs leading down. He felt apprehensive.

As Bucky entered, he was struck violently and painfully in the ribs with a tire-iron. His ribs broken, he tumbled to the bottom of the basement stairs of the mystery house. Son-of-a-bitch! Who's doing this to me? thought Bucky. And why?

Bucky fell to the floor in pain, clutching his side, enduring intolerable pain. The tire-iron came down again, smashing the side of his face. He flinched and moved his head just in time. The tire iron caught him only a glancing blow. Still, the pain flashed to his brain. A lightning bolt of pain. Excruciating! He heard himself screaming as he lay on the floor, bleeding badly, his face half-crushed and battered.

A man stood above him. Jesus H. Christ! It's that fucking faggot British singer. That son-of-a-bitch Benedick! Dante Benedick. The One. Realizing this, Bucky's lips twisted with

265

rage, but he remained mute.

The One loomed above him, holding handcuffs. Dante cuffed Bucky's hands behind his back.

"It's almost show-time, and you have the best seat in the house." Benedick intoned.

Bucky looked up. He was lying on a cold, dirty concrete basement floor. He saw two young girls and an older woman on the staircase above him. He had a hard time recognizing them with blood pooling in his crushed eye socket, but he knew. He smelled the perfume. Renee's favorite perfume: Adrienne Vittadini. Renee, Kaley and Isabella together again. But how? How was this possible? Bella was dead. The hairs on the back of Bucky's neck rose. He appeared terrified. Something was very, very wrong.

Dante Benedick stood on the steps above Bucky, his voice low, controlled. He spoke, "You miserable excuse for a human being; you've done enough harm to your family, to your country, to the world. I'm going to make sure that you never hurt anyone again. I'm here to make it stop forever. First, I'm going to take your family. Then, I'm going to fix things by fixing YOU!"

Through bleary eyes, Benedick saw a garden shears in The One's right hand. Dante leaned down and cut Bucky's Jockey shorts from his body. Finally finding voice, Bucky screamed, " God! No! Not that! Don't cut that!"

The pain was indescribable. Blood everywhere.

Bucky screamed in agony. His wife and daughters watched silently, as though paralyzed, forming a silent tableau. Renee smiled wanly. The girls looked away. Before Bella turned her head, Bucky saw hollow eye sockets. Her face, a leaden blue, had begun to decompose.

William Bellwood awakened.

As he reached consciousness, Bucky grabbed his crotch, to ensure that the crown jewels were still intact.

'Bucky' Bellwood, the Leader of the Free World, appeared at the door of the Oval Office, disheveled, disoriented and scared witless. The dream had been so real.

"Nailer. Where's my wife? Where's my daughter? Where did they go?" Suddenly realizing that his pants were unzipped, he reached down to pull the zipper up.

266

"Sir, we've lost track of Mrs. Bellwood. She left the White House after Isabella was pronounced dead. She was last seen with Kaley and Dante Benedick."

"Fuck!"

Agent Nailer ducked, or the ashtray would have nailed him.

"Our lives are filled with love and hate.
There is no way to make Death wait.
'Why?' is the thought that haunts us still,
'When?' is unanswered. We know not, till
He calls for us on that dark night,
To take us on our final flight."

—*Swan Song*, The One

CHAPTER 41

The Funeral (Part 2)

11:00 a.m.
Monday, November 22, 2010
Arlington Cemetery

The mourners gathered at Arlington. Hundreds were there on this bright, chilly fall day. The wind had picked up.

Mia Akaihane-Black, the Vice President, gave her husband Roger a poke and whispered, "Do you have a tissue?" The Vice President's nose was running in the November chill.

"No, Precious," said Roger, ever the docile servant.

"Great," said Mia in a surly tone under her breath. Leave it to Roger to be totally unprepared.

The Bellwood family wasn't holding up well. Kaley was a mess, crying and shaken. Renee Bellwood was in stoic mode, eerily reminiscent of Jacqueline Kennedy. A veiled chapeau concealed her tear-ravaged face. The President looked ashen. He seemed totally out of it. Kaley Bellwood was sobbing hysterically. Her mother's arm around her shoulders did little to assuage her grief.

Lucas Racine, the Secret Service man assigned to Bucky spoke into his earpiece, "Hawk One looks more like Chicken Little and as though he's ready to fly the coop. He's not doing well. Watch him."

"Roger that, Lucas," Paul responded, from the far left of the crowd.

To the President's left, Mia Akaihane-Black stood stiffly, sniffling and clutching the arm of her husband, Roger Black. Mia appeared very strained and preoccupied. She was stylishly attired in a black Gucci suit, with satin spiked heels that were sinking into the not-yet-frozen ground of the cemetery. She

269

was upset that her brand-new Jimmy Choo shoes were never going to be the same. *Thank God I didn't wear the Manolo Blahniks*

It was expected that the mourners would be upset on this sad day. This was, after all, the burial of a twenty-one-year-old girl. Even Mia Akaihane-Black, Bitch Black, appeared sad and pensive.

Celebrities in abundance were present, most of them foreign dignitaries: Princess Stephanie of Monaco; the young Windsors, the children of Princess Diana and Prince Charles, themselves no strangers to untimely death; the Prime Ministers of France, Italy, Canada, Mexico, Germany, Sweden, Brazil and China; ambassadors from various United Nations countries. Turbaned sheiks and caftaned dignitaries galore.

This is a regular United Nations of mourners, Dante thought, as he scanned the crowd.

Dante just looked immeasurably sad. The sun was behind him in such a way that a nimbus of light radiated from behind his thick light-brown hair. Mirrored sunglasses hid the pain in his eyes. Every so often, The One would glance towards the First Lady, darting a furtive glance to see how Renee was bearing up.

Under her veil, Dante knew, Renee Bellwood would be as white as paper, as white as snow, as white as the clouds scudding by above them on this glorious fall day. But he also knew that her face would be tear-ravaged. What hell the woman must be going through! The twin sister, Kaley, was the most vocal of the three immediate family members, since William Bellwood had chosen the stoic route, barely showing emotion of any kind. Bucky was wooden. Kaley was sobbing almost hysterically. Rhythmically. Gutturally. Especially as the white hearse bearing Isabella's body approached the gravesite.

Kaley held her mom's hand. Renee felt if she didn't clutch her daughter's hand, she'd totally collapse. Renee's twelve hours of functional ability were over. The First Lady knew she had to be strong, not just for her family, but also for her country and the world. The world was watching. All the television networks were carrying the service. CNN was live.

Press was everywhere.

The coffin was of rich mahogany, with yellow roses bearing a yellow ribbon. The message on the ribbon spelled out "Beloved daughter and sister." Dante wondered if the yellow roses had been chosen because they were Isabella's favorite flower, or if William 'Bucky' Bellwood had ordered them because of the Yellow Rose of Texas, his home state. If Renee had been functioning in her normal, tasteful, efficient manner, she would have over-ruled Bucky and ordered Isabella's favorite flowers: orchids and lilies. But, today, Renee was running on empty. Functioning was too kind a word for the Xanax-induced stupor in which she was moving.

The minister rose. "To conclude the service today, The One has graciously consented to perform Isabella's favorite song." The selection would not have pleased the President, had he known the lyrics beforehand. *Words*, Dante's song chosen by Kaley, suited Isabella's vision of Washington, D.C., perfectly, as she had become more and more disenchanted during her father's second term in office. Her view of politics as a career had been extinguished by his greedy profiteering while in office. Lawyer, maybe. Politician? Never. She had developed a very low opinion of her father's policies and of politicians, in general. This was why Dante's song *Words* had particularly amused her.

The man in white stood next to the casket, holding his white acoustic guitar. He began strumming, singing softly:

> *"If fewer words were spoken,*
> *If fewer words were said,*
> *If deeds, alone, were the mark of a man.*
> *Not the "catch" of an eloquent pledge.*
> *If fewer words were spoken,*
> *If fewer words were said,*
> *If, for all the fake forensics,*
> *There were simple words, instead.*
> *And a man stated just what he started to state,*
> *Without false fuss or further ado.*
> *If you weren't a politician*
> *I'd probably listen to you.*
> *Words, words.*

Only words.
Words, words.
Only words."

Dante stopped and looked down at the coffin with infinite sadness. He knew that the Secret Service men were going to arrest Zuma shortly; he knew he had to do something to prevent it before that happened. He had to act quickly. "I'd like to bring someone else up to say a few words in memory of Isabella Bellwood," he said. "Please listen to the eulogy of Mosuma Hamad of the Syrian Royal Family, a friend of Isabella's from Georgetown." Everyone swiveled to scrutinize the figure approaching the microphone from the left.

Mosuma was surprised. How did a British rock star like The One even know his name? Nevertheless, he walked to the microphone when summoned.

"Isabella was my friend. We met at classes at Georgetown. We became friends and stayed good friends after our classes together ended. I loved her. I will miss her very, very much every day of my life." Overcome by emotion, he stepped away from the microphone. A murmur of voices buzzed throughout the assembled crowd. *Who was this young man? What was his relationship to Isabella Bellwood? Why had none of them ever heard of him before?*

Dante put his arm around Mosuma, leading him from the gravesite. They exited together.

History had just been changed.

"Did Prometheus Bound, his liver devoured each night by vultures as punishment for giving fire to man in defiance of the gods, this punishment repeated each torturous day...Did Prometheus feel his unendurable pain was appreciated? Did he regret his rash actions?"

—Ever since that time: Burn! Burn! Burn!

CHAPTER 42

Burn! Burn! Burn!

12:25 p.m.
Monday, November 22, 2010
Near Georgetown University

The white limousine stopped in front of a white townhouse in a neighborhood of identical white townhouses. "This is the place," Dante said. "Zuma lives here. It's not too late. You can still back out if you want to," he said to Kaley and Renee. "We weren't able to save Isabella's life. In order to stop the attack, we must stop Mosuma from carrying it out. Maybe he'll have mellowed after Isabella's funeral. This time, he wasn't humiliated with the world watching." Kaley and Renee looked at Dante. Their apprehension about what was to take place was palpable.

Renee shook her head no, meaning that she was going to go through with it. Kaley stared blankly at the townhouse, fear coiling, snake-like, in her belly. She thought of an Edna St. Vincent poem about the belly of the beast. What beast awaited them inside? Reluctantly, she showed support for her mother's decision to approach the townhouse door.

"Okay. If you're going in, Mom, I'm going in with you both," said the frightened girl.

It had all started after the funeral.

Renee wanted to thank Dante for singing "Words" at Isabella's funeral. She'd insisted that Kaley accompany her. Renee didn't want to be alone with the singer. The One had acted so strangely at the hospital, said so many wild things. Instinctively, Renee wanted a backup, a chaperone. Perhaps part of her reason for wanting Kaley along was the way being in Dante's presence made her feel. She didn't trust herself to be alone with him. When she was with him she felt giddy, like a schoolgirl with a crush. Renee smiled and thought to herself, *Kind of funny. My daughter chaperoning me, rather than the other way around.*

"Thank you so much, Mr. Benedick, for singing at Isabella's funeral. It meant a lot to our family." She choked up as she finished her simple thank you speech.

"You don't need to thank me. You just need to believe the things I've told you. Believe me and help me. We must get to Mosuma Hamad. He's planning to return to Syria. If he does, events will be set in motion that will cause the death of thousands of people. Please help me." He added, pleading, "I have to stop him. Will you help?" His urgency carried the day and here the three of them were, with Joshua Gottlieb chauffeuring them.

* * * *

Dante rang the doorbell of Zuma's brick townhouse.

Zuma cracked open the door, safety chain still in place. Zuma recognized Dante from the funeral, but kept the chain latched, door ajar. Dante seized the opportunity to insert his foot in the opening. Dante began speaking to Zuma, quickly, intently. All the while, Zuma was peering at him suspiciously through the cracked door.

"Don't go back to Syria. The lives of many people will be in jeopardy if you return to your homeland, including your own life and that of your brother Zacarias."

"What do you know of my brother Zacarias? How do you even know his name? What will happen to my brother?" Zuma's voice trembled.

"Can we talk about this inside?" Dante asked.

Zuma opened the door to allow them entry. Dante, Renee and Kaley entered the foyer of Zuma's townhouse. Joshua waited outside at the wheel of the car.

"Once you return to Syria, your brother will kidnap you. You will be instrumental in the hijacking of an Airbus A380 with eight hundred passengers aboard. Horrible things will be done to you and to those passengers. You'll go down in history as just another terrorist murderer, when you are so

276

much more than that."

"Liar!" Zuma shouted.

"If I'm lying," Dante said calmly, "why are your bags packed?" He pointed to the luggage on the foyer floor behind Zuma.

Zuma was too angry to answer. A shiver went down his spine like a corpse's embrace.

"I didn't want to come here," Dante said. "Renee and Kaley should not be here at all. We came to try to save you and to try to save the world."

"I grow tired of your lies. Leave!" Zuma shouted. He seemed to be losing control. He slammed his fist on the hall table. "Leave immediately!" As he spoke, Zuma was fumbling with the pull to the drawer of the hall table in the foyer.

"We're not leaving until you promise us that you won't return to Syria." This from Dante in a calm, low, insistent voice.

Zuma opened the drawer of the hall table. In his hand the trio saw the steely glint of a 38-caliber revolver, reflecting the dim light.

"I said leave." Mosuma's hands were shaking, but he was pointing the pistol's barrel squarely at Dante's chest.

Dante took a step closer.

"Don't come any closer. I will kill you. I'll kill all of you."

Dante took a tentative step closer, all the while thinking, *Where are Renee's Secret Service men when we really could use them?*

"Dante, don't!" Kaley screamed. "Stop! Let's just leave," she urged. The fear in her voice was unmistakable.

Zuma's attention was distracted by Kaley's scream. Dante grabbed for the 38 and struggled with Zuma. There was a moment when it was difficult to tell which man was winning the struggle. Grunting. Groaning. Then, a loud explosion. Zuma fell, gut-shot, the bullet entering his stomach and exiting through his back. He lay on the foyer floor, bleeding profusely, moaning in pain.

"Burn the papers. Burn the secrets. Burn Bella's secrets." Zuma's voice was weak. His color was ashen, gray. He relaxed his grip on the gun, his fingers twitched. "Make sure that the government doesn't find out Bella's connection to the papers that are in that drawer." With his last ounce of strength, he pointed to the drawer of the hallway table and muttered, "Burn! Burn! Burn!" Those were Zuma's last words.

* * * *

The papers were incriminating. Photos, plans, and documents of proposed nuclear power plants. Other diagrams linking both Vice President Black and Isabella Bellwood in obtaining classified documents of the layout and operations of the Beaverton Nuclear Plant. Some of the documents appeared to have been taken directly from the Oval Office.

"That's how Faris and Bahar were able to plan their attack on Beaverton so successfully," murmured Dante, as he hastily examined the papers. "Quick. We don't have much time." Dante was gathering all the papers and maps and hurriedly stuffing them into Zuma's nearby briefcase. He had unceremoniously dumped the previous contents of the briefcase on the floor. A small mountain of papers had formed as Dante jettisoned the briefcase's prior contents. Turning his attention to Kaley and Renee, Dante said, "We need a place where we can examine these documents and plan our next move. We haven't much time. We should also try to get your friends, Agents Paskvan and Savage, to help protect us. They could have been useful just now."

"They're just around the corner where I told them to wait," replied Renee, "but I'll get them on my cell." She dialed, telling the agents to join them as they attempted to make the airport.

"I'll be boarding a private jet with Kaley," Dante heard her say. "You two are to take Kaley and me to the plane. It is Mr. Benedick's plane, but don't let anyone know our destination or that Kaley and I are onboard. Mr. Benedick will come along by himself, in his own car, right behind us. Please pull up to the white townhouse where you see his car. Now!"

Dante continued giving the women directions for their safe escape. "You two can't stay in Washington DC. It's too dangerous. I have a friend, a country and western star, Kenny Golden. He lives about thirty minutes south of Nashville on

I65, in Franklin, Tennessee and I have a key to his place. We can stay at his place until we figure out what to do with this information."

"Will Mr. Golden mind?" Renee asked.

"He's on tour. Besides, he owes me a few favors."

* * * *

"We have to get out of here," Renee said. "We really have no other hiding place where your father won't be able to immediately find us. If we can get to Nashville, we can figure out how to handle this information about Isabella, before the FBI is involved. If we don't involve your father, as President, he can't be implicated."

* * * *

Kaley and Renee had already boarded Dante's plane after being driven to the airport by Agents Savage and Paskvan. Both agents had gone aboard to provide protection and both agents had taken care of concealing Mosuma's body rather leaving a corpse in the foyer of his townhouse. It would eventually be found, but they took it to his garage and covered it carefully with a tarp, wiping the area clean of fingerprints and cleaning up the blood. Dante followed the women in his own car, which attracted two familiar faces. He saw Nailer and Racine tailing him in his rear-view mirror when he was halfway to the airport, after Kaley, Renee and the two agents were already safely aboard.

Secret Service agents Nailer and Racine pulled their car up beside Dante's on the tarmac near the plane. They screeched to a halt. Since Kaley and Renee had a ten-minute head start, the agents didn't see Kaley and the First Lady climb the steps to the small plane, nor were they aware that Agents Angel Savage and Jack Paskvan were aboard. All they knew was that Dante Benedick, their nemesis, was about to board his private Lear jet.

"The President wants you to leave town. Now," Racine said unpleasantly.

"That's what I was about to do," Dante said.

279

"I hope you aren't planning on leaving the country," Nailer said.

"What if I am?" Dante asked.

"The President wasn't too pleased with that song you sang at his daughter's funeral," Nailer said. "He'd rather you stay in the country while he's dealing with the fall-out. There may be some repercussions for you on your work permit and your green card."

"I was only playing what the First Lady requested," Dante said. He seemed nonchalant in the face of their threats, rather than defensive.

"I don't care if it was a request from the Virgin Mary. You should've known better. What's your flight plan? Where are you going?" Nailer was asking questions in staccato bursts. Unpleasant little staccato bursts.

"The Keys."

"Remember: stay in the United States until you have clearance from the President to leave," Nailer said. "We'll be keeping our eyes on you."

Dante looked at them, amused. "The hand can be faster than the eye, boys. Remember that. Keep your eyes on the prize."

He climbed the stairs, pulled the door to the jet shut, and waved as the Lear jet began to slowly taxi down the strip for take-off.

"This anonymous identity
That fate's assigned me here
Does not promote tranquility
But makes me crazed, I fear."

—*Crazed,* The One

CHAPTER 43

Crazed

2:00 p.m.
Tuesday, November 23, 2010

The flight to Nashville from DC didn't take long. Kenny Golden's place was not technically in Nashville. It was in Franklin, thirty minutes south of town.

The estate that Kenny had built with the proceeds from his first gold record, "Golden Dreams and Silver Wishes," was remote. The land and original buildings, bought by Kenny's family, had cost only $30,000 dollars back in 1959. The ranch had several acres of land and sat on a hill with a curving road leading up to the antebellum-pillared mansion, straight out of "Gone with the Wind".

Kenny had built the house after he began to achieve fame, and it had been enlarged and modernized as he became more successful. The size of the estate was amazing. The house, itself, was much bigger than the Graceland mansion that Elvis had called home. The kitchen, alone, looked as though it could turn out dinner for one hundred people without any problem, while Graceland had a very ordinary knotty pine small kitchen that looked more like it belonged to small-town America. In 2010 dollars, the estate, with all the improvements, was easily worth hundreds of million dollars. The special amenities that Kenny had added increased its value. All improvements were one-of-a-kind.

There was a racquetball court, bowling alley, enclosed underground swimming pool and large Olympic-sized outdoor swimming pool, landscaping, stables, ten-car garage for Kenny's car collection, private recording studio and private screening room. But still there was a comfortable homey feeling to the place. It felt like a working ranch where someone lived; it didn't feel like a rich man's trophy house.

When Renee, Dante and Kaley arrived, Kaley went exploring immediately, almost like a small child on a treasure hunt. Her excitement was contagious. Renee and Dante decided to explore the private screening room. It was exactly like a small-town movie theater, lacking only the popcorn.

Dante turned to Renee, "What's your favorite movie?"

"That's a hard one. You first."

"*Somewhere in Time*," said Dante. "It starred the man from all the Superman movies."

"Christopher Reeve?"

"Yeah, that guy," Dante said. "He died on my birthday, a long time ago. It's strange thinking back on it now how a guy who played Superman became an invalid, crippled in just a fraction of a second. What if he hadn't gone riding that day? What if the horse had cleared the jump? What if the EMT's hadn't administered CPR so efficiently? You realize how split seconds of time impact on your life. How things could be so different, if just a few things surrounding the event went haywire." Dante seemed lost in thought, contemplating this for a moment. Then he asked Renee, "Now, your turn. Your favorite film?"

"I'd say *The Lake House*, with Sandra Bullock and Keanu Reeves." She lapsed into silence. The theme of both movies was similar. Star-crossed lovers separated by time. "Funny. Both movies have lead actors with almost the same last name. They're different, but alike."

Dante said, "Like us?" His smile melted her heart.

Dante put his arm around Renee as they sat side-by-side in the back row of the small twenty-row theater.

"When I was a kid in Chislehurst, this is how a sneaky chap would try to cop a feel ..." He feinted towards Renee's right breast, stopping short of actual contact, eyes twinkling.

In spite of herself, she laughed. Dante was so surprising. One moment, he was discussing philosophers. The next he was talking about techniques boys used to grab a girl's breast.

She felt flirtatious, herself. "Why? Do you *want* to cop a feel?"

"Every boy does," Dante said.

"Yes, but you're a man, not a boy."

"You can take the man out of the country, but you can't take the boy out of the man."

"You made that up," she exclaimed, laughing.

"Yes, I did, and it stinks, doesn't it?" Dante smiled. A genuine smile, filled with good will and humor.

"Let's order up a flick, shall we?" said Renee.

"Let's not and say we did," responded Dante, this time trying the reach-around-the-girl-to-touch-her-breast technique for real. Renee returned his kiss, as he leaned in. They sat there, necking like high school kids in Kenny Golden's private screening room for thirty minutes. His kisses were soft, tender, and passionate. His hand was caressing her right breast, moving towards the buttons of her baby blue cardigan sweater, lightly caressing her neck. He turned in his theater seat and took her face in both his hands, looking deeply into her dark brown eyes, and said, "I have a better idea than a movie. Come with me."

Renee rose to follow Dante from the screening room, completely entranced. Finally, she felt no guilt, only anticipation. She deserved this attention and respect from a loving man.

They climbed the staircase towards the largest bedroom in the house. They could see Kaley, the animal-lover, outside by the stable fences, feeding the horses. A groom was speaking to her. Dante and Renee were finally alone. The Secret Service was checking the house and setting up a communications room. The couple had time to themselves for once.

Dante unbuttoned the first button, the second, the third button of Renee's cardigan. He removed the pale blue cashmere sweater that Renee had worn on the flight over. Underneath the sweater, her chest was ample and her breathing deep. Her lovely breasts rose with each intake of breath and fell with each exhalation.

Dante slid his right hand under the thin fabric of the shell she was wearing beneath the light blue cardigan sweater. He felt a lacy bra and, instinctively, moved to unhook the hooks in the back. But there were no hooks in the back. This was a front-closing bra, and, finally, laughing slightly, Renee guided his fumbling fingers to the front-closing mechanism. When that, too, presented the rock star with difficulties, she reached up herself to undo it and released the most perfect breasts Dante Benedick had ever seen.

He lowered his head to nuzzle them, taking the nipple and aureole of each perfect breast into his mouth. Sucking. Suckling. Moaning slightly with pleasure, his erect penis growing harder and harder. Renee was enjoying it as much as he was. Her lips were parted slightly in pleasure.

They were still very much alone. It seemed as though this might be the only time in the world that they could count on being alone and uninterrupted. Usually, time worked against them. They had enjoyed such a brief time together, and almost none of it alone. Time was their bitter enemy. Their times together were always being interrupted by one cataclysmic catastrophe after another.

They lay on the bed together, Renee nude from the waist up. Dante's throbbing organ strained for release from his white jeans. He removed his jeans, while simultaneously pulling at Renee's slacks, which she had unbuttoned at the waist. Because the room was chilly, Dante pulled back the covers of the deep gold coverlet with the maroon damask stripes, revealing the gold satin sheets beneath, and the two of them slid under the covers together, bare chests meeting for the first time. Heaven. Dante was now completely nude. Renee soon would be, as she wriggled free of her slacks and panties and threw them to the floor by her side of the bed.

This man knew his way around a woman. She moaned slightly, thoroughly enjoying the attention.

Then, in a reversal of expectation, Renee turned and mounted Dante, poising above his erect cock. Her womanhood dripped wetly on his erect penis, teasing it, teasing him, wanting him, but wanting him to want her more. She moved down the shaft slightly, ever so slowly, ever so slightly. She withdrew. She threw her long tawny hair to one side. Her tongue protruded from between her full lips, while her eyes were half-closed. Still, she watched to see that Dante was with her, that he was following her lead, that he was enjoying this moment. She settled slowly, slowly, slowly onto his maleness. His shaft slid smoothly into the jellied bliss awaiting it. Both moaned as he entered her. She again moved upward, to repeat the motion. Over and over, like a rider on a horse.

As Renee rode Dante, he touched her clitoris with his hand, rubbing it in a circular steady motion, exciting her even more, almost more than she could bear. Renee was totally into the moment, as was Dante. She began riding him, more and more quickly, more and more expertly, faster and faster. They were on the edge. They were almost there. They would fall off the cliff together.

"I can wait," came between his gasps of pleasure.

"I don't want you to wait. I want you NOW!" and, with that signal, both of them came, together, in a cataclysmic, moaning, endorphin rush. He moved from side-to-side. He touched her even more after he had climaxed, bringing her to a second and a third orgasm.

Hours later, she would think back to these stolen moments and secretly smile. She had never felt so mellow in her life.

* * * *

At 3:00 a.m. on Kenny Golden's ranch, Kaley was awakened by the sound of a locomotive passing in the distance. The sound of the dead. Images of a death train filled her head.

The train of the dead.

The sound of the train faded. She still couldn't shake the feeling of dread left by its passing. The abyss of night is when ghosts from the past come back to haunt you. When Kaley was a young girl, her family used to vacation in Westerly, Rhode Island. It was a common vacation destination for wealthy commuters from Connecticut, where they lived at the time. Their cottage in Westerly was not far from a railroad crossing.

One night, when she was seven years old, a train derailed at the crossing. The twin girls heard a horrible screeching of metal on metal, a terrific impact. Neighbors began running to the scene of the horrific accident.

Since most of the commuters were families coming to the beach for the weekend, many children were crash victims. Kaley would never forget their cries or their bloody corpses

287

being pulled from the wreckage of the burning train. Bones broken. Dolls crushed underfoot. Hysterical parents. What she had seen that night wasn't a dream. It was a nightmare. Now, every time she heard the lonely whistle of a passing train, her mind hurtled back to that humid summer night, crickets chirping and the brackish water in the nearby pond lurking green and scummy. Some of the children's broken bodies had to be removed from the pond, their bodies as lifeless and crushed as rag dolls.

Men, women, and children roamed up and down the railroad intersection, searching for their missing loved ones. Most were incoherent. The passengers were covered in blood and grime. Broken bones protruded from arms and legs. Screams filled the night. Some victims wore the dazed look of the walking dead. All were in shock. The accident had taken place at three in the morning. Ever since that night, Kaley often awakened at three in the morning. Whenever she did, her mind involuntarily returned to that horrible night.

Lying restless in the middle of the king-sized guest room bed, she knew that sleep wouldn't come. She slipped on a blue terry cloth robe, got up, walked to the darkened living room upstairs. Curling up on the couch, she turned on the television set. The TV screen was the only source of light in the room, a dim greenish glow.

Late night on the tube offered nothing but infomercials, sitcom reruns and mediocre movies she wouldn't even watch during the daylight hours. She really wasn't able to concentrate on the dreck on television at this hour.

She turned on her iPod. Joss Stone was singing. That music was followed by some jazz. Kaley began to drift off. The first three songs flowed together like a quiet creek. Her eyelids grew heavy.

Just as she was drifting into sleep, a Miles Davis trumpet solo on the fourth song, sad and hollow, Miles playing "Round Midnight." The haunting solo reminded her again of a train whistle; all her bad memories came flooding back.

The Dead Train Is A Coming, Up Around The Bend.

The image of a train loaded with the dead, with corpses, filled her with dread. She was tempted to go to her mother's room and see if she was awake.

What if I find Mom with Dante? The thought flitted through Kaley's mind, spreading like an evil stain, darkening her mind-set, and disturbing her. *Naaaah. Mom wouldn't do that. But Dante seems to really like Mom.*

If she found her mother with The One at three o'clock in the morning, the dark night of the soul, it would break her heart. She tried to push the image from her consciousness. It was her sub-conscious that kept resurrecting it, like a ghoul rising from the graveyard to stalk her sleep.

Don't let my mother steal the man I love. Don't let Dante like her more than he likes me.

The mournful whistle sounded once more in the distance. Kaley shivered and headed back to her lonely bed.

"One is the loneliest number…"

CHAPTER 44

Return to Georgetown

Wednesday, November 24, 2010

A little after 4:00 a.m., Kaley wanted to get out. She'd been lying in the king-sized bed, sleepless, tossing and turning, her mind filled with visions of her mother locked in Dante Benedick's embrace. She didn't know if her fears were true. All she knew was that she didn't want to hang around and find out.

Gathering up her few belongings, she quietly descended the staircase to the communications center established by Angel Savage and Jack Paskvan. Angel was her favorite agent. She knew he would help her.

"Angel, I really need to get out of here. Now."

"Is it okay with your mom?" Angel asked the question while snuffing a cigarette in a nearby ashtray. He'd been smoking steadily since 3:00 a.m. in an effort to stay awake on his shift.

"Sure. We talked about it before I went to bed. You know I always have insomnia. I just really need to get out of here. Now." Kaley shifted nervously from foot to foot. "The airport is only four miles away. I'm sure there's a commercial flight I can catch."

"I can probably handle that. Mr. Golden's got several vehicles in his garage, all of them with the keys in them." Angel smiled a radiant Hispanic smile, showing beautiful white teeth. "They're inside that fancy garage of his on the grounds. Do you prefer a Rolls or a simple Mustang for your trip to the airport?" he asked, smiling. He gave her an inquiring look with his large liquid deep-brown eyes.

"Nothing fancy. The Mustang will do," she said. "Let's get out of here ASAP." With that, Angel Savage left the slumbering-on-the-couch Agent Jack Paskvan to guard the First Lady for an hour as he escorted Kaley to the Nashville airport.

* * * *

When dawn broke, Renee and Dante woke with it, entwined in each other's arms and made passionate love again. It was as though they knew this opportunity might not come again for a long time.

"You're like the Energizer Bunny," Dante teased. "But my batteries need recharging. For one thing, I'm hungry!" Both realized that they were ravenous.

"Let's go downstairs. I'll see if I can rustle up something for the three of us to eat," Renee murmured in Dante's ear, as she nibbled on his left ear lobe.

"Careful. That ear is not breakfast. Not even an appetizer. And you'll need to fix breakfast for five unless you want two very unhappy Secret Service agents."

"Right. For the five of us. I sling a mean frying pan full of hash browns. I make 'em with green pepper and onion. My scrambled eggs aren't too shabby, either." As she spoke, she kissed him lightly on the reddened ear. She was pulling on a white terry cloth robe that hung in Kenny Golden's closet to wear downstairs.

The two descended, sleepily, to the immense kitchen below. Renee checked the Sub-Zero refrigerator/freezer for the ingredients she needed. Luckily, Kenny's staff had them on hand. When the feast was nearly ready, she turned to Dante. "Go tell the agents and Kaley that everything's ready." The table was set, white dishes against a blue-and-white checked tablecloth. The country atmosphere was inviting, and the smell of hot coffee and maple-sugared bacon filled the air. The small alcove in which the table sat made the immense kitchen inviting.

Dante strolled into the communications room, where the agents were taking turns dozing on a couch. "Breakfast is served," he said to the sleepy agents. "Seating for five. Right this way." He gestured as though he were a headwaiter, ushering customers to their table.

"Four, you mean," said Angel Savage, rubbing his eyes.

"Well, Kaley isn't down, yet. I'll go knock on her door and get her up." Dante headed for the stairs.

"No. I mean, Kaley left. Last night. Or, really, this morning. About 4:00 a.m. She couldn't sleep. She said her mother had approved an early return. By now, she's probably back in her Georgetown apartment. Or else at the White House."

Renee was so shocked when she overheard this that she dropped the frying pan of scrambled eggs she was carrying to the already set table.

"Why did you let her go? Why didn't you let me know?" Renee demanded.

Angel Savage looked sheepish. "She said you already knew. That you had okayed it. It was four o'clock in the morning!" It was obvious from the startled, shocked look on Renee's face that she had not approved Kaley's departure for home.

Renee said nothing. She left the kitchen and raced upstairs to dress. She knew that as soon as Kaley returned to D.C., Bucky would find out where they were and he would be livid. She must return immediately, in order to minimize the fall-out.

Dante, just as surprised, followed upstairs more slowly, his booted feet taking the steps with measured precision as he, too, thought of this repercussion. Agent Paskvan took a look at the juice, bacon, hash browns on the table, stepped over the eggs on the floor, and helped himself to what was left of the food. He sat down to eat. Angel shrugged and joined him.

* * * *

"So, the return of the prodigal daughter," William Bellwood snarled at his daughter. "Where-in-the-hell have you been? And where's your mother?"

"We've been in Nashville. I should say, outside of Nashville, in Franklin, on I65 South. We only spent the night there. I came back early because I had insomnia. I just couldn't sleep. So much happened. There was a Syrian guy. He was shot during a fight with Dante Benedick at this townhouse in Georgetown."

"What? Dante Benedick? The British singer?" Bucky's hackles rose. "Not him again."

"Yes. He was with Mom and me. We went to Franklin and stayed at a friend's house there. A friend of Dante's, I mean. We didn't know what to do after the shooting. It was a complete accident, but we knew that Mom couldn't be found there. That it would be bad in the press, and, well, there were complications. There were some papers that implicated both Mia and Bella in something bad. After I couldn't sleep, I decided that Agent Savage might as well put me on a commercial flight back home. I was sort of the fifth wheel, anyway. Mom and Dante Benedick were in the private screening room the last time I saw them. I think they were going to watch a movie. I've brought the papers that we took from that townhouse where the Syrian guy was. I think you need to see them."

Kaley handed her father the briefcase that she had surreptitiously removed from the communications room as she left.

"I'll just bet they were watching a movie," Bucky muttered. "Probably *Last Tango in Paris.*"

"We tried to help Mr. Benedick convince Mosuma Hamad not to go back to Syria. It was something Mr. Benedick felt very strongly about. I didn't understand it all. All I know is that everything ended badly. The guy pulled a gun on us. There was shooting. He gave us papers implicating Bella in a terrorist event and told us to burn them. Why would Bella do something like that? We took the papers to Nashville to destroy them. We thought that if we could take care of it without your knowledge, it would protect you by keeping you out of it. You wouldn't need to know, and you would have deniability if it ever came out. But, when I couldn't sleep, in the night, I thought about those papers.

"I think you need to see them, yourself, before they are destroyed. I brought them for you to see, Dad. I think you need to know that Mia Akaihane-Black was scheming, behind your back, to have you take the fall for the terrorist hijacking.

She and Bella also stole plans, diagrams of the Beaverton Nuclear Facility. Plans for nuclear sites out of the country. I think she must have stolen them from your office. Bella had to have helped her. They were giving them to Syrian terrorists. I just don't understand why." Kaley's eyes were wild with fright and disbelief.

As his daughter spoke, disjointedly, out of breath, with haste and urgency, warning him of the Vice President's treachery, Bucky Bellwood felt his face growing flushed. His blood pressure shot up by at least ten points. He was livid.

"That bitch. Who does she think she is? *I'M* the President of the Goddamned United States. She's just as useless as teats on a boar, and about as important. Thanks for letting me see these papers, Little One. You did exactly the right thing. You run along now. I'll take care of it. I have some discussing to do with the Vice President."

Kaley was whisked to a car and driven to her apartment, where she remained sleepless despite her best attempts to finally end the restlessness of the night before.

Meanwhile, Bucky Bellwood was stewing over the treachery of the Vice President. *That little bitch! How dare she attempt to pull something like this and then blame it on ME! What does she take me for? Some silly fool like her husband Roger? She'll pay, She'll pay dearly.*

His lips twitched in an ugly grimace.

When Mia Akaihane-Black arrived at her office around eight a.m., Bucky had been thinking about the best course of action for nearly two hours. He was thinking, but not clearly. He had had a few belts of Jack Daniels. *A little Jack Daniels helps you think. Good ol' Jack.* He downed his third glass of straight bourbon. While he was drinking, he twirled the pearl-handled Colt pistol that his Great Great Grand-daddy Ben Bellwood had given him. Ben Bellwood was also known as "Belly" Bellwood, because of his tremendous beer gut. *Truth be known, it was a bourbon gut, but who really cares?*

This particular pearl-handled Colt revolver had been inside William Bellwood's desk ever since he had assumed office. He had it in his pocket when he took the oath of office, in fact, on the old family Bible that belonged to Ben Bellwood and his wife, Nora. The pistol was a family heirloom. It was engraved with the date of the battle of Shiloh. His great great grand-daddy had fought and died at that bloody battle. This pistol was a genuine family memento.

By the time Mia arrived in her office in the morning, completely unaware that she had been discovered in her duplicity, Bucky had devised a plan. He had been thinking and drinking for at least three hours. The plan was pretty simple. Kill the bitch. However, there was literal killing and figurative killing. If he threw her to the wolves that were always at the Presidential door, in a live press conference, the woman wouldn't have a chance to cook up an alibi.

"Anna, buzz the Vice President and tell her to get in here right away, will you?" Bucky's words were slurred, but that was nothing new. His Texas drawl was almost indistinguishable from his bourbon slur, anyway.

Drinkin' and thinkin'; thinkin' and drinkin'. I like the sound of that. I do some of my best thinking when I've had a few. The invasion of Namibia. Figured that out while I was high, and now look: we control ALL their oil.

Bucky straightened his shirt collar, unconsciously, an old habit from his glad-handing running-for-office days.

"Yes, Sir, Mr. President." The elderly secretary buzzed the office of the Vice President.

"The President would like to see you at once," Anna Ferdinand relayed.

There was a long sigh on the other end of the line. "All right. I'll be right there." Mia was thinking, *The man's an animal. I haven't even had my morning coffee and HE'S ready for sex.*

She had already had to put up with Roger for their once-a-month joyless coupling this morning. Now this. She tried to think of an excuse to avoid reporting to Bucky's office right away, but it was so early in the morning that no other appointments could be used as an excuse. She slipped her high heels back on, from where she had kicked them off under her desk, and trudged wearily to the President's nearby office.

When she entered the room, the stench of bourbon rolled off Bucky like the smell of tar off a blacktop road. *He's plastered! At eight o'clock in the morning! Drunk AND horny! What a combination!*

But Bucky didn't seem his usual jovial self. What Mia thought was going to be a leetle ol' roll in the hay, turned out to be a curt discussion about a live press conference Bucky wanted held that very evening.

"I have a few things of national importance that I think the public has a right – in fact, a need – to know," Bucky drawled. "I want you to be there right beside me. As long as the shit is hitting the fan, you can help deflect it. You've heard the expression 'catching shit,' right? Well, Mia, that's what I want you here for tonight." He smiled, but his smile lacked even artificial warmth. Oddly, it even lacked Bucky's usual quota of horny, which Mia found off-putting.

"Okay. What time?"

"6:00 p.m. We'll interrupt the dinners of Americans everywhere." As Bucky expressed that thought, he smiled.

"Right. Well, send the briefing memo over to my office, so that I'm up-to-speed on all topics to be covered," said Mia, in her most professional tone of voice. It seemed a bit unusual for Bucky to want to share the spotlight, but, if, as he said, there was blame to be spread, he would be likely to want to do that.

"Oh. I'll be sure to do that, darlin'," Bucky said.

And with that, Mia Akaihane-Black left the President's office as acting Vice President for the last time. The next time she was physically present in the Oval Office, she would be placed under arrest, charged with treason, handcuffed, and escorted to a cell. But Mia was not fully aware of the evil that lurks in the hearts of men as intrinsically evil as William 'Bucky' Bellwood.

Bucky just sat there, eyes glazed. He poured himself yet another finger of bourbon after Mia's departure.

Agents Racine and Nailer entered. "Get my press secretary. I want a live press conference from the Oval Office at six p.m. tonight. All major networks. Have Anna set it up pronto. And, incidentally, haven't you heard? The wife has had a complete breakdown over the death of Bella. Renee's addicted to prescription drugs, sleeping pills, you name it. Nuttier than a fruitcake. Just plain bat-shit. Needs Xanax or Prozac or both. She's going to need to dry out for a spell in Silver Springs and get some therapy." Bucky laughed maniacally and poured again. "Make the arrangements. As soon as the First Lady arrives here, off she goes. Have the men with the butterfly nets and the white coats waiting."

"Yes, Sir," the agents said.

* * * *

It was only moments after Renee's return to the White House that the attendants from Silver Springs, Jim Robinson and Henry Hook, had Renee restrained in a strait jacket, sedated, and headed for the Silver Springs, Maryland, Mental Health Facility.

"Garrett," Bucky had said on the phone to Dr. Garrett Shields. "I've got another little favor I have to ask of you. You know I'll make it worth your while."

"What's that, Bucky?" Garrett was, himself, not quite sober. He had been popping pills most of the night.

"Well, it's the Little Woman, again. My lovely wife, Renee. She needs some major therapy. I'm thinking some shock therapy, possibly followed by a lobotomy chaser."

"What's in it for me?" said the always-chivalrous Dr. Garrett Shields.

"One hundred thousand dollars," said Bucky. "We'll be there within the hour." The President hung up.

* * * *

Garrett put down the telephone receiver and said, out loud, "That cheap-ass son-of-a-bitch. This is the fourth time since his election that I have had to do him a 'little favor.' And how does he treat me? Like dirt. Does he ever say, 'Thank you, Dr. Shields. I appreciate your help, Dr. Shields.' No. He treats me like a hired lackey. And, with the money he's got, he could pay me a lot more than what he's offering. Does he appreciate all I do for him? No. Does he appreciate all I *HAVE* done for him, ever since college? No. He does not. I've pimped for him since we were eighteen, and he's never been the least bit grateful. That man needs to learn some humility, and I might be just the one to teach him some." Garrett popped another pill and ended his soliloquy.

Dr. Garrett Shields of the Silver Springs Psychiatric Facility was not a happy camper.

"The whispering just gets louder
It echoes in my head
I hope I find the answer
Before I wake up dead"

—*Damaged Soul,* The One

CHAPTER 45

Escape from the Darkness

7:00 p.m.
Wednesday, November 24, 2010,
Silver Springs, Maryland

Renee Bellwood regained consciousness more quickly than the ambulance attendants had anticipated. She'd always had a high tolerance for anesthesia. The OB/GYN doctor had discovered this when delivering the twins by C-section, twenty-one years earlier. Renee had come out from under the anesthesia before the doc was done tugging the girls' tiny little bodies from her womb. The doctors were really tugging and pulling with vigor; it was no delicate, gentle delivery. She remembered that the entire process had been excruciatingly painful. Now, this idiosyncrasy of her physical system – her high tolerance for painkillers – might actually prove useful.

Renee lay on a gurney in the back of a Silver Springs ambulance. Alone.

"After all. She's out like a light. It's not like she's sick or anything," Henry Hook said aloud to his driver partner, Jim Robinson. Henry and Jim were often paired for pick-up of various psychiatric cases. Sometimes, it was a two-man struggle to get the patient into the vehicle, especially if it was a male paranoid-schizophrenic. Renee's pick-up was a piece-of-cake. In fact, Jim was planning on eating a piece of cake: birthday cake that he had brought with him from the funny farm.

It was his forty-third birthday, and his wife, Mrs. Robinson, Katie, had sent him to work with a homemade chocolate cake. No way was Jim leaving that cake behind for all those suckers on duty at the funny farm to eat while he and

301

Hank made this run. He'd slipped a couple of pieces of cake onto a paper plate when he and Henry got the call. Those pieces of cake were now calling his name. His and Henry's, that is.

"I'm sitting up front. We're celebratin'! Crank a CD." And so Hank and Jim rocketed through the night, listening, ironically, to a song by The One, talking, and cramming huge pieces of messy chocolate cake into their mouths.

If Renee's memory served, she was on her way to the Silver Springs Mental Facility, where Dr. Garrett Shields, an old friend of Bucky's, burned the midnight oil performing a variety of grim and ghastly tasks, by request. She'd made this trip before. Never willingly, never happily, and never in the dead of night.

Silver Springs had been a mental health facility since 1888. It was a looming Gothic building that rivaled the set of any horror movie. Tan bricks and mortar. Pillars. Gargoyles. The whole nine yards. All the grounds of Silver Springs needed was a thunderstorm, with lightning zigzagging from the heavens to the timbered grounds and thunder booming to remind of classic horror flicks like "Frankenstein." *Maybe Bride of Frankenstein would be more correct.* It was a horrible-looking ancient set of buildings, mostly abandoned now with recent advances in modern psychotherapy.

There was a winding circular gravel driveway that led to the front steps of the large structure. It was ringed on all sides by trees, the kind of trees that made you think of the old days at Caesar's Palace. Or, at least, they made Jim Robinson think of Caesar's, because, last year, he had spent his birthday in Vegas and the massive yews that had always reminded him of Hadrian's Villa near Rome were gone.

In its heyday, the hospital had housed up to two thousand inmates who actually had jobs: a dairy farm, a vegetable garden, plowing, planting, milking cows. With the advent of anti-psychotic drugs, most of those troubled patients were pumped full of thorazine – or whatever more recent drug-of-choice yielded the best results – and put back on the streets. Released to society. Left to their own devices. Abandoned, some might say. They could be found in the larger cities, mumbling to themselves and panhandling. Paranoidschizophrenics talking to God. The rest of the weirdos talking to strangers, trying to bum a dollar to buy food or booze.

Beneath Silver Springs lay an elaborate labyrinth of catacombs. Some of the catacomb-like tunnels housed the regular things that any building needs: electrical conduits, underground telephone cables, plumbing pipes. But much of the maze was meant to provide a quick quiet way out for the failed human experiments that Dr. Shields and his predecessors caused, ruined bodies, carted anonymously, to the nearby Potter's Field.

That particular piece of real estate – Potter's Field – was located near Acorn Road. Spooky place, too. Garrett Shields was fond of saying, "That's where we bury the nuts," and then laughing. A brutal laugh, for such a weasel of a man. He would add, "But mighty oaks from little acorns grow, and Acorn Road is very near." Tired old joke. Jim thought of Garrett's indifference to human life. He shrugged. *The guy is probably crazier than most of his patients. He's gotta' be certifiable. If people only knew!*

If a person ended up in a state mental facility like Silver Springs for life, he or she probably didn't have a family that was really all that interested in how the patient's sorry life was going to end. This facility was the end-of-the-road in more ways than one.

Dr. Shields disliked climbing down into what he called "the Tombs," but the tunnel, that ran for almost five miles to a nearby rural road, had been useful over the years. Records had disappeared through these tunnels, after one particularly vigorous investigation led by none other than Geraldo Rivera in his early days as an investigative reporter. Bodies had been carted through the tunnels. The pipes underground were always damp and dripping with mold. The entire tunnel smelled of mildew, rat feces, and despair. It was not a pleasant place, even for the rats.

Fortunately for Renee, the attendants had neither noticed nor taken her cell phone. They weren't getting paid overtime for this run, and both of them were wise to the benign nature of the call. They only had to work till eight o'clock tonight, and they were already mentally off-duty and glad of it.

"Old Bellwood wants to put the fear of God into his

wife, again," Jim Robinson said to Henry, as he gunned the engine preparatory to driving to the White House for pick-up. He sighed. Last time, Renee had been their "guest" only for a long weekend.

"Probably seemed longer for her than it did for us," they snickered.

Jim had accidentally smeared some cake on the steering wheel. He was intent on wiping it off with his sleeve so that the gooey frosting didn't stain the seats. The lumbering vehicle was weaving across the centerline, and Henry hoped that Jim would stop soon. He had never liked Jim's driving, sober or drunk. While Hank was worrying about Jim's driving, Jim was thinking, *Wouldn't do to piss off old Garrett Shields. Lord knows what he might do. He's about as batty as they come.*

Neither Frank nor Henry wanted to find out what sort of punishment Garrett Shields might devise, if they were to destroy asylum property. Once, Dr. Shields had made a particularly stupid orderly scrub the entire west wing armed only with a toothbrush and a bucket of sudsy water. That orderly was one tired and crabby employee by the time the week ended, when Shields added cleaning all the toilets with the same toothbrush to his list of assigned duties.

Finding that she was unsupervised and in possession of her cell phone, Renee snaked the cold metal object to her mouth. She realized, with a faint flicker of hope, that she could call Dante Benedick for help. Whispering with urgency, she dialed the only man in the world she knew who could help her. And got voice mail.

"Dante. This is Renee. I'm being held prisoner. I'm being transported to the Silver Springs Mental Facility in Silver Springs, Maryland. Get hold of Dr. Garrett Shields, its Director. Offer him anything; he can be bought. Kaley should be able to help you. She'll be on the visitors' list. Just help me. Please. Get me out of here. Before it's too late."

Whispered into the message function of Dante's unanswered cell phone, Renee prayed that her message would reach the only person in the world who might have the money, guts, brains, and willpower to save her. She knew that, when Dante heard the message, he would enlist Kaley's support.

The One would try to help her escape what would almost certainly be a black fate. She trusted Dante like no one else in her life. She felt that he cared for her. That he wanted her to be happy. That he would do anything he could, anything within his power, to help her when she was in need. She only hoped that what she was now asking him to do *was* within his power.

As Dante put down the cell phone, listening for the third time to the saved message, he was already dialing Kaley at her Georgetown apartment.

"Kaley, your father has had your mother committed to Silver Springs Mental Health Facility in Maryland. Do you know where it is?"

"What? Why? Why would he do that?" Kaley was shocked. She responded with questions rather than answers. She only belatedly realized this. Kaley made herself focus on the question Dante had asked, "Yes. Yes, I do know how to get there. Dad did this to Mom once before, but she was back home after a weekend of what Dad called 'R&R.' I can lead you there. You sound very concerned." Kaley waited for Dante's response.

"I *am* concerned. I don't trust your father where your mother's welfare is concerned. I don't know what has happened to cause him to do this to her, but I know, from talking to your mother, that it wasn't pleasant the last time he sent her there. Were you allowed to visit her when she was confined previously?"

"Yes. I was on the visitors' list. Dad told me to go visit on the Saturday, but she was only there over a long weekend." Kaley set down the glass of Diet Dr. Pepper she had been sipping as she cleaned her apartment.

"Well, this may or may not be a long weekend stay. It sounds as though your mother is terrified. Last time, they gave her electro-shock treatments. Have you ever seen what an electro-shock treatment does to a patient? It isn't pretty. Who knows what your father did or said when your mom returned to the White House?" A beat. "How did he seem when you saw him?"

"He was upset about the espionage, about the treason of the Vice President," replied Kaley. "But he didn't mention Mom, except to mutter something under his breath about the movie I mentioned you guys were watching at Kenny Golden's place."

"What do you mean?"

"Well, when I said that you were thinking of ordering up a movie, he said, 'Probably Last Tango in Paris.' Something like that. I don't know that movie. Is it any good?"

"Depends on what you mean by 'good,' Kaley. It's a very old film, with Marlon Brando. I think it proves that your father was very displeased with your mother. We have to assume that he is sending her to Silver Springs to punish her, not because she really needs to be sent there. We have to get her out of there. Fast! You have to help me."

"Of course I'll help. Just let me know what you want me to do." Kaley began grabbing for a lightweight jacket to throw over the jeans and sweatshirt she already was wearing, even as she finished her answers to Dante's questions. She had been doing some light cleaning of her apartment. She was dressed in tennis shoes and old dark grubby clothes, which would be perfect for the night's activities.

"Can you somehow contact the doctor in charge, Garrett Shields?"

"I can. I'm her next-of-kin. You might have trouble getting in to see her or even talking to Dr. Shields, but I'll be on any visiting list. I'll call right now. Dr. Shields is a real squirrel, though." Kaley made a face as she thought of the sweaty little man with the pencil-thin mustache who never raised his eyes above chest-level when speaking to her.

"Okay, okay, just so you know, I've done some research on the Silver Springs facility," Dante said. "It seems that there is a very helpful underground passageway, a catacomb like tunnel, that runs beneath the institution and comes out on Acorn Road, about five miles to the west, near a soybean field. If you can get to Dr. Shields, offer him whatever amount of money you need for directions and safe passage through the underground tunnel. See if he's open to helping us disappear his star patient. I think Dr. Shields is a businessman. If I'm right, he'll be open to the possibility of helping us with a blueprint. Hell! Maybe he'll even offer to act as our Indian guide, if the price is right. Tell him that there is some mistake. That your parents are divorcing, your father is being vindictive. But make sure that you make it worth his while. He's an old chum of your father's from college. In order for him to turn on your dad, the money has to be right. You know that I'm good for it. I'll do anything, pay anything, to help your mother."

"Yes. I can see that. I know that," Kaley said simply. Her heart missed a beat as she thought of how much she cared for Dante and how little he realized it. It was like a little death for her to hear the affection in Dante's voice when he spoke so warmly of Renee.

She hung up the phone after talking to Dante and dialed information for the Silver Springs Mental Health Facility in Silver Springs, Maryland.

"Tis now the very witching time of night,
When churchyards yawn and hell itself breathes out
contagion to this world."

—*Hamlet, Act III, Scene ii,* William Shakespeare

CHAPTER 46

Nick of Time

9:00 p.m.
November 24, 2010,
Silver Springs Mental Health Facility
Silver Springs, Maryland

The dank smell of dead and rotting rodents offended their nostrils as Dr. Garrett Shields heaved open the massive metal door to the Catacombs. The Tombs. The door creaked as though it had been months since it was used, although it had been opened just one hour prior by two orderlies.

Renee was supported between Kaley and Dante, their arms around her waist. Dr. Shields didn't seem to feel any need to help physically support the drugged woman, even for half a million dollars. Although she was quickly regaining consciousness, Renee was still weak and mentally fuzzy. A short staircase led to the depths below.

It had taken Dante and Kaley less time to get to Silver Springs than anticipated. The field near Acorn Road was a perfect landing place for his helicopter. Dante had always loved risky hobbies. Flying was one of them. He was qualified on many types of aircraft, but, in his opinion, flying a helicopter was one of the more difficult flying tasks. Depress the left pedal and you need to compensate with a deft twitch of the cyclic stick. Move the cyclic back, and you need to increase power with the collective. Helicopters are very complex aircraft, requiring a great deal of coordination. Every control input requires an accommodation in some other area. Dante's Messerschmitt Eurocopter BK117 was one of his indulgences.

After Kaley's initial contact with Dr. Shields, arranging

Renee's escape had been only a matter of meeting the good doctor's price. Shields was more than a little greedy. He saw a chance for sale to the highest bidder. A bidding war. A whose-is-bigger contest. Although he did not realize Dante's true identity – and Dante was doing his best to disguise it, with a black stocking cap and dark clothing – Shields knew the President's daughter could probably get her hands on a few dollars.

The doctor held out for $500,000 for Renee's release. In return, Dante and Kaley demanded that Garrett Shields, himself, lead them out of the hellhole in which Renee was being held prisoner. Garrett would have to traverse the Tombs with them, guiding them as part of their Four Musketeers quartet. Too bad Shields had been popping pills all day. He was neither totally sober nor even halfway coherent.

The first thing they noticed when they opened the heavy-as-lead door was the smell. It was a fetid smell. Their flashlight beam revealed old standing pools of water. Dead rodents. Festering evil. The cobwebs that drifted from the pipes overhead were works of art, spectacularly large and interwoven. Kaley thought to herself, *I hope I don't see any of the spider's that made webs this big!* She was doing her best, trying to be brave for her mother's sake.

Dante was supporting most of Renee's one hundred and ten pounds, but Kaley had one arm slung around her mom's waist to help stabilize the woozy woman. The knockout drugs Renee had been given had really done a number on her. Although she had recovered enough in the ambulance to contact Dante, once the doors were opened upon arrival at Silver Springs Renee was shot full of a whole new array of tranquilizers. She had struggled, briefly, although she knew it was hopeless. Her Rolex watch and other valuables were confiscated. Luckily, there had not been time for more than this, as her call for help had been heard and acted upon.

Please, God. Let Kaley and Dante find me! she prayed before losing consciousness. *If I make it out alive I'll never make the mistake of wasting a single moment of time again.*

After twenty minutes of strenuous labor, half-walking, half-dragging the nearly comatose form of the First Lady of the United States, Kaley stumbled and fell. The ground was littered with old glass from syringes; broken glass from beer bottles; cans and bottles abandoned by partying orderlies. This was a popular after-hours spot for drinking, on or off the job. Secluded. Seldom visited. It fit the bill nicely. Kaley inadvertently let out a shriek, a high-pitched scream, as she reached out to break her fall with only one palm. Her other arm was around Renee's waist. Kaley's blue jeans were ripped at the knee. Now, the entire knee of her jeans gave way, exposing a bloody kneecap with ground glass embedded in it as a result of her fall.

"Kaley, can you go on? Do you need a minute?" Dante was concerned.

"Just let me rip the lower cuff of my blue jeans off," she said, between gritted teeth. "Having this thing dragging on the ground will only slow me down. Mom always said I was a klutz." She smiled up at Dante through red-rimmed eyes as she worked on ripping the denim fabric. Her nimble fingers shredded the lower ankle portion of her already-distressed jeans. "I'll be right in style, now," she said with spirit. "Denim and plastic covers on CD's: the world's two toughest materials to cut through or remove." An appreciative chuckle from Dante.

"No kidding. Don't worry. We can put some disinfectant on those cuts when we hit New York. We still have time, but we have to make it from here to New York City within the next three hours."

"New York City? Why are we going to New York City?" Puzzlement showed in Kaley's tone.

"There's no time to explain it all to you now. When we're aloft, I'll explain about the Gray Wolf Coffee Shop and its importance. We have to make it back there. There's a time limit on how long we have. We must be there before midnight. After midnight, all bets are off."

Just as Dante uttered his brief explanation to Kaley, that midnight was the bewitching hour for all of them, and the last chance they would have to use the time machine, the quartet rounded the corner of the Catacombs and stumbled upon Jim Robinson and Henry Hooks.

The birthday boy hadn't wanted to stop celebrating his 43rd birthday with just Katie's chocolate cake, eaten in the car while on the job. Jim had suggested to Henry that the two of them duck below ground into the Tombs and have a beer or two or three before they ended their shift, before Jim's natal day was over. The Tombs were a well-known place to party, whether that meant booze or other illegal substances that might occasionally fall into an orderly's hands while on duty. *So many drugs; so little time*, had been suggested as the motto for Silver Springs by one employee.

"After all, you only have a birthday once a year, right? If you play your cards right, that should be enough. Let's take Samuel Adams with us for a short celebration, shall we, Hank?" Jim addressed Henry Hooks with a grin, as he hoisted two full six-packs of the cold bottled beer that he had stashed in his van for the occasion.

Jim and Henry had been seated on two dusty concrete blocks, having a fine old time for forty-five minutes, ever since they got off their shift at eight p.m. If truth were known, they had started celebrating at 7:45 p.m., but who was keeping track, really? Sam seemed to be having a good time, too. Only two full bottles of the brew remained. Samuel Adams was, indeed, popular. Five beers apiece for the cake-loving duo. They were feeling no pain. The two were experiencing few inhibitions at this point, either. They had been actively trashing their boss, Dr. Garrett Shields, for the last half hour.

"That guy gives me the creeps," Henry said, taking a swig of Sam Adams. "What's with that weasel-boy mustache? It makes him look like a bad imitation of those old Art Fern skits that Johnny Carson used to do on the *Tonight Show*. 'Go to the Schlossen Freeway and cut off your schlossen,' " Jim said this last in a high mimicking falsetto. Both men roared with drunken laughter.

"And the three-day stubble looks like Ryan Seacrest on season two of American Idol. I hate that guy," added Henry.

"What guy? Shields or Seacrest?" Jim clarified.

"Both of 'em, really," responded Henry, taking another swallow. "May they both rot in hell."

Into all this illicit merriment stumbled the First Lady and her companions, Dante, Kaley and Dr. Garrett Shields.

Jim and Henry rose clumsily to their feet. Their response time was a bit slow, after ten beers in forty-five minutes. They shielded their eyes from the blinding light of the four hand-held flashlights aimed directly at them by the approaching party. Jim and Henry had brought down a small camping lantern, but its gentle glow had been hidden by the bend in the Tombs tunnel just prior to this halfway point.

"What's going on?" asked Jim Robinson in a bewildered tone of voice. "Dr. Shields, we can explain. But what are *you* doing down here at this time of night with these three?" Recognizing the patient they had just transported to Silver Springs, Jim said, "Hey, we just delivered Mrs. Bellwood. She should be upstairs in Ward C." The two orderlies took a threatening step towards the four people headed in their direction.

Shields just stared blankly back at his orderlies. The drugs in his own system from this afternoon had slowed down his thought processes. He had no well thought-out explanation for his presence in the Tombs after hours. He had no thoughts, at all, if the truth were known, beyond what he planned to do with $600,000 dollars.

Dante quickly sized up the situation. These two are drunk. He smiled to himself at the phrase "drunk and disorderly." *No. In this case, just drunk orderlies.*

Like most rich rock stars with time on his hands, Dante had dabbled in the martial arts. He was no black belt. Hell! Steven Seagal or Elvis could take him. He chuckled at the thought of that unlikely duo fighting him. Two fatties punching his lights out. What Dante had was street smarts from his hardscrabble adolescent kid-from-the-gutter youth. He could handle himself in a fair fight. Or, if needs be, in an unfair fight.

They're both drunk. The one guy's gotta' be at least forty. The other one's pushing fifty. I can take 'em if I have to, but the best thing to do would be for Dr. Shields to talk our way out of this. Dr. Shields seems to be on mute, so maybe I'll give it a try.

Dante spoke.

"Gentlemen. Steady, guys. Obviously, Dr. Shields has okayed this transfer. We're just trying to cut down on any possibility of media coverage of the First Lady's departure from the asylum by taking her out the back way."

313

Jim looked at Henry. Henry returned Jim's skeptical gaze.

Henry Hook was getting angry. "Since when is there media hanging around at 9:00 p.m. at night? Especially when they don't even know the patient is here yet. What you say may be true, but this facility has certain procedures. Certain standards. Patients don't go out the back way to avoid media fifteen minutes after they're admitted. This particular patient's rather prominent, wouldn't you say?"

"Procedures? Standards?" Dante snorted derisively. "I can see that this is a tip-top facility, all right. Two of its finest are down here sloshed, drinking on duty." Fire flashed from Dante's eyes as he delivered this message.

"Now, just a minute, whoever you are. We're *NOT* on duty. We got off at 8:00 p.m., right after we delivered Mrs. Bellwood to Ward C, and we want to know why she isn't *IN* Ward C right now? I'll bet the President of the United States would like to know, too!" This from Jim in a belligerent tone of voice. Jim didn't like this guy's attitude. *Who does he think he is?* thought Jim. *Somebody rich and famous?* The birthday boy was sulking.

The two orderlies had actually left their posts at 7:45 p.m. to come down and hoist a few, but it was nearly 9 p.m., now. Jim felt he was safe in proclaiming their innocence. *But what about these guys? What are they up to?*

It would be just like Garrett Shields to be up to no good. There's probably money in this for him somewhere. That last thought – the money that he and Jim might make by safely returning First Lady Renee Bellwood to her husband, the President of the United States –is what started the trouble.

Garrett remained mute throughout. It was as though he were contemplating his own navel. He was as much help as a blind seeing-eye dog.

"You four had better come back to the Main Administration building with us," said Jim, dusting his hands off from the accumulated soot, dust, and gravel of the Tombs. He tried to muster as much officious authority in his voice as he could. He also made a big show of beginning to gather up the previously jettisoned Samuel Adams empties. He was carefully placing them back in their cardboard containers.

Wouldn't do to let Garrett think that we were coming down here to drink AND litter, thought Jim. *As for the drinking, it's my Goddamned birthday, for Chrissakes! And we're off-duty!* Jim was growing more belligerent by the moment, something that the only stone cold sober man in the group could sense for himself. Dante was good at picking up on vibes from his audience.

These guys aren't going to let us through quietly. And Garrett has clammed up. I'm going to have to take them out, thought Dante.

With that thought, Dante quickly kicked out the lantern and swung his torch at Henry Hook's head. The flashlight struck Henry a glancing blow on his left temple as he stared stupidly at Jim's janitorial efforts in picking up the Samuel Adams empties. Hank never knew what hit him. He lay face down on the tunnel floor, temporarily unconscious.

Seeing his partner's fate, Jim backed off, six-pack of empties in his hand. He skittered away from Dante, crab-like, edging behind The One back towards the Main Administration buildings from whence the quartet had come.

Jim's final brave act, before throwing the six-pack of empty beer bottles in Dante's direction and running for his life was to say, "Hey, Mister! I'm a lover, not a fighter. We just wanted to have a couple of beers on my birthday, okay? I don't want no trouble. Take her. She's yours. Just leave us be." With those parting words and a weak-wristed toss of a six-pack of good old Samuel Adams in the direction of Dante's head, Jim Robinson was gone, scurrying through the Catacombs like a rat through a maze. The rough lip of one of the glass bottles caught Dante on his right cheek inflicting a slight cut. Nothing serious. A small trickle of blood dribbled down Dante's chin.

"We've got to move. Fast. That guy will pull the alarm and cops in three states will be hunting for the escapees from the Mental Institute as soon as he does." Dante gathered Renee in his arms like a limp rag doll.

"Thanks for all your eloquent help, Garrett, Old Boy," Dante said, sarcastically.

"You're welcome," Dr. Shields mumbled.

Kaley regained her feet from the floor where she had

remained crouched throughout the encounter. The four set off at a military trot. The struggle to transport Renee Bellwood to safety continued, with the very discombobulated Dr. Garrett Shields remaining a very unconcerned, very uninvolved, but very rich, Boy Scout guide.

When they reached the short staircase leading upwards to the waiting helicopter, which Dante himself had piloted to the field, Shields asked, "Are you flying that thing?" It loomed large and yellow in the field.

"Yup," said Dante, as he assisted Kaley in shoving Renee through the open door to the seating behind the front two seats. The helicopter was a Messerschmitt Eurocopter BK117. As the President's daughter, Kaley had ridden in helicopters before. For a cautious girl who didn't even like to ride on the Ferris Wheel, riding in this helicopter was going to take every ounce of courage she could muster. Kaley had already displayed massive amounts of courage tonight. Dante was impressed. She was not about to let Dante Benedick or her mom down now by announcing that helicopters terrified her.

Kaley and Dante climbed into the two front seats of the big yellow copter after Renee was safely buckled up in back. The three were airborne in moments. The rotors kicked into gear, making a familiar whining roar, and debris exploded everywhere. Below, as the rotors kicked up dust obscuring the fading form of Dr. Garrett Shields, Dante muttered, "Good riddance to bad rubbish."

Then he turned the copter towards New York City and a destination that might mean safety. Peace. Salvation. Maybe they could attain all three in the nick of time.

"In the middle of the journey of our life, I came to myself within a dark wood where the straight way was lost...Here must all distrust be left behind; all cowardice must be ended...Into the eternal darkness, into fire and into ice...without hope, we live in desire."

—*The Divine Comedy,* Dante Alighieri

CHAPTER 47

Into the Eternal Darkness

11:00 p.m.
Thursday, November 24th, 2010,
Thanksgiving
The Gray Wolf Coffee Shop
453 East 56th Street, Manhattan, New York City

Pier 86 on the Hudson River lay directly below the Messerschmitt Eurocopter BK117. The choppy water of the turgid dirty brown river was churning violently from the rotor wind. The yellow copter struggled in the grip of crosswinds, seeking safe harbor below.

Beneath the helicopter loomed an 898-foot, 42,000 ton landing space: the black deck of the Endeavor aircraft carrier. Now retired and used as an airplane museum for tourists, the Endeavor housed famous planes such as the Concorde and the Stealth bomber. The gigantic landing deck, which had actually been used during World War II, had ample space for one additional plane, the small helicopter piloted by a famous rock star. The One, Kaley Bellwood, and Renee Bellwood hurtled toward their destinies.

Dante didn't have to worry about shearing off power lines or hitting trees, which would have been problematic for him if he had selected his second choice of landing sites, Central Park. "And we stand a reduced chance of being mugged", Dante had said to the women, with a twinkle in his eye.

Dante carefully navigated using the various pedals and cyclical sticks, fiddling just enough with the collective, moving that control just the few centimeters necessary to accommodate and adjust for the copter's gradual vertical descent.

It was difficult to talk above the noise of the copter. Dante shouted above the din, "We've got to hurry. We're running out of time!" If they weren't at the Gray Wolf Coffee House and ready to time travel before midnight, the Time Machine would automatically travel back to the year 2025. Like the old Michael J. Fox title, it would go "back to the future" without them. It was pre-ordained. Like a homing pigeon returning to its coop, their means of escape to the future would be lost and they would be abandoned in the past.

Dante, who had lived in both times, did not think this was as dire a predicament as Dr. Dunne had suggested it would be. Dante had been younger and healthier in 2010. More handsome, too. The world was also younger, healthier and more handsome in 2010.

But in the future, there would be no William Bellwood, Leader of the Free World. There would be no threats of nuclear holocaust. If there had *been* a nuclear holocaust, it would be over. They would be its survivors. Dante knew that there was only one time travel machine. He banished from his mind the image of who would be in that seat when midnight struck.

The women did not know the specifics of why or where they were hurrying. It had been too noisy to converse in the helicopter to explain things to them completely. They didn't understand what Dante meant when he talked about "running out of time." The exact science of time travel eluded them.

However, they shared his sense of urgency, without knowing the reasoning behind it. It was in his voice and actions. All distrust had been left behind. All cowardice was abandoned. The straight way was lost, but if the crooked way led to a future with hope and happiness, both women were prepared to sacrifice the present and the past for the future. The trio lived in desire. They would follow Dante into fire, into ice, into storm, with hope or without hope. They both trusted Dante Benedick completely and would follow him through hell. Where he sought to take them, they would willingly follow. They both loved him. "Whither thou goest, I goest," Kaley whispered under her breath, quoting Scripture.

Dante continued attempting to explain things to his

puzzled passengers. "The time machine had to be pre-programmed prior to my departure from the Year 2025. Our opportunity to use the machine runs out at midnight tonight. We have to get from this docking point to The Gray Wolf Coffee Shop in the 400 block of East 56th Street in Manhattan before midnight. It's 11:04 p.m. Let's go!"

"How are we going to do that?" asked Renee, shaking off her grogginess. She glanced at her wrist, searching for the correct time on her Rolex. Her wristwatch had been taken from her back at Silver Springs. She'd never see that particular bauble again. Kaley checked her own inexpensive silver-and-gold Anne Klein watch.

"It's 11:05 p.m. right now. Is that enough time? Can we make it?" Kaley's wild eyes said it all.

Dante pulled upwards softly on the lever that settled the huge landing gear gently on the deck, ignoring her question. The entire maneuver was accomplished with no more force or difficulty than tapping an egg against the side of a frying pan.

"How much time do we have?" Kaley asked. She was confused. Her questions and tone of voice gave her away.

Renee was now fully conscious. She seemed almost back to normal again, although grim and concerned.

Eternal darkness blanketed them. They stepped onto the deck of the huge aircraft carrier, surrounded by the ghosts of all who had gone before. Eerie. Silent, now that the rotors had ceased. Calm. They looked out at the reflected lights on the Hudson. Echoing in Renee's mind were the words of another Dante, "I came to myself within a dark wood where the straight way was lost." *Were* they lost? Could they make it in time?

When Dante had completed all landing maneuvers, he answered Kaley's question. "It has to be this way. We have to go. Now!" He assisted the two women, as they climbed from the aircraft.

"I notified Joshua to be waiting here for us before I left for Silver Springs." He smiled, "That was a long time ago. Let's hope the poor bloke hasn't fallen sound asleep. If he has, I have the second set of keys to the car. I can activate the horn by pushing the button, so we'll know where it's parked." He smiled at the thought of Joshua rudely awakened by the honking of his own car horn. He could just picture Joshua's mussed hair and bleary eyes, if he had, indeed, been asleep these last few hours, waiting in the parked vehicle.

It was after-hours at the Museum. In October, after the tourist season, the entire place had been shut down for repairs and updating. It would not re-open again for another two years. Only a skeleton crew guarded the boat. The two crew members were below deck enthusiastically watching a football game between the New York Giants and the Chicago Bears.

The trio scrambled from the copter's interior and took off at a trot for the gangplank leading to the streets of New York.

"Be careful!" warned Dante, as a variety of cables came into view, most of them tethering famous planes to the deck. They passed the supersonic Concorde; the immense, deadly, secretive Stealth Bomber, which, true to its name, was painted Darth Vader black. It was barely visible in the dubious moonlight.

Just as Dante had predicted, the car was not instantly able to be located. Dante hit the "horn" button to pinpoint the parked vehicle. A silver Mercedes, one block to the east, blared. Enough noise to wake the dead. Or, at least, to wake the sleeping Joshua, who started the vehicle and pulled up to collect the exhausted trio.

"Anyone want to go for a cup of coffee?" Joshua asked.

All three were tense when the Mercedes stopped outside 453 East 56th Street in Manhattan. Canopies of nearby apartment buildings welcomed residents into lighted lobbies manned by doormen in uniform. The Luscious Donut Shop spewed a wonderful aroma into the night air, tomorrow's batch of morning goodness being prepared at this late-night hour.

Next to the Donut Shop, the green awning of The Gray Wolf Coffee Shop, with its half-filled coffee cup icon, looked like an abandoned storefront. It was almost 11:30 p.m. They had one-half hour to gain entrance to the locked building, find the time machine, make the necessary preparations, and send the time machine's passengers into the year 2025.

Dante ran to the door, with Kaley and Renee close behind. The realization that it was locked, shuttered, and dark temporarily startled him. He looked dismayed.

Thinking quickly, he removed one of his shoes, smashed through the glass window pane of the front door, and opened the door from the outside. No alarm. Lucky.

"It's downstairs!" shouted Dante. The trio followed his lead. He struggled with the heavy door to the basement stairs. It was pitch black. Dante only belatedly remembered to trigger the light switch. The light, coming from fluorescent lights hanging from the ceiling of the floor below, gave a sickly glow upwards to illuminate the concrete steps they took two at a time.

There it was. A chair with straps. Brutal headpieces. It looked like a high-tech electric chair. The clock on the wall read 11:55 p.m.

"Take off your clothes!" Dante shouted with great urgency. He unbuttoned and unzipped his white jeans, throwing aside his underwear and shirt.

"Why do we have to take off our clothes?" This from Kaley. Renee echoed the question. "And, there's only *one* chair: who's going? Who's staying?"

"Ladies, nobody's going if we aren't totally and completely starkers, strapped in that chair, and ready to roll when it strikes midnight. I'm the one from the future. My mission is to return to the year 2025. I have to be ready to rock and roll when it strikes the midnight hour. One of you can join me. We can try to take two carbon-based organisms through, one atop the other, but the clothes have to go. All of them." He continued removing his clothes, his Calvin Klein underwear kicked aside. He was totally nude. Beautifully naked. He looked like an advertisement from a high-fashion magazine. Perfume. Shirts. Whatever product blatant sex would sell. There were several magazines aimed at men that would kill for a picture of Dante Benedick taken right now.

"I have to go back to my time, if I can," Dante said. He sat in the chair. He began strapping himself in. "I have to face my destiny, face the future. I have to try to make this happen. I promised Dr. Dunne that I would return."

"Dante ... I ... I can't go with you," said Renee. "I can't leave. I made my choices when I was Kaley's age. Those choices can't be undone. I would never do anything to intentionally hurt Kaley." She ran to him, hugged him, her

323

eyes wild, her cheeks tear-stained. "I can't go. Take Kaley. Save Kaley!"

Renee didn't articulate what she and Dante both knew: Kaley was hopelessly in love with Dante. Both women loved this man. If Renee left with him now, it would break Kaley's heart, something Renee would do anything to avoid. But if Kaley left with Dante, Renee would lose her last and only living child forever.

Dante looked deeply into Renee's troubled brown eyes. He gave Kaley a searing look.

Renee tried to reason with him one more time, mustering all her control.

"Dante, all we have on Earth, any of us, is each other. We only have one another. Please don't go. Please don't leave us."

"Renee … I …" His eyes pleaded with her; his eyes said it all. He knew he loved Renee. He knew that she loved him. What they had shared in Franklin, Tennessee couldn't be faked. But he knew that Renee was loyal, first of all, to her children. She wouldn't do anything to hurt her child. Dante realized, with an abrupt upheaval of emotion, that the Sophie's Choice here was not his to make, but Renee's.

With just the slightest of hesitations, Dante unbuckled the straps and leapt from the chair, escaping the Time Machine, which would automatically activate at any moment, taking him far, far away forever.

There was a sudden powerful surge of energy. It was as though an unseen hand had thrown an electrical switch. They felt it more than saw it. A humming sound could be heard, subliminally. Short flashes of light. Charges of electricity. The chair was almost pulsating. Intense glowing light surrounded it. Sound. Heat. An odd smell, like ozone after a storm.

Just as quickly as the noise and pulsating and the mysterious ozone odor ended, the mechanism disappeared. The chair was gone. No one was in it when it retraced its journey. Release into 2025 was no longer an option for any of them. There was no trace of the Time Machine in the now-empty basement room. It was as though there had never *been* a Time Machine. Nothing occupied that space. Nothing occupied that time.

Renee quickly grasped the significance of what had just happened, although Kaley did not. She ran to Dante, standing nude in the center of the room, clung to his waist, savoring his nakedness, holding on to the man she knew she loved. She had followed Dante's directions more quickly than Kaley, but not quickly enough to join him. And, really, *could* she join him, knowing that it would break Kaley's heart? Knowing that she would never see Kaley again? Renee was totally naked as she clung to the waist of the man she now knew she loved with all her being. Renee and Dante had reveled in each other's nakedness in Nashville; it was not shocking or embarrassing for her to disrobe in front of him. It was not the first time, for Renee.

But for Kaley, it had all been too confusing. It had all been too embarrassing, too sudden. The fact that Dante was staying was partially because of Kaley's hesitation. Kaley had thwarted Dante's one chance at time travel, because of her delay, her hesitation. They would all have to stay in this time, in the year 2010. There would be no escaping to the year 2025.

Kaley, the younger and more reluctant and confused of the two women, had removed only her upper garments. Her time-consuming questions about the process had played a part in dooming Dante's jump to the future.

"Dante, what will happen to you? Will you die if you missed this chance to return to 2025? Please tell me that we haven't condemned you to death..."

Renee was in tears. Kaley was whimpering like a small animal. A newborn mewling puppy.

"I don't really know. Dr. Dunne spoke of violating the space-time principle paradox ... time-shifting ... a ripple in the space-time continuum. But I seem to be all right. I feel all right." He sounded surprised when he said this. Dante was just as unsure of the ultimate effect of being abandoned in the year 2010 as the puzzled women. Only time would tell.

"What does all this mean? For you? For us?" Kaley asked.

"Damned if I know," said Dante, sliding his white jeans on, sans underwear. He stood there, chest gleaming, naked from the waist up, flushed, tired, dirty, sweaty, bloody where the Samuel Adams had taken a chunk out of his right cheek, his right arm around Renee's naked waist. His left arm around Kaley. He laughed.

Both women laughed, incongruously. They were near hysterics. The tension and stress they'd been under for so long had gotten to them. Either they had to laugh or they would all cry.

"Will something blow up? The world? This room? New York City?" This question from Kaley, very naively posed with wide child-like eyes. She was now hugging Dante, positioned on his left side, her naked bosom pressed against his left side. Dante noticed that having two naked women as attractive as Renee and Kaley stuck to him like glue was not a totally unpleasant sensation, even if it did mean that they had missed their chance to return to the future.

"Logic tells me it will take more than a chair disappearing to destroy New York City," smiled Dante. "I honestly don't think that anything dire is going to happen right now. Who knows about the future? Who-in-the-hell knows anything about the future?"

Actually, I do know a bit about the future. He smiled to himself at this thought.

Kaley seemed to be losing focus. She was apologizing for the questions, asking if they had fatally delayed their departure. Dante and Renee knew better.

"I'm so sorry. Was it my fault?"

Dante hushed her. "Shhhhh, Little One. 'Theirs not to reason why. Theirs but to do or die." He didn't add the next Kipling line, "Into the Valley of Death rode the six hundred."

Dante enfolded both women in his strong arms, hugging them both, comforting the frightened Kaley, feeling very fortunate to have two such lovely women within his warm embrace. *Some men would die happy at a moment like this*, he thought.

He didn't know what had just happened. He didn't know what *would* happen. He had no answers for the frightened Kaley or the befuddled Renee, but he did have feelings for them both, and they for him. That was the only thing he knew, for sure.

He quoted his namesake, Dante Alighieri, one of his

favorite quotes: "In the middle of the journey of my life, I came to myself within a dark wood where the straight way was lost." He said, "This is a divine comedy all right. It must be someone's idea of a perverse joke to let us get this close, and then come up short. A divine comedy, for sure."

"But, who would have gone, Dante?" asked Kaley. "There was only one Time Machine."

"You know what they say, Kaley: necessity is the mother of invention. One of you lovely birds might have had to sit on my lap, naked as a jaybird." He grinned. "Which one of you would have volunteered?" Trust Dante to joke at a serious moment.

The image of a nude woman atop a naked Adonis, tethered to what looked like an electric chair amused Dante. Although he was marooned here now, in this time, in this place, while with these two lovely creatures, he felt no sadness or fear.

The One spoke. He quoted Dante Alighieri. "Into eternal darkness. Into fire and into ice." He added, "With or without hope, we live in desire."

Looking at the two lovely creatures clinging to him, he added, "That's my namesake: Dante Alighieri. He's right. We live in desire. We live on. We will survive. All we have now is time and each other. Nothing but time and each other."

ABOUT THE AUTHORS

Connie (Corcoran) Wilson graduated from the University of Iowa (English & Journalism) and earned a Master's degree from Western Illinois University (English & Education), with additional study at Northern Illinois, Berkeley, and the University of Chicago. She's taught writing at six Iowa/Illinois colleges, and wrote for five newspapers, and five blogs, (including her own blog – www.weeklywilson.com).

An active member of the Horror Writers Association, her stories have appeared online and in print. Her work has won prizes from "Whim's Place Flash Fiction" and "Writer's Digest," and she has published two books, with 3 upcoming.

She's reviewed films and books for the *Quad City Times* (Davenport, Iowa) for 12 years, taught for 36 years, founded 2 businesses, functioned as their CEO, and wrote humor columns, as well as conducting interviews for the (Moline, Illinois) *Daily Dispatch,* and three other newspapers.

Connie's interviews with writers such as Kurt Vonnegut, Jr., William F. Nolan, David Morrell, Anne Perry, Joe Hill and John Irving have appeared in "SciFi Weekly," "Reflection's Edge," "The Brutarian," and a variety of other online and print magazines.

Mike McCarty has been a professional writer since 1983, and he is the author of over 10 books (fiction and nonfiction), plus several hundred articles, short stories, and poems.

He is the 2008 David R. Collins' Literary Achievement Award winner, from the Midwest Writing Center. In 2005, he also became a Bram Stoker Finalist, for the Nonfiction Book of The Year, *More Giants of the Genre.*

He lives in Rock Island, Illinois, and is a former stand-up comedian, tried his hand as a musician, and once worked as managing editor of a music magazine. Currently, Mike is a staff writer for "Science Fiction Weekly," the official website of the SCI FI Channel.